COLD PRESS

David Bradwell

purefiction

A Brilliant Debut Novel.
This is a great beside the pool, at lunch, at the Spa, back by the pool, outside my room, at dinner, bedtime book, yes I read it in 24 hours because I literally could not put it down! As I now eagerly await the sequel I recommend you buy Cold Press, read it, love it and then pass it on!
- CF Sherwood, Amazon

Put the kettle on and lose yourself in this amazing mystery thriller
I loved this book right from the very first chapter. The style of writing gets you involved very quickly and draws you in, so much so that you feel the excitement, the tense tingling sensation of mystery and the shock at 'I didn't see that coming'. A great read and one I would highly recommend. I very much look forward to the next book.
- Amazon Customer

COLD PRESS

Packed with intrigue, twists, conspiracies, and dark humour, Cold Press is a hugely entertaining mystery set in 1993.

Clare Woodbrook is the enigmatic head of the Special Investigations Department at Britain's leading daily tabloid. Her exposés are legendary, but she's not without her enemies. Now, on the verge of unveiling her biggest-ever scoop, she arranges to meet her researcher Danny Churchill, to reveal all over lunch.

But Clare never shows, and later that day her car is found abandoned on the hard shoulder of the M25. Worse still, the enquiry is being headed up by DCI Graham March - the embodiment of police corruption, and the subject of one of Clare's current investigations.

Danny sets out to find Clare, and enlists the help of his friend and flatmate - fashion photographer Anna Burgin. But as they embark upon an explosive trail of murder and intrigue, they realise they're not alone in trying to find Clare.

And soon their own lives are very much on the line.

ABOUT THE AUTHOR

David Bradwell grew up in the north east of England but now lives in Letchworth Garden City in Hertfordshire.

He has written for publications as diverse as Smash Hits and the Sunday Times and is a former winner of the PPA British Magazine Writer of the Year Award.

Aside from writing, he does the occasional bit of screen acting and runs a hosiery retail company with web sites at www.stockingshq.com and www.tightsandmore.com.

For more information, please visit:
www.davidbradwell.com

... and join the mailing list for updates, competitions, free things and more.

COLD PRESS
A Gripping British Mystery Thriller - Anna Burgin Book 1

First published in 2017 by Pure Fiction

Copyright © David Bradwell, 2017
www.davidbradwell.com

Printed and bound in Great Britain by Clays Ltd, St Ives plc

For Keir and Isabella. With love.

PROLOGUE

Monday, July 6th, 1985

IT was too late to waste time forming first impressions. She accepted the handshake, made eye contact and confirmed her name. A chair was waiting on the far side of the table. She took it, and placed her bag on the floor. It was time for the show. It was time to change the world.

Her preparation was flawless. Her instincts alert. She could sense the cynicism, the stress, fatigue and fear. He opened a file containing her CV. She could see his confusion, giving way to dismay. She knew he would do everything to keep the interview short. To take the first opportunity to send her home. Exactly as she'd planned.

Stephen Robinson looked tired, jaded by long hours. He seemed like a decent man, she thought, an editor for whom the news mattered. For whom the local people mattered. But his job prospects were about as robust as a cobweb in a hurricane. Local evening newspapers, once the centrepiece of the community, were under pressure. The Evening Herald was suffering, under competition from the widespread availability of television news, local independent radio, and then the arrival of the free weeklies. Now there was a new threat. The Morning Gazette had extended its distribution to cover the former Herald stronghold, and readers were deserting. It was grim.

It was perfect.

If at first you don't succeed, think laterally. Clare Woodbrook looked up at Robinson and the man alongside him, the Herald's news editor Martin Goodyer, awaiting the first question. She knew that in terms of experience, her CV was weak. After leaving school she'd found shop work and signed up with a temping agency. But, two years ago, she'd come to understand where her true vocation lay. She enrolled on a journalism course and subsequently graduated with the highest marks of her intake. It hadn't been easy, doing it with no family, no support. But she'd immersed herself in the work. She'd learned how to write, both news and features. She'd embraced the inverted pyramid, the structure of the classic news story. She'd learned how to investigate and communicate. And she'd mastered the art of influence and persuasion. It was time to make her case.

The other candidates didn't stand a chance. The editor didn't stand a chance. Not for the last time, she was in control.

Pleasantries over, Robinson spoke.

"Everyone who walks through that door tells me the same. Everyone. You know what they say? 'I've got unrivalled enthusiasm.' Of course you have. So's everyone else. Complete nonsense. Of course you're enthusiastic or you wouldn't be here in the first place. They say, 'I'm the best writer. I'm tenacious. I'm full of passion. I'll work through the night and every weekend. I'm so committed.' I'm full of bollocks, if you pardon the subtext."

Clare smiled.

"I'm looking at your CV and, not to overstate the issue, but it's on the cusp of minimalist, not to say non-existent in terms of actual newspaper experience." He lit a cigarette, shaking out the match and snapping it into an overflowing ashtray. He offered the packet but she shook her head.

"It's... sparse. Agreed. But experience isn't everything. I'm not here to waste your time..."

"You've done nothing," Goodyer interrupted. "NCTJ diploma fine, shorthand fine, but everyone's got those. What have you actually done? We're not looking for a new starter that I've then got to handhold because they've never seen a courtroom before. I don't have that luxury."

Clare looked into his eyes.

"I understand that. And I understand that on the face of it I'm lucky you even agreed to see me. I probably shouldn't even be here."

"So why are you?" Robinson again, speaking through smoke. "Not wanting to be too abrupt, and I appreciate you coming in, but we get a hundred applicants for every position here. Probably more. We're interviewing all day. And I'm not actually sure how you made the shortlist, if I'm brutally frank."

He turned to Goodyer, who took the opportunity to join in.

"You're what? Twenty-three? And you've never written a published story. Maybe you'd be better off going to work on a weekly to learn the trade, sharpen up your skills, learn what the business is all about. And then come to see us again in, I don't know, a year or so, when you're more the finished article."

"To use a newspaper term," added Robinson, with something approaching a smile, split between encouragement and dismissal.

Clare looked at the men in front of her. Robinson would never see sixty again. He hadn't aged well, with years of deadlines and nicotine chiselled on his face. Goodyer was younger, maybe mid-forties, but looked like a maths teacher in an ill-fitting jacket over a striped yellow shirt and loose-fitting tie. She was half-inclined to check his cuffs for chalk dust. She regarded them both, clasped her hands together and leaned forward so she could lower her voice but leave no doubt about her message.

"What's the problem?" she said, with the cool, calm confidence of someone beyond her years. "You know I can write. You can see that from the college work. And yes, you could give this to someone with more experience, but why? Isn't this about the words that have yet to be written, rather than those that have gone before?"

She paused to give them both a chance to acknowledge the point, but neither man spoke.

"You need something new, Stephen, if I can call you Stephen. And you, Martin. Likewise. Not somebody who has had their inspiration and fight removed by the drudgery of reporting on the local Women's Institute and lollipop men celebrating thirty years of service. No disrespect to either.

"I don't need that sort of experience to work on the Herald. What I like is real news. Stories of local interest that really matter. Stories of national interest. International. Why stop? Real stories. Something with bite. Something to get this paper back on its feet again. With all due respect, the very fact I haven't worked on a weekly paper is the main reason why you ought to give me this job."

Robinson looked at her. And then at Goodyer, who was nodding, despite himself.

"Hmmm..." he began, and then paused, trying to compose his thoughts. He looked past her to the car park outside, where a lorry was reversing its load of two giant reels of virgin newsprint toward the press hall. "You know, I've been in this business since I left school. I deal in words, but I'm struggling to find any on nodding terms with appropriate just now."

His eyes flicked up, as though searching for a moment of clarity. As though trying to regain his trust in his instincts. After a moment he brought his focus back to the interview.

"You make some valid points. It's something to consider. I can say that I genuinely admire your passion. And yes, it does seem genuine. I think if you can keep that spirit intact then you can have a great future and you could go far. And I admire that, and I wish you well. But this can be a tough place."

He paused again, as if giving himself time to reach a final conclusion.

"I'll speak to Martin, and we'll consider you, but I do worry that this is a step too far for you at this point in your career. I'll tell you what I'll do. I think maybe we should keep in touch. Maybe you can come in occasionally. Some freelance shifts. Learn the ropes and work your way up, and when we get another opening perhaps in a year or two, you'd be perfect. I think we... well, I think we need time to think. If that's not tautological."

Across the desk, Clare looked calm, eyes alive, still in control. She fought the urge to smile. Everything was going exactly as she'd rehearsed.

"We've still got other people to see," Goodyer added. "We've made a note of the points you've made, Miss Woodbrook, and we'll be in touch."

Clare collected her bag, stood up and shook hands with both.

"Thank you for the opportunity," she said. "And thank you for making the time to see me. It's been a good learning process if nothing else." She turned to leave, but then paused, and took a manila folder from her shoulder bag, passing it across the table.

"What's this?" Robinson asked.

"A report on the misuse of funds by the local authority

13

housing department," she said, with the same cool, detached voice. "It's one hundred per cent accurate. All the quotes are verified. Dynamite, if I say so myself. Call it a present to remember me by."

She remained standing. Unmoving. Robinson took the folder and glanced at its contents. Goodyer took a page and started reading, transfixed. His chief reporter had been working on this story for two months and had yet to deliver a sentence.

"Unless, of course, that changes things. Maybe now you believe I can do the job. Or would you rather I walked straight out of here and into the position I've been offered on the Morning Gazette?"

She could see from his face that Robinson knew he was outplayed. Of course this changed things. He was not to know that the alternative job offer was as much a figment of her imagination as the story on the desk was hard truth. The decision was made for him. Putting down the folder, he gestured for her to retake her seat. He looked at Goodyer again, but his news editor was still engrossed.

"All right," he said at last. "You're good. We'll give it a go."

The men exchanged glances.

"I just want you to promise me something," he said.

"What's that?"

"You've got to keep honest to yourself. You've got to be prepared to learn. You're bright, no question. And if you work hard and you're not afraid of seeking advice when it's needed, I think you could have a very bright future. You can rise to the very top of this profession. You can go far if that's what you choose to do. Just keep that passion. Keep that focus. Work hard and don't waste your talent."

"I promise," she said.

"That's not the promise," he continued. "I've been around a long time, and I know I'm not going to be here forever. The greatest satisfaction for me now is recognising talent. Nurturing it. I can't make you a great writer, but I can encourage you and help you if you're open and willing to be helped."

"I'm willing."

"And I'm... well, I'm going to take a chance on you, but I think you've earned it. One day you may be on my side of the table and you'll know how this feels. But please, for me, take the baton. And one day, maybe in many years to come, you'll know when it's time to hand it on. One day you'll meet somebody you believe in and who you'll have the power to help. They may need your encouragement, but give it to them and they'll go on to equal greatness. Promise me that and the job is yours."

"Is that it?"

"Yes."

"Okay, I promise that as well."

The Evening Herald's newest reporter stood up, shook her editor by the hand, and turned to leave. Exactly as she'd rehearsed.

CHAPTER ONE

Wednesday, February 10th, 1993

HER voice carried through the open doorway. Inside the office his heart skipped a beat, as it always did at this time of the morning. He didn't know it would be for the very last time.

Two back-to-back oak desks dominated the room, battle-hardened through years of use. Behind them a reference library packed overflowing shelves. Clare's large leather chair obscured a stack of newspapers and magazines. A French phrase book rested on top of the overnight bag, in turn packed ready for emergencies, still with the airline tag from the last time. Rain lashed against the window. The February sky was grey, menacing.

She breezed through the doorway, and the butterflies returned.

"Hiya Danny." He loved the sound of her voice. She removed

her long grey coat and rested her umbrella against the wall, dripping collected rain onto the corded floor. "It's freezing out there." She took her chair, swung round to face him, past her Atex terminal screen, and closed her eyes, head back as though exhausted. "What have we got?"

Until recently he would still have blushed. He couldn't take his eyes off her slender fingers as they played with her Ceylon sapphire ring, twisting, turning. On some mornings he still found it hard to believe he was here, sharing her office, her trusted colleague, her chosen partner in uncovering crime. She was the perfect boss: fearlessly pursuing justice, upholding values of integrity and respect.

Outside their room, the main news floor of the Daily Echo was buzzing with the usual mid-morning intensity. Suspended TV screens relayed the latest breaking stories as reporters went to work, fuelled by nicotine and caffeine, against a constant hum of activity, searching for new angles, chasing leads, writing the next day's headlines for Britain's biggest-selling quality tabloid. But behind the smoked glass door of the Special Investigations Department there was a rare sense of relative calm. Those who knew better knew not to ask.

Danny took the pile of paper from his in-tray and started to go through it.

"There's nothing, really," he replied. "Press releases, mainly, but I'll pass those on. Two invitations to the same party next Thursday - one faxed, both from different agencies, so we'll have to work out a way of going twice. There's one from a magazine asking for permission to quote from the Ravenscroft exposé, but I'll pass that on to syndication."

"Good." She sounded tired. "Anything else?"

"Well, talking of Ravenscroft, we've had another letter."

Clare groaned.

"For heaven's sake. What is wrong with the man? Accept when you're beaten. Is it bad?"

"Just more of the usual."

Danny passed across an A4 sheet, with anonymous text from a dot matrix printer. Jimmy Ravenscroft was six months into a twelve-year sentence and seemingly not taking things well. His trade in fake pharmaceuticals had been uncovered by Clare when he took her into his confidence, mistaking her purely professional interest for something more. He'd lost his livelihood, his liberty, and his partner of seven years, Sophie Lambert, who'd wrongly been convinced that Clare had only got close to Ravenscroft by seducing him. In truth he'd have been more than amenable, but Clare didn't operate like that. She didn't do kiss and tell. Ravenscroft had a reputation for brutality second only to his callous disregard for morality and had vowed revenge. He was safely locked away but others previously on his payroll were still at large, still suffering financial pain, and apparently still seeking retribution on his behalf. And after the court case the anonymous threat letters had started to arrive. For Clare it was all just another manageable risk. She faced danger every day, but didn't succumb to intimidation. Danny found it harder to conceal his concern.

Clare scanned the letter, and placed it in a filing tray to the right of her screen.

"If they are from Jimmy, the man needs help," she said, rubbing both temples with outstretched fingers. "Tell me that's everything."

"There's just one more," Danny continued. "It's just a personal one - someone saying he admired the interview you gave on Carlton last week."

"That's nice," she said. "Always good to be appreciated. Makes a bloody change. Not, however my finest hour."

Danny had learned not to question her occasional self-deprecation. For all the success, she had periods of extreme frustration and there seemed just the faintest hint of insecurity at her core. She divided opinion across the newspaper world.

Respected by most. Feared by a few. And an irritant to others who didn't share her opinion on the importance of integrity.

Danny continued to relay Clare's messages.

"That's it on the post. Aside from that, a man called and asked for you. Said he wanted to meet you. Wouldn't leave his name. He asked if you were around this afternoon but I said I didn't know."

Clare looked puzzled.

"God. Well, there's nothing much on. We need to go through the latest on the Easter Bunny. But otherwise I'll be here, quietly fuming. There's no way I'm going back out in that rain unless I have to."

"What's up? You sound stressed."

"Oh, nothing. Just editorial differences. What did the mystery caller sound like?"

"East London accent, mid-twenties maybe. Hard to tell. Possibly older. Quite roughly spoken. No message aside from that, just that he'd call back later."

"What time was that?"

"Just after nine."

"Well, we shall wait in anticipation." She groaned. "Hopefully it's a nice man from the Lottery."

"You and me both. Oh, and Derek called from the subs. He wanted to thank you for his birthday card."

Clare smiled. It was always good practice to nurture relationships with sub-editors. They wrote the headlines and edited the text, bestowing the gift of column inches.

"Nothing much then, all good. No nasty surprises. Pass me that letter about the Carlton interview then. I may as well read it. Who's it from?"

"I'll check. Er, Benjamin Serraillier. I think that's how it's pronounced. It's on paper from the Mowbray Hall Hotel somewhere. Is that Streatham?"

"Let me see."

She reached out her hand for the letter. She skimmed it, then folded it up and tucked it away in her Filofax. Danny was surprised that she didn't make any comment. As she moved to hide behind her screen he thought he saw a rare look of fear in her eyes.

Danny reached for Clare's phone. It was part of their routine. She had two on her desk: a black one for incoming calls via the switchboard and a red one for personal callers who she trusted enough to give her private number. The black one was ringing but Clare immediately shook her head and mouthed "I'm not here" as Danny made excuses on her behalf.

She leaned back in her chair, looked up at the clock on the wall beside them, and reached for a Silk Cut from a packet she kept in her top drawer for emergencies. She threw the rest down on her desk, lit the cigarette and inhaled, blowing smoke into the room. Danny wished she wouldn't smoke, but he stayed quiet.

"Everything okay?" he asked, after replacing the receiver. "You look tired."

She paused for a moment to flick ash, giving herself time to answer.

"Mmm. I'm fine. Just a few late nights catching up."

She looked away, reaching for a ring binder. Danny knew better than to ask what she'd been up to. But he was attuned to her moods and he could sense something wasn't quite right.

She replaced the binder, picked up the black handset, and was just starting to dial a number when the office door flew open. Mike Walker, the Echo's editor, didn't need to knock.

"Clare, darling, I need a word," he said, giving Danny little more than a cursory glance. "Easter Bunny? Any progress?"

Clare put down the phone and turned to her editor. Easter Bunny was the ironic code name given to their current five-month investigation into the extracurricular activities of a powerful, high-ranking member of the Metropolitan Police, DCI Graham March.

"We were just discussing that," she said, nodding in Danny's direction.

"And?" Walker continued, looking at Clare as though Danny didn't exist. Danny, in turn, got up to shut the office door.

"Well, we're getting there. He's a hard bastard to pin down."

"Where are we?"

"We've been interviewing. We've got him on vice for definite. Evidence removal. Pretty sure about protection, but you can imagine what it's like. Getting anyone to talk on record is proving a challenge."

"Can you have it for conference tomorrow?"

"Tomorrow? God no. Sorry."

"When then?"

"Next week? End of, probably."

"Fuck. Really?"

"Sorry, Mike. But honestly, we're on it."

"Soon as you can, please. Keep me updated. Tomorrow would be better." He patted her shoulder, turned and left, closing the door with more vigour than seemed strictly courteous.

"Christ. That's all I need," said Clare as the sound of the slam subsided.

"I'm doing what I can," said Danny.

"I know you are. But tomorrow's conference? Not happening. I'm not turning up till it's ready. Dotted, crossed, everything." She closed her eyes, and let out a deep breath.

"What's up?" he asked again. "Are you sure you're okay?"

"Yeah," she said eventually. "I just... Oh I don't know. I'm just worn out. It's age." She sighed. "I'm going to be thirty-one next month, for God's sake. Halfway to sixty-two. So old! I think I need a holiday."

Danny laughed. "I can imagine you at sixty-two. You'll be the wise old lady of Fleet Street, commanding minions from a golden throne. Or the agony aunt." He winked. She rolled up a Post-it note and threw it at him. They both grinned. But it didn't last long. A serious expression returned.

"I don't know. I just have a daydream. I'd just like to set my own deadlines. Not have to deal with people letting me down all the time, making life a misery. Not you, obviously, but everyone else. Go to work when I want to and say sod it when I don't. Get two dogs and take them to the beach and shout at the sea without worrying about affording a mortgage and how to pay for two weeks away every year."

"Start a family?"

She just raised her eyebrows, shrugged and looked away without comment.

"I thought you were happy here."

"Oh, I am, it's just... sometimes I feel like I want to work for myself, not some editor or publisher or the shareholders. And I could do without death threats from idiots." She nodded in the direction of the latest, started typing, logging in to her terminal, and then paused. "Oh, just ignore me. I just need an early night. Or lots and lots of wine."

After a few minutes she returned to her theme.

"You know what? Nothing lasts forever. You'll be fine, though. My rising star. One day, all of this will be yours." She cast her arm around the room.

Danny couldn't imagine life without her. In his own personal daydream they'd be together forever, but he knew that one day she'd get another job or maybe get married and move away. Clare rarely talked about the future, less still about her personal plans. Once, after a particularly lively evening, she'd confessed a secret desire to open a restaurant, but he'd put that down to the meal they'd just had, and its myriad shortcomings.

It was time to change the subject.

"Oh, I nearly forgot, we had a call from..." Danny began, but at that moment the red phone rang and Clare answered it before he'd had time to react. She took a pen from her desk tidy and scribbled notes in shorthand on the pad in front of her. She ended the call and swore. She tore the page from her notebook, and rose from her chair.

"I'm going to have to go out for a while," she said as she reached for her coat. "Despite the weather. Hold all my calls. Say I'm in the building if you like, but you don't know where to find me."

"Okay. But where are you going?"

"Don't worry. It's just something that's come up. It's nothing to worry about, but I'm needed urgently."

"Anything I can help with?"

"No, not yet." She paused. "Look, I can't tell you yet. It's a bit risky. Well, more than a bit - but I'm sure it's fine. It's just... It's just something I've had a hunch about. What are you doing for lunch?"

"Nothing yet."

"Then meet me. Say Brannigan's, 1.30? I'll tell you more then if I can. Hopefully we'll all be sorted by then and we can look at it together. It could be the biggest story ever. I've just got a couple of loose ends. Don't worry, you'll be the first to know."

"Okay. Brannigan's. But..." He trailed off. They worked on everything together. They didn't have secrets. "Are you *sure* you're okay?"

"Me? Yeah." She tried to give a reassuring smile. "Look, don't worry - it's nothing too exciting. I'll bring you up to speed over wine and pasta."

"Well, just be careful anyway. I'll book a table. Oh, before you go, we had a call from..." But it was too late. The door was already closing behind her. It would have to wait. He sat back in his chair and sighed, lost in thought, trying to stem the gathering sense of unease.

CHAPTER TWO

BRANNIGAN'S was the sort of bistro favoured by media hacks and resting actors. Everything about it had just the right amount of pretension to attract a regular semi-celebrity clientele. Even on a Wednesday it would be packed at lunchtime and bookings were advised to guarantee a table.

As Danny looked for the number in his Rolodex, he reflected on the hasty exit of his boss. Normally she'd come to work at 10am, read the papers and catch up on events before starting anything new. She rarely made appointments before lunchtime except in an emergency, and never without telling him where she could be reached. But today it was different. Barely through the door and she was out again.

Was it the call? It must have been. But then she'd looked unsettled by the letter too, although that was just fan mail. Wasn't it? He tried to remember its contents, but it just seemed harmless, even if perhaps a little unusual. She'd seemed okay until then though. Friendly enough. Maybe not quite her usual self, but then she'd had a couple of mornings like that recently.

Actually, probably more than a couple. Thinking about it, she'd seemed vaguely out of sorts since Christmas. Not all the time, just occasionally. He hadn't worried at first. He knew she didn't like Christmas with no family of her own. And after that she'd complained of a winter cold. But there was the odd late morning with no real explanation. He didn't like to ask.

Normally they'd work together on everything, but a couple of times now she'd mentioned a story without saying anything more, just that it could be huge but may come to nothing, and she didn't want to say anything to anyone until she knew that it was worth following up. He never saw her make calls about it, and yet what were these appointments? He'd tried to probe but she told him not to worry. If it stood up, as she hoped, he'd be the first to know. It was strange that she wouldn't confide in him. She always had before. But she must have her reasons.

He wondered about the possible exposé. What could be so big? Mafia links with the royal family? Third world drug links with a leading government minister? But he had no evidence to support either. In fact he had nothing at all. He made the appointment at Brannigan's and looked forward to the big reveal. But he couldn't shake an edge of concern.

Normally when she went out, Clare would take her mobile phone and tape machine. She had a tiny camera she could conceal in the smallest inside pocket of her coat, but at various times she'd left all three. Three days previously she'd lost the mobile phone when her car was broken into, and it was yet to be replaced. It was taking an unnecessary risk for her to go alone into potentially dangerous situations, but Clare was a woman of great resources.

He thought about following her, but that would be pointless. She was a master at disappearing into crowds and reappearing in remote places. Even if he managed to follow, he was unlikely to discover much, and if she should see him? Well, that would be a breach of trust and he'd be in danger of losing her permanently.

He'd first spotted Clare when she appeared on television at the time of the St James scandal, back in 1988. It was one of her first big exposés after moving to London. At first he just noticed the beautiful woman on the TV screen, but as she spoke, the mere physical attraction was eclipsed. He detected a faint accent. Like him, she came from Sunderland - a city in the north-east of England that worshipped the heroes it produced. But as he listened to her speak, he was captivated. It inspired him to give up his job at Nissan, the local car factory, and a promising sideline as the keyboard player in local band Flag Day. He returned to college to become a writer, moving to London in the process.

He fell under Clare's spell, both physically and professionally. He never thought he would meet her but he started to follow her career with ever-intensifying interest. She was his role model. His inspiration. He dreamed of the day he could follow her career path and maybe one day achieve a tenth of her success.

In his final year at college, she was booked as a guest lecturer in the second term. He was first to turn up that fateful morning, and took his position at the front of the class. He taped every word of her lecture, and at the end he asked her countless questions while the other students urged him to stop so they could retreat to the bar.

At the end of the period he moved towards the door of the lecture theatre, glancing in her direction as he left the room. She was deep in conversation with the college professor, but at that moment she looked up and caught his eye. He thought he detected a smile, but dismissed the idea as fantasy. He found himself drawn closer to her, until suddenly he was right there with her. The professor packed up his things and left the two of them together. Danny lost his voice, blushed and felt his strength drain away. It was the biggest moment of his life, but the words wouldn't come.

The silence was broken by Clare. He was sure he had heard her ask him a question, but he still couldn't speak.

"Canteen?" she said again.

"Er, yes, this way..."

They left the room and took the lift to the basement.

Once in the canteen, she bought the drinks and they took a table in a darkened alcove. She offered him a cigarette, but he refused. Gradually the words returned.

"Sorry for asking all those questions. You sure you didn't mind?" he asked.

"Not in the slightest," she replied. "It's nice to know that someone shows an interest."

They chatted about her work for a while. Then, in the dim light of the polytechnic canteen, it all poured out - how he'd watched her, read her books, followed her career and tried to emulate her style in his college projects.

"A true fan," she smiled. "I don't think I've ever had a fan before."

He looked at her - the shape of her face, framed at the time by shoulder-length blonde-highlighted hair.

He couldn't believe she was here. Talking to him. Her words caressed him - no longer from a printed page or in front of thirty other students in the lecture theatre - but one to one. For those few precious, dreamlike moments he held her attention and she talked freely about her work. She even offered to show him her office. They found they had much in common - places and even some people they both knew. Landmarks from their mutual home town.

She left him an hour later with a handshake and her private office number written in ball-point on a polytechnic napkin. Call me, she said, if you'd like to come to see me.

He didn't sleep much that night. The next day he could think of little else. He was aching to call but couldn't face using the phone for fear of rejection. When he finally plucked up the courage she was on another line, in a meeting, or out of the office - avoiding him maybe? Two days later, he got through and she was as keen and helpful as he'd remembered. Yes, she'd love for him to come in and see her. Next Thursday perhaps?

He turned up early, palms sweating as though on a first date. But once inside the office of the busy daily newspaper, he felt that he was at home. Terminals all around the huge, open-plan, air-conditioned office flashed stories in various states of preparation. Journalists pounded keyboards, with telephone receivers lodged between shoulder and ear, smoke from overflowing ashtrays clouding the air. Clocks displayed the time in various major cities around the world. Copytakers with headsets typed stories onto large black screens. So many people, he thought. How many of them were journalists that he'd heard of? What would he give to swap places with them?

A secretary showed him through to Clare's office. He was entranced. So this is where it happens, he thought. This is the actual keyboard. Clare showed him round the building. They went out to an interview together. They came back and both wrote stories - hers precise, articulate, his too long and wordy, and missing the central point. Everybody starts somewhere, she encouraged him, it all comes with practice.

From there they kept in touch. Occasionally he would ring her for advice with projects. She would ask him to help with some research. The next summer, he graduated - he was Danny Churchill, with a certificate from the National Council for the Training of Journalists. He went to work for her full time, freelance at first, then as part of the staff. He proved his worth. She looked upon him as her protégé. Still he found her alluring, but now she was a colleague rather than just a figure of fantasy. As they worked together, so their friendship grew. She could be tough - he found that out the first time he did wrong, failing to cross-check a source - but she was always fair, and she would put her reputation at risk to protect her own. But romance was out. He knew where to draw the line. He hoped that one day he would be able to do something that would make her notice, and of which she would be proud.

Danny made his way to Brannigan's at lunchtime with an eager sense of anticipation. He always looked forward to lunch with Clare, watching other people turn their heads as they walked into the restaurant, feeling special because she was with him. And today of all days was extra special. He'd find out what was going on. Soon, he expected, she would tell him all about some high-level corruption, with international implications while all around them other diners would be discussing football or the casting of a TV sitcom. At precisely 1.30pm he made his way to the table and ordered drinks - white wine for each of them. He sat down and waited. And waited. At 2pm, when she was half an hour late, he was still waiting, watching the minutes pass. A waiter came twice to take his order, but both times he waved him away. It was unlike Clare to be late, especially without leaving a message. He recalled her words and the anxiety started to bite, so strongly that it wiped out all feelings of hunger.

"It's a bit risky," she'd said. "Well, more than a bit."

At 2.30pm he spoke with the waiter again and called the manager over to see if there had been any messages. There hadn't. The bistro started to empty as the world went back to work. At 3pm he stood up and walked to the till. Unsure of what to do, he paid for the drinks although her glass had remained untouched. He left a message in case she should call and made his way back to the office.

Must have been held up in traffic, he reassured himself. He arrived back and called the switchboard, but nobody had been trying to reach him. He couldn't concentrate on work. Where was she? Terrible images flashed through his mind. But no, he said to himself. I'm sure it's fine.

Time passed slowly as he stared at the phone, desperately urging it to ring.

Five o'clock came with no release from the mounting tension. He called Clare's flat, and left a message on the answering machine. He felt empty and his mouth was dry. He knew the name of her neighbour so called directory enquiries to get the number. No, she hadn't been seen for days. He called the police, but there were no traffic delays, and no reports of any accidents. By 6pm there was still nothing. He moved to her desk, and sat in her chair. Where was she? Why didn't she call? He tried to tell himself there was no need to panic and that it must be something routine. Maybe she'd gone on to another appointment. He looked in her drawer and found her desk diary. The afternoon was blank. He looked out to the street below, convincing himself that he would see her down there, walking towards the office through the wind and rain. "Sorry about that. The car broke down and I couldn't find a callbox," she would say. But there was nothing but water in the gutters and the urgency of a thousand commuters all making their way home.

He waited for another hour and then packed up to go home. Maybe she would try to call him there. He left the office and walked slowly to the car park, hoping to meet her at the lift on the way down. Once in the basement, he found his car and without thinking, got inside and started the engine. He edged out of the car park, but once he was into the traffic he couldn't wait to get home. He cursed other drivers, and the cruel change of the traffic lights. He drove too fast, hardly concentrating.

Once home, the feeling of worry got even more intense. Panic was starting to set in. He couldn't eat, and kept checking the phone to see that it wasn't off the hook. He called the operator to see if there was a fault on his line, but then a call came through for his flatmate. Anna was out, probably at her studio, taking pictures or preparing the next shoot. He switched on the news but there was just the usual politics and death. At nearly midnight, he went to bed but couldn't sleep. He looked at the books. He remembered the way she used to laugh and the many good times they'd shared. Why was he worried? He tried to reassure himself that morning would come and she'd be there as usual, sharing the office as she always did.

"Hell of a day. Sorry about lunch, but wait till you hear about this..."

Morning came, and he went to work. He got there early but Clare wasn't there. No need to worry, he thought. She never comes in before ten. At quarter past he tried her home again but there was still the same answering machine. He brightened at the sound of her voice, but depression set in as he replaced the receiver. He left a message with the secretaries and made his way to her flat. Looking through the letter box, he saw post piled up inside. She hadn't been home.

When he returned to the office, there was a message for him to call the police. That night, a black Lotus car, registered in Clare's name, had been found abandoned, unlocked on the hard shoulder of the M25. There was a sign of forced entry but no news of the driver. The police would be round soon to take a statement and Clare's name had been added to the missing persons' list. But there was no news about where she could be. Danny felt physically sick. He could think of nothing as he waited for the police to arrive. They were there within the hour.

First through the door was the Easter Bunny himself, Detective Chief Inspector Graham March.

CHAPTER THREE

Thursday, February 11th, 1993

DANNY'S shock gave way to a sense of foreboding. He accepted the handshake as an automatic courtesy, but felt repelled by the clammy touch of the older man's skin. March was an eighteen-stone, greying veteran of twenty years' police service, but had long applied his own order to the business of law. His presence dominated the room.

March introduced his colleague, Detective Constable Amy Cranston. Danny offered chairs. Cranston accepted, taking Clare's, but March chose to stand. Danny returned to his own desk, on edge.

"Talk me through yesterday," March began, in what Danny perceived as an attempt at a reassuring voice. "Everything leading up to the moment you first thought she might have disappeared. Every detail. Everything you can remember."

Immediately he was on the defensive. He didn't want to even talk to the man, and yet he knew that he didn't have an option. For Clare's sake. Despite everything he knew, DCI March was there to help. Or at least he hoped so. To be fair, the detective had a decent track record in clearing up cases. Clare had crossed paths with him on a couple of previous unrelated enquiries, although Danny knew she loathed everything he stood for. Ironically, DCI March was familiar with her work and seemed to think she was a friend. He couldn't have been more wrong.

Danny thought hard and tried to be thorough in recalling the events of the morning. The messages. The letter. The phone calls. The final call on the red private phone. The lunch appointment at Brannigan's where she didn't show. The DC took notes as he spoke.

"And you've got no idea where she was going?"

Danny shook his head.

"She said she was going out to meet somebody and that she could tell me all about it later, over lunch."

"Did you always discuss things over lunch? A plate of scampi help the conversation?"

Why did it sound like an accusation?

"No, in fact rarely... normally if one of us is going out we'd discuss it here in the office. I don't know. I suppose that was a bit strange, but we do meet for lunch occasionally. I didn't really think about it."

"Okay. So, going back. She left for a meeting. Any idea who or why?"

"No idea. She said it was dangerous but no more than normal. Oh, she said it was urgent. That she was needed urgently. And then she was gone."

"Straight after the call?"

"Yeah, definitely. In fact she'd just said she was expecting a quiet day and didn't want to go anywhere outside because the weather was filthy. It was freezing yesterday. And lashing down."

33

"It's trying to snow out there at the moment," DC Cranston confirmed. Danny didn't give a fuck about the weather.

"She didn't give any indication of what she meant by danger?"

"No, not at all. I think the exact term she used was 'risky'. I can't remember exactly. There's often an element of risk in things that we do, as you know. But it's usually more talk than anything. She said something about loose ends I think, but that was all."

"And again, she didn't give any clue about who she was meeting? She's a lovely lady. Could be a boyfriend? And maybe the risk was because he had a kinky side."

Danny gave a look of distaste.

"No, not that," he said. "No idea who she was meeting, nor where she was going. One minute she was on the phone, the next she was out of the door."

"You don't know who the call was from?"

Danny hated being civil to the man. Why did he keep asking the same question? He shifted uncomfortably in his seat.

"No. She wrote something down in her notepad, but that was all. Then she went. I've checked the next sheet to see if she left a trace of a message but nothing came through."

"Does she often go wandering off on her own? Staying out longer than you'd have expected? Maybe she's just insatiable."

"No, not really." He ignored the innuendo and decided not to mention the morning appointments.

"How did she seem? In herself."

Danny took a moment to consider.

"She seemed okay when she first came in. But, I suppose, tired perhaps? Maybe worried. No, that's probably too strong. Hassled maybe. We've been getting anonymous threat letters ever since Ravenscroft was put away but she'd said it was best to ignore them. You don't think..."

"Old Jimmy? Nah. He's safely out of reach. Do you have the

34

letters?"

"They're in a tray." Danny indicated Clare's desk. DC Cranston leaned forward and took a pile of paper from one of the filing trays.

"Are these them?" she asked. Danny nodded and she handed the letters to March, who started to look through them.

"Well, they're not nice," he began, "and the grammar isn't up to much. But if Jimmy's behind them there's nothing really to worry about. He's all mouth but it's going to be a while before he's any risk to anybody. So, she was hassled? Who was hassling her?"

"Oh, I don't know. Again, it's just been mad busy. She said she was tired. Needed an early night. It's that, I think."

March looked at DC Cranston who nodded and continued to make notes.

"I think she was probably a bit nervous about the story as well," Danny continued. "She said it was possibly the biggest story ever." Bigger even than uncovering large-scale police corruption.

"But she gave no clues to what it was all about?"

"No. Like I said, she was going to tell me everything over lunch."

The DCI frowned, and considered for a moment. Suddenly, the charm fell away.

"You look nervous," he said.

"Me?"

"Yeah, you." He paused, fixing his eyes hard on Danny's face. "Is there something you're not telling me?"

"No, of course not. Jesus. I just want to find her. I'm worried. I'm telling you everything I know."

Danny was on edge. He suddenly felt like he was under suspicion. He wasn't shocked by the sudden change in mood; he was aware of March's reputation. But it was no more welcome for that.

DCI March walked over to the window, looking out over the grey city. After a moment he checked his watch and turned back.

"So talk me through yesterday. What did you do after she left?"

"I just, well I just waited here till lunchtime. I made the reservation and then carried on with work. Then I went out just after one, to go to Brannigan's."

"And had lunch?"

"Well, no. I just had a drink while I waited, but she didn't ever come."

"Are you aware that it's against the terms of the licence for a restaurant to serve drinks without food? It can be a fairly serious offence."

"I..."

"I'm just messing with you. And after that?"

"I came back here."

"What time was that?" There was a subtext of menace. And then, with a steel edge to his voice, he added: "Just filling in the blanks."

Danny didn't like this. He felt out of his depth.

"I don't know. About 3.30 I suppose. I must have left Brannigan's about three."

"Can anybody vouch for that?"

"Er, yeah, I suppose. I came in through the main office. Anybody there would have seen me."

"And then what? You just waited here, playing games on the computer all afternoon because the boss was away?"

"What? No, of course not. I... well, I made phone calls. I expected her back at any minute but when she didn't come I called her flat, then tracked down her neighbour and called him, but nobody had seen her."

"So from the time you say you went for lunch to the time you say you came back, you were out for what? Two hours?

Three?"

"About that."

"But you didn't actually have any lunch?"

"No, I told you. I got the drinks. I waited. I didn't order any food. I was going to do that when she arrived."

"Ok. So after the lunch that wasn't a lunch, you were here all afternoon. Not playing games, but making phone calls. We can check that. And then you left? When?"

"About seven, I think."

"That's late."

"I often work late. But last night I was waiting here in case she came back."

"And you went where?"

"Straight home."

"Do you live alone?"

"No, I share a flat with a friend."

"Girlfriend?"

"No, just friend."

"Boyfriend then?"

"No, just friend. From college. A girl but not a girlfriend."

"No, you don't look like the type to have a girlfriend. So, can this 'friend' confirm what time you got back in?"

"Anna? God. No. Sorry. She was out. Why does it matter? Surely you don't..."

"No, no, of course not. Just trying to see as much as I can. You'd be amazed how often we find the answer by looking at those closest to the case. But you were home all evening?"

"Yes, from then onwards."

"Alone?"

"Yes, alone."

"Okay." The detectives exchanged glances. DC Cranston closed her notebook and made to get up.

"She's out there somewhere," said March, more to himself than Danny, returning his attention to the view. "Somebody

37

knows where she is." He turned back to Danny. "Have you got any questions for me?"

Oh, if only you knew, thought Danny.

"I just want to find her," he said. "Have you looked round her flat?"

"Not personally, but a couple of the lads went round this morning. They're probably still there. I hope they're being respectful."

"And? Have they found anything?"

The DCI shook his head.

"Not as far as I've been told. All as it should be, apparently, last I heard. There was no sign of forced entry, but by the same token there were no clues. It would help if we knew what we were looking for. If we had a body we could look for a murder weapon and then a motive."

March caught Danny's eye. It was an unfortunate turn of phrase, but Danny thought he saw a flicker of amusement. The DCI seemed to be enjoying this. But then he relented.

"Look, I didn't mean to alarm you. I'm sure she's safe. I'm sorry."

But no amount of apology could remove the doubt from Danny's mind. What if she had been killed? What if whoever had been sending the letters had actually acted on them? What then? How would he cope without her? If only he could wind the clock back twenty-four hours to the time she was last in this office, and stop her from going out. But it was no use thinking like that now.

"Listen Danny," March continued, his hard face softening. "I'm going to make you a promise. I will find Clare. Whatever it takes. Even if it means I've got to work every minute of every day from now until Christmas. And I've got the delightful DC Cranston with me, so rest assured I will be happy to work through the night if the situation demands it, if you catch my drift. I know how much she means to you. But believe me, she means as much to me as well. She's done work that we were unable to do and uncovered crimes where as far as I was aware, none existed. But more than that, she's a good friend, and I'll put myself out from here to heaven to find her, because I know she would do exactly the same if it were me."

Danny couldn't decide if March was just completely ignorant or toying with his mind. Or what if he knew he was being investigated and he'd had some part to play in Clare's disappearance? It was too much to take in. Either way, he couldn't wait for them to leave.

"If I find anything I'll let you know," he said, his confident voice masking the uncertainty that was beginning to overwhelm him. "If I come across something after you've gone."

"Yes. You do that. Keep us informed and we'll work on this together. But we will find her. Whatever it takes. Perhaps there'll be a story in it for you."

Danny fought hard to contain a look of deep distaste.

"Perhaps," he said. But at that moment a story was furthest from his mind.

CHAPTER FOUR

WHEN the detectives finally left, Danny drew breath. He was overcome by a sense of confusion, fear, panic, and shock. It was mentally and physically draining. All just so hard to believe. While there were no clues to tell them where she'd gone after leaving the office, there was no solid evidence of her disappearance, apart from the abandoned car. And why were they asking so many questions about him? Surely they didn't think he was in some way responsible?

DCI March said he would also ask Northumbria Police to keep a check on the house she kept in her home town, Sunderland, in case she should turn up there. She had no next of kin to notify. Because of the delicate nature of Clare's work, it was agreed that the press should not be informed - including colleagues at the Echo. If anybody called, she was away on business. Danny hoped it was that simple.

Alone in the office, he made his way to her chair and sat down, thinking through the previous day's events again and again. There was something he'd forgotten to tell the police.

There must have been. He thought back over the last few weeks. Nothing sprang to mind. He tried to call home to hear the reassuring voice of his flatmate. To ask her advice. But there was no one there.

Benjamin Serraillier. The fan letter. Clare had taken it. She hadn't looked too pleased. Where was it he worked? Some hotel, in Streatham.

Danny walked over to the bookshelf and took down the South London Yellow Pages. Hotel Mowbray something. It wasn't much, but it was the nearest thing to a lead that he had. Danny found the number and dialled.

"Mowbray Hall Hotel, Julia speaking, how can I help you?"

"Oh, hi. Can I speak to Benjamin Serraillier please?"

"Certainly sir. Do you know his room number?"

"Room number? I thought he was a member of the staff."

"There's nobody of that name working here, sir. Hold on, I'll check the guest list for you."

Julia disappeared. Half a minute later she returned.

"I'm afraid we don't have any guests of that name either. Are you sure you have the right hotel?"

"Yes, I think so. Nobody by that name has moved out recently, have they?"

"I'll check. One moment."

Danny frowned. This wasn't going to plan. It was probably nothing anyway. But still... The receptionist came back on the line.

"Not recently, I'm afraid. He may have done at some stage, but not within the last month."

Danny thanked her and hung up.

Something jarred in his mind. He was sure he had the right hotel. Which meant Serraillier either worked there or had used the stationery. But if he wasn't a guest, then what was he? Or was it just an old piece of paper from a previous stay? Danny had many pens taken from hotel rooms over the last year or so.

41

But the paper as well? And yet he'd read the letter, and it didn't seem unusual. It wasn't threatening and didn't seem to give any obvious cause for concern. But if that was the case, why did he think he'd seen fear cloud Clare's eyes as she'd read it? And why had she taken it in her Filofax rather than just putting it back in a tray?

Danny tried to think harder still. The receptionist had been adamant. But what if she'd been mistaken. He thought of calling her back, but knew it would pointless. The answers would just be the same.

In the absence of anything better to do, but not really knowing why, he decided to visit the hotel in person. Maybe if he spoke to someone else he'd get a different answer. It wasn't anything tangible to go on, but what else did he have?

And at least he'd feel like he was doing something.

He thought about calling DCI March, but thought better of it. He just couldn't trust the man, and as yet he didn't know that they were on the same side. And anyway it was probably nothing. Except... He closed his eyes. How he wished Clare was here. She would know what to do. He decided to trust his instincts.

He made a note of the address of the hotel: Silver Street in Streatham, south London. He left the office and made his way to the underground car park.

**

Elsewhere in London, a man let himself into a 1960s concrete tower block and brushed the worst of the rain from his shoulders. The cold had permeated his leather jacket but he didn't seem to notice. He didn't bother with the lift. It wouldn't be pleasant, and anyway he only had six flights of stairs to climb. He was in no rush.

On the third floor he left the stairwell, and walked through the dimly lit corridor to flat 35. He unlocked the door and pushed it open. There was no need for particular stealth but he hardly made a noise. Force of habit.

At the end of the hallway he turned left into the sparsely furnished living room. An ageing, sagging sofa, dust-covered portable TV and a desk with a black fabric swivel chair. Foam showed through where the covering was frayed. It wasn't a big room. It wasn't a big flat.

He eased off his jacket and threw it on the sofa before taking the chair by the desk and flicking on the lamp. He had work to do. Unlocking the desk's only drawer, he removed a Nokia 1011 mobile phone. The buttons were unfamiliar, but he found the numbers stored on the internal memory and transcribed them into a spiral-bound notebook. Then he looked at the recent calls list and wrote those numbers, too. He compared the lists. Which contacts had she called recently? Now he knew their names. Some of them were familiar. He smiled. Job well done.

When he was satisfied there was nothing more to learn, he switched off the phone. He'd take it back outside and leave it somewhere. It didn't make sense to have evidence at home. You could never be too careful.

For now, though, he just wanted a small celebration drink. She couldn't say she hadn't been warned. Now she'd paid the price. Tough.

He opened the drawer and placed the phone back inside, on top of the notebooks and the London A-Z street atlas in which he'd already highlighted the location of her flat. He'd deal with the notebooks soon but the flat was next. He felt a sense of justice being done as he reached for the bottle.

***

The Mowbray Hall Hotel was set in a tree-lined street away from the main shopping area of Streatham, on the road to

Crystal Palace. Danny parked his car in the gravel car park and made his way to reception. It was a grand entrance for an out-of-town hotel, dominated by twin marble pillars which led through to one of the bars.

"Good afternoon, sir," said the woman behind the desk, who was in her late twenties and wore the hotel uniform of a white blouse with a large blue bow and black skirt. Her nameplate was pinned to the blouse, and from it Danny could see she was Julia, the assistant manager. He assumed she was the woman he had spoken to on the phone. "Are you checking in?"

"Er, no... no. I was wondering if you could help. I'm looking for my friend Benjamin Serraillier. I believe he's staying here?"

"That's funny," she said. "You're the third person to ask for him in the last hour. But no, I'm afraid there's nobody here of that name."

Third person?

"Three? Who were the other two?"

"I don't know. Just a couple of phone calls. Are you sure you've got the right hotel?"

"I thought so, but I may not have. I'm sorry to bother you." He turned to leave, then reached for his wallet.

"One more thing," he began. He withdrew a photograph that he always carried, of himself and Clare from an awards function the previous year. It was their first big night out together. The first time he really felt part of her trusted inner circle, and the first time he felt part of her success. "Do you recognise this person? I believe she may have been here yesterday morning, meeting somebody perhaps?"

Julia looked at the picture and then back at Danny.

"Are you the police?" she asked.

"No, just a friend. Well, boyfriend, actually." He paused. "Look, to be honest, we've been going through a rough patch and I'm just worried she may have been seeing someone else. She didn't come home last night. I saw the name of this hotel

44

in her diary and I thought it was worth a try." He paused again. "It's only half a chance, but it's all I have. I love her. I want to find her. I want to bring her back."

At least the last bit was true. The rest was wishful thinking.

Julia looked up at him with a sympathetic smile.

"What was she wearing yesterday?" she asked, her voice softening.

Danny thought hard to remember. The vision was still clear in his mind, but events were conspiring to blur it around the edges.

"Black dress under a long grey coat. She would have been here about 11.15, possibly slightly earlier."

"And she was meeting this Mr Serraillier?"

"Yes. I think so." Danny blushed.

"Hold on a moment. What's your name?"

Danny told her. Julia took the picture, left the reception and spoke to a colleague in the office behind. She returned a couple of minutes later.

"I'm sorry, Danny," she began. "But yes, a woman looking very much like your girlfriend was here yesterday. Late morning. We think so anyway, but of course it may not have been."

Danny's heart skipped a beat.

"Did she book into a room?" Maybe she was here. Maybe at this very moment she was sleeping off a hangover in one of the rooms upstairs, and would wake up wondering what all the fuss was about. Although that wouldn't explain the abandoned car. Maybe it had been stolen.

"No, she wasn't a guest, I'm afraid. Although that's probably a good thing if she's your girlfriend. She had a drink in the cocktail bar with someone. I've had a word with the barmaid, and she remembers them because they'd only just ordered their drinks before they left, all in a bit of a rush."

"Did you see where they went?"

"No, sorry. They left together, though. Sorry."

Danny thought for a moment.

"This man. Did you get a look at him? Is there anything you can tell me?"

"Hold on, I'll get Carol." She turned to the back office and called for her colleague.

A small woman in her fifties appeared. She, too was dressed in the hotel uniform, but with an apron over the front. Julia made the introductions.

"Yes, love, I remember them," said Carol, "although they weren't here long."

"Can you remember what he looked like?"

She thought back.

"Not really. Sorry. Quite tall I suppose, dark hair. Maybe mid-thirties. He had a very smart suit. Navy, I think."

"I wonder," began Danny, remembering his cover story. "I think I know who he was. Had you ever seen them before?"

She shrugged.

"It's a public bar. We don't ask them to sign in. But... well, I'm not sure that I should say, really."

"No, honestly, it's okay. I'd rather know."

"Well, I'd be lying if I said no, my dear. They've been in a few times."

"Recently?"

"Over the last few weeks."

Maybe he was an actual partner. Maybe Clare had been having an affair. Maybe she was keeping it secret because he was married or just because she never really discussed her private life anyway. And if so, then maybe they'd had a falling out and she'd been upset and gone away to drown her sorrows. But why would he send a letter on hotel paper rather than just call? And how did that explain the car? It just didn't seem like Clare. In any case she'd said she was working on a story, so how did he fit into that?

"Thank you. You've been very helpful," Danny continued. "One other thing. You didn't see his car, did you? Assuming he drove here."

Carol thought for a moment.

"I did, actually. I'm not great with cars but it was very nice. Dark blue I think. Quite large but very sporty-looking. They both left in it. It made quite a noise. The windows were shut, obviously, but I could hear it as they went."

"You don't know the make?"

"No, I'm sorry. I'm not an expert. But it was unusual. Looked expensive. I'd never seen it before."

"Did you see the number plate?"

"Oh dear, no, not especially. I'm sorry."

"Not to worry. Did you see another car here yesterday, a black Lotus? Quite small but sporty too."

"Doesn't ring a bell. But the car park often gets quite full at the front. It may have been parked at the back but I only see the front from the bar."

Danny paused to take it all in.

"You've been a magnificent help," he said. "Just one more thing before I leave you to get on. I wonder if you'd mind showing me which table they sat at."

"I suppose so. Follow me."

Carol led him through to the empty cocktail bar. There were no customers and so the bar was closed.

"It was that one over there," she said, pointing to a small marble-topped table in the corner. Two large, comfortable armchairs stood beside it. Danny tried to picture them there together. Who was he? What did he want with Clare? "Look, can I get you something? A coffee? We're officially closed but my husband cheated on me, the bastard, so I know what you're going through. It's just not right."

Danny thanked her but declined.

"You didn't hear what they were talking about I suppose?"

he asked, fingers crossed.

"No, not really. She got here first and had a drink. Then he showed up a few minutes later. They weren't here much longer after that. Just ordered their drinks and left. Didn't even touch them. The one thing I did notice was his voice. It had an accent."

"What sort of accent?"

"French perhaps?" She shrugged. "I don't know. He seemed European, but that's about all I can tell you, I'm afraid."

"How were they acting together? Did they seem good friends?"

Carol hesitated.

"Yes, I suppose they seemed to know each other. They weren't holding hands or anything, mind. They were very quiet, though, as though they were nervous - waiting for something to happen. Perhaps... perhaps they thought that you were coming. It seems wrong."

"Mmm, maybe. Listen, I must thank you, you've been a big help," Danny was growing fond of the woman. She seemed decent and honest. He felt for her. He thanked her again for her trouble. She assured him it was nothing and said she'd leave him alone to think in the bar.

He sat in one of the two armchairs and began to ask himself questions. Which chair had been hers? She'd been here, but where did she go to next? His mind was devoid of possible solutions. If the two had left together, what had happened to her car? And how did it end up on the M25?

He began a more detailed search of the cocktail bar. Always check everything thoroughly and always make meticulous notes, Clare had told him. Repeatedly. He began by jotting down the layout of the room, and searched the carpet, the backs of the chairs, down the side of the cushions. He was almost at an end when he felt something hard wedged deep into the body of the chair, down the side of the cushion. He squeezed his fingers down the gap and gradually eased it free. A platinum ring, with, as its centre stone, a large Ceylon sapphire. It was Clare's ring. The one she always wore. The one she played with to help ease stress. The one he had watched her remove and replace so many times.

He pocketed the ring and quickly scanned the rest of the bar. He nodded to the receptionist on the way out.

"Thank you very much," he said. "I'm sure I'll find her."

Julia smiled, and raised an eyebrow.

"I'm sure you will," she said. "Good luck, Danny."

Danny couldn't face going back to the office. He walked to a callbox across the road and left a message to say he was going to spend the rest of the day out on business. He checked his watch. It was still too early to ask the police the result of the tests on the Lotus, even assuming they'd tell him. He got the impression they weren't going to be as cooperative as DCI March had suggested.

He needed to talk to somebody. He needed Anna. He got back in his car and set off for home.

CHAPTER FIVE

STRANGE as it may sound, I was examining a bra strap when I heard the familiar jangle of Danny's house keys. Not my bra, I hasten to add. It was a tiny detail on a 35mm transparency, face up on my light-box. I was pleased with the shot. The model had a tremendous sparkle in her eyes - the result of a multiple flash set-up I'd designed after reading an interview with the brilliant John Swannell. I'll probably get a bad back one of these days, bending over, examining pictures all the time, but hey, I'm still young, so I'll worry about that another day. There were bigger issues just now.

I rushed out to meet Danny, arms extended. Any excuse for a hug, normally, but this time it was a mercy mission.

"No news?" I asked as I wrapped my arms around him.

Danny's silence gave me all the answers I needed. I tightened my grip.

"Come on in. Let me get you something to drink. Are you hungry?"

Danny and I live together. We have done, in one place

or another, since we met as students and became the best of friends. We're not a couple, alas, although I don't think he's aware of my disappointment in that regard. He's too fixated on his boss.

I led him through to the front room, and reached over to turn off the television. He accepted a can of Michelob, but said he wasn't hungry. Nor did he seem to want my sympathy. Sympathy implied failure. He wouldn't want to contemplate being beaten. I know what he's like, probably better than anyone.

"So, what's happening? She's got to be back soon."

He recounted the day's events. How he'd met the police and felt that he was somehow under suspicion. The visit to the hotel. And finding the ring.

"The ring?"

"The one she always used to wear. At least we know that's where she went. We just don't know why, or who she was meeting. Was he a boyfriend? A source? We still don't know if she's run off, been kidnapped, or she's just in a hotel somewhere and doesn't even know her car's been stolen. It's all a mess." Danny clearly felt the hollowness of despair and I could see tears just below the surface. Tears of frustration. Of loss. Of fear.

I was secretly quite excited by the thought of Clare running off with a boyfriend, but kept this to myself.

"Have you told the police?"

"Not yet. I was going to call them today. It's just knowing what to say. They kept suggesting I was keeping something back from them, which I wasn't. But now I've gone off somewhere and found her ring, which won't sound great if they start asking questions."

"But you've got to tell them."

"I know. I just... I don't know. I just want her back."

"Wait there."

In truth, he wasn't going to do much else. I went to my desk and got a notepad and pen. Luckily I'm fairly resourceful in moments of crisis.

"Okay, so where are we?"

"How do you mean?"

"Well, let's think about this. Let's make a list. Come on, Poirot. Where could she be? And why? Who do we think is involved?" I think it got on his nerves when I called him Poirot but I was past caring.

"It could be anybody. She could be anywhere."

That wasn't much of a start.

"Come on," I said, trying to encourage him to think logically, but aware of his sensitive state of mind. I could only imagine the panic he was feeling. "Who was she meeting?"

"Benjamin Serraillier."

"And what do we know about him?"

"Not much. Drives a blue sports car, foreign accent, maybe French. They've met a few times. Oh, and he sent her a fan letter on headed paper from the hotel."

"Okay, good start. Weird but good. We'll leave him there for a moment. Next?"

"Next? Well, I suppose Jimmy Ravenscroft."

"What? I thought you'd had him put away."

"We did. He's down for ages but ever since the court case we've been getting anonymous death threats."

"Jesus."

"I know. Not good."

"How's he doing that if he's in prison? Don't they check the mail?"

"I assume so, but presumably he's got someone on the outside doing it for him."

"Okay. Do we need to take him seriously?"

"I think so, but the police think not. Oh, that's a point. DCI March."

52

"Who's he?"

"He's the detective who came to interview me, in charge of finding Clare."

"Right. So one of the good guys."

Danny just looked at me. Took a deep breath and shook his head.

"No, definitely not one of the good guys," he said with a sigh.

"How come?"

"You wouldn't believe. He's a bent bastard. Been on the take for years. We've been investigating him."

"And he's in charge of finding Clare?"

"I know. Not great. And yet, of everyone we know so far, he's probably got most to gain from her disappearance. Although presumably he'd need to get rid of me, too. Jesus."

"Let's not think about that."

We both stopped for a minute. This was a lot to take in all of a sudden.

"Are your files safe?"

"Yeah. We both keep copies. I'll go through them."

"Okay. Make sure you do. And then photocopy them again. Urgently. Anyone else?"

"We had a phone call. Some bloke, maybe from the East End, wanting to meet. But that was probably nothing. I can't remember now. I remember telling Clare but can't remember how she reacted. I wasn't really expecting any of this. But we don't know who he was. He was supposed to be ringing back, but hasn't as far as I know."

"Okay, a mysterious man. Anyone else? Anything else we should make a note of?"

"No, I can't think of anything. I mean it could be anyone she's written about over the years. She's made a lot of enemies - nature of the job - but none I can think of who would go that far. Although she did have her car broken into."

"Really? When was that?"

"A few days ago. Sunday, I think. Yes, Sunday. Her phone got stolen and a few other things. Some notebooks. She said they weren't anything important and it would have all been in shorthand anyway, but that was a bit odd."

"Okay. Car theft. Although she's presumably fairly used to that if she comes from Sunderland." Not my finest attempt at humour. Luckily Danny seemed not to notice.

"And things have been a bit odd since Christmas. She's been late in a few times, which seems a bit unusual, but again it's probably nothing."

"Strange. I'll write it down. Anything else, at all?"

Danny shook his head.

"Right. Well, that's a start. We'll get there. She's out there somewhere."

"That's what March said."

"It's true. Got to be."

Danny looked up at me and I could see the pain in his eyes.

"Thank you," he said. I put the pad down.

"I'll get the phone so you can call the police and tell them about the ring. Unless, of course..."

"Unless March is behind all this and it makes things worse." Danny finished my thought.

But before we could do anything else, the handset started ringing. I rushed to the table where it sat in its base station. I answered, looking at Danny. But he was lost in thought, looking like he was fighting feelings of desolation. After a moment, I passed him the receiver.

"It's DCI March," I said, looking concerned and distasteful in equal measure. Danny took the phone, while I sat on the arm of the sofa, my hand resting on his shoulder.

"This is Danny," he said, and then paused, listening. Finally he turned to me.

"Yes, of course. I'll come in now." He pressed the button to end the call.

"News?"

"They've finished searching the car. I've got to go in and answer more questions."

"More questions? What sort of questions?"

"I don't know. They just said I was needed, at my earliest convenience. Implying if I didn't go now they'd come and find me."

"I don't like the sound of this." Then I thought I should at least attempt a brave face for Danny's sake. "But hopefully it's good news. Hopefully they're onto something. Come on, I'll take you down and we can decide what to do about the whole hotel and ring thing on the way."

"Cheers, Anna," he said, sounding braver than I suspect he felt. We got up and headed out into the early evening traffic, driving through lashing rain, heading for Danny's second police interview of the day.

CHAPTER SIX

ONCE at the station, Anna waited in reception while Danny was shown through to an interview room by a uniformed PC. He was asked to take a seat on one side of a Formica table and then left alone to wait. And wait. Time ticked on, but nobody came. He got up to walk around and inspect his surroundings, but eventually returned to the hard plastic chair that was screwed to the floor. From the other side of the two-way mirror, DCI March watched him closely, with DC Cranston alongside.

Eventually, after almost an hour, March and Cranston entered the room. They didn't apologise for the delay. March sat down opposite Danny, while DC Cranston remained standing, expressionless.

"Danny, thank you for coming," March began. Danny nodded in acknowledgement. He knew better than to voice his frustration. "Interview started at 18:50 hours on Thursday, 11th February 1993. For the tape, can you please confirm your identity."

Danny did so, but alarm was spreading through his veins.

"Okay," March continued, "again for the tape I will confirm that also present are DCI March, that's me, and DC Cranston, which is the delightful Amy over there. Danny, you are here voluntarily and are free to leave at any time, although I would strongly advise against that until we've finished asking a few questions. You have a right to have a solicitor present if you would like one. If you do not have a solicitor we can appoint one for you."

"A solicitor? Are you charging me with something?"

"Should we be?" March stayed silent, looking for a reaction.

Danny could feel his skin prickle. The room suddenly seemed uncomfortably warm.

"Of course not. I just want to help you find Clare. Have you found her?"

"All in good time. For the tape, Mr Churchill has declined the offer of legal representation."

"I..."

"Danny. Shut up, and listen. You could be in a lot of trouble here so I suggest you answer the questions. Tell me the truth. Don't leave anything out. And if all goes to plan we'll be out of here in time for last orders. Now, where's Clare?"

"How do I know? I... Have you found something?"

"Have we found Clare? No. Have we found her car? Yes. And have we searched it? Yes. Can you tell me where you were between the hours of 1pm and 4pm on Wednesday, February 10th."

"You know where I was. I went to meet Clare at Brannigan's but she didn't show up."

"Okay, and for the record, you previously stated you then returned to the office where you stayed on your own until 7pm, before returning home, again alone."

"Yes, exactly."

"You see, that gives us a problem, Danny. Clare's gone

missing and you don't have an alibi for most of the day. Have you got a driving licence, Danny?"

"Yes, you know I have."

"And have you ever driven Clare's car?"

"Clare's car? No, of course not."

"And yet, Danny, we found two sets of fingerprints inside the car. And I think one of them is yours."

The warmth was getting oppressive. Danny began to feel nauseous.

"Well, that's possible I suppose. I've been in the car, but not yesterday."

"So you say."

"I haven't!"

"Okay, calm down."

Danny was beginning to feel a rising anger and resentment. What the hell were they playing at? Why were they wasting time on this and not out there looking for Clare?

"I am calm. This is just a complete waste of time. I don't understand what this is about. You want to be investigating Ravenscroft, not me. Nobody wants to find Clare more than me."

"Hmmm, so you say."

"Yes, so I say. Jesus."

"Okay. And don't worry yourself about old Jimmy. He's turned a corner now. Couldn't wish to meet a nicer man. But while we're discussing the things you say, what would you say if we told you we found a notebook in the car in which Clare made it very clear that she thought you wanted to take over her job?"

"What?"

"What would you say, Danny?"

"That's madness. I mean, yes, we have discussed that. In fact we talked about it yesterday morning. She said one day I would take over, but..."

58

"But you didn't think to mention this in our earlier conversation, in which I specifically remember asking you to tell me everything that had happened yesterday morning."

"Well no, because it's..."

"It's what? Not relevant?"

"No. Exactly that. It's got nothing to do with anything."

"I think you should leave me to be the judge of that." He turned to DC Cranston before adding: "You know what I hate? Jumped-up wet-behind-the-ears journalists who think they're God's gift to investigation because they once played a game of fucking Cluedo, and who think they know better than the professionals who do this for a living." He turned back to Danny. "So anything else - any other vital piece of information that you suddenly remember not telling me earlier?"

Danny shook his head. He was pretty sure he wasn't going to tell DCI March anything at all unless specifically asked, and sod the consequences.

March took a set of keys and put them on the table.

"Do you recognise these keys?"

"Yes."

"We found these in the car," he said. "I wonder if you could help me work out what they open. The Yale key opens the door to Clare's flat, and the car key fits the Lotus. There's a back door key and a garage key, but the other three are a mystery."

Danny looked at the collection. He identified them as one for the office, one for the filing cabinet, and one for Clare's desk. He handed them back.

"Do you know anybody who may have a spare key to Clare's flat?"

"I've got one... but apart from that, no, no one that I can think of. Neighbours maybe."

The DCI nodded.

"Do you often go to Clare's flat?"

"No, not really."

"But you wish you did?"

"How do you mean?"

"Are you in love with Clare, Danny?"

Danny just blushed. He was tempted to say "no comment" like he'd seen on countless police dramas, but his complexion gave him away.

"I'm going to be watching you, Danny," March continued. "I don't know what you're playing at but I know you're playing at something. Clare is a very good friend of mine. If I find out that you have anything - anything at all - to do with her disappearance, or you have done anything at all to cause her any harm, I'm going to have you. Let me leave you in no doubt about that. Your life as you know it will be over. Interview suspended. You're free to leave. For now. But you'd better hope she turns up soon, or you're going to have to tell me where you've hidden her body, and if you don't I'll personally crucify you."

And with that the two detectives left the room. Danny sat in shocked silence until a uniformed PC returned to escort him back to reception.

***

If I could put aside my petty romantic jealousies, I'd have to admit to liking Clare, and having a huge respect for her professional achievements. Big "if" though, in fairness. I once offered her my services as a photographer, hoping for the byline "pictures by Anna Burgin" in the national press. It would have done wonders for my career, but I don't think she took me particularly seriously. She's a bit cold sometimes but a brilliant journalist and a fantastic teacher. I'll give her that. And Danny's misguided affection isn't her fault, as far as I can tell. I'm not even sure she's aware of it.

He looked as pale as a badly overexposed snowscape when

he returned to reception. He didn't speak and I didn't really know what to say either. I asked if he was okay but he just shook his head and indicated for me to follow him back outside.

Once in the cold night air he relaxed, but he still looked older and more serious than I'd ever seen him.

"They think it's me. The absolute bastards think it's me," he said at last. And then he gave me a short summary of the interview, adding some fairly choice swear words that were, it has to be said, entirely justifiable.

"What next? Back to the flat?" I asked, once we were back inside my car. I fired up the engine and turned on the heater to attempt to de-mist the windscreen.

"I think... oh, I don't know," Danny began. "Can we go to Clare's flat?"

"Of course, but you'll have to direct me." I kind of knew it was in the Docklands somewhere but I'd never been invited.

"It shouldn't take long. Head east and I'll show you." Danny took a bunch of keys from his coat pocket as I turned on the wipers in a rather futile effort to help clear the screen more quickly. "I've got a spare set of keys from the office. We can have a look around, see what we can find. I don't trust March and God knows who he had in there searching the place. We'll see what they've missed."

Danny looked through the keys and then stopped.

"That's different," he said.

"What is?"

"There's an extra key. March had the original set and asked me to identify them, but these are the spare ones she kept in her desk. There's an extra one."

He flicked on the interior light to take a better look. The key in question had a green plastic cover at the hub which featured a large, distinctive embossed letter R. It was unusual. Similar to the front door key but slightly smaller and bright silver in colour. Inset into the green plastic was the number 1196. It looked new.

"What's that for?" I asked. It was a fairly stupid question, given that he'd just noticed it.

"No idea, but we're going to find out."

The windscreen had cleared well enough that I could see to drive, so I pulled out and headed towards the exit of the car park.

***

They hadn't noticed the person in the black Sierra taking photographs as they left the station. And they didn't notice the same car set out to follow them as they pulled out of the car park, heading east.

CHAPTER SEVEN

WITHIN forty minutes we were pulling up outside an impressive block of flats in the Isle of Dogs, close to the Thames in the Docklands area of London. It was an up-and-coming part of town but felt a bit like a building site, with cranes and scaffolding masking a lot of the construction. As we walked through the entrance lobby, the concierge nodded and said good evening. It was like the reception of a smart hotel, oozing calm and sophistication. And money. Danny led the way to the lift and pressed the button for the seventh floor. Other buttons offered a swimming pool and a gym. It was all right for some. We found Clare's flat and Danny opened the door. I couldn't help feeling a tinge of jealousy.

"Nice place," I said as I surveyed the living room. The flat had all the hallmarks of newly acquired wealth. It was expensively furnished but in a modern rather than classical style. There was a thick pile carpet underfoot. The room was dominated by a cream leather suite which curved round in the shape of a horseshoe. A wineglass stood next to a couple of magazines and an empty ashtray on the large glass-topped coffee table. An expensive-looking hi-fi and Nicam stereo television stood against one wall. There was a faint smell of stale cigarettes.

I moved over to the large picture window and admired the view across the Thames. A small boat headed upriver far below, but the sound of the outside world was muffled. Rain clouds obscured most of the moonlight. It appealed to my sense of dramatic lighting.

Danny, meanwhile, checked both of the bedrooms and the bathroom for any sign of life, or at least recent habitation. I tested the sofa, and, with a professional eye, picked up a copy of Company magazine from the table. The Christmas theme of the cover lines told me it wasn't a recent issue. Danny emerged.

"Anything?" I asked.

"No, not really. It doesn't look like she's gone away through choice. There's a toothbrush and toiletries, and there's a case in the spare room that's still half packed, but nothing seems obviously missing. I don't know. It just feels weird."

We both headed to the kitchen which had colour-coordinated Poggenpohl units and a host of integral appliances. Like the living room, it was clean, but there was a thin coating of dust on the surfaces. I opened the fridge. There was a bottle of semi-skimmed milk in the door, long past its best before date, and inedible-looking food next to two bottles of wine on the glass shelves. Danny indicated a pile of post that lay opened on the kitchen counter.

"This was on the doormat when I looked through yesterday," he said. "Presumably the police have gone through them."

I felt uncomfortable going through someone's private mail, but it had to be done. I picked up the first envelope. It had been carefully ripped open. Inside was a credit card statement. There were no new items on the bill, but the outstanding balance was £860. The minimum payment had doubled because nothing had been paid the month before.

Three other letters were junk mail, with offers of free gifts if Clare would accept catalogues or goods on approval. Danny made a comment about the state of the Brazilian rainforests and how many trees were felled each year to produce letters that nobody read. He opened a gas bill and a red reminder from the electricity board.

"Looks like she hasn't been paying anybody this month," he remarked. He looked at the postmarks on the envelopes. Some were dated January.

"She's not been here, has she?" he said. It was looking that way. But more than that, it looked like her entire life had been put on hold. I shuddered. It was like going through the belongings of a dead woman.

The last letter was different to the others. It had a handwritten envelope and was slightly larger than A4 size. The stamp was French. Inside was a catalogue from an art gallery and a compliments slip, signed simply "as requested, Dominique". The gallery - La Galerie du Châtelet - boasted of sales offices in Paris, Geneva and New York. Danny put it back down on the counter.

"No clues," he said, frustration showing itself in the weary tone of his voice. "I'll check the answering machine."

He went back into the front room and found the machine, but I'd checked it earlier. It was left in the "at home" position, and didn't even have a tape, so that wasn't much use. Nothing else in the room seemed unusual or out of place. I glanced into the bedrooms just to double-check. The main room had a large double bed, with what looked like clean linen. A couple of novels stood next to a lamp on the bedside table. The tiled bathroom looked clean. I checked a sponge in the shower but it was hard. It hadn't seen water for a while. Bottles of perfume and moisturiser stood next to the sink.

The spare bedroom had been turned into an office. There

was a single bed, made up presumably in case of guests, but beside that was a black ash desk, facing the window, complete with an Ambra PC. Danny came to join me but there wasn't much more to see. We returned to the living room, closed a few of the curtains, and made our way out.

"Where to now, Poirot?" I asked as Danny opened the front door.

"Back home, I suppose," he replied. "I just don't get it. She's been missing for a day but, from the looks of things here, she's been staying elsewhere for weeks. But where? And why? Oh Clare, Clare, Clare. Where the hell are you?"

We headed downstairs and returned to the car. I opened my door and got in, and then reached across to open Danny's door.

"Central locking's gone funny," I said, by way of explanation. "Sometimes it does, sometimes it doesn't." I'd bought a Honda Prelude because they were supposed to be reliable but it wasn't without its foibles. "Come on. Let's get back, we'll give it some thought and I'll do my best to cheer you up."

Back in Camden, Danny called the night desk at the Echo to see if there were any messages while I went to the kitchen. I struggled to choose between alcohol and tea but then opted for the latter. I got a sense it was time for a clear head. When I returned to the front room, he was just replacing the receiver.

"Nothing there," he said, accepting the mug I'd made him. It was a slow news day, and for a journalist there was nothing more frustrating, especially when you're at the centre of the story. I switched off the light-box, where I'd been working before heading to the police station, and phoned out for a takeaway. I had no idea when Danny had last eaten. Okay, so I didn't think either of us would have much of an appetite, but it just felt like a positive thing to do. I didn't know what to do for the best. I decided to give Danny some time to process everything while I waited for the pizza man, but once the food was served I joined him on the sofa and gently coaxed him into conversation.

"I don't know what to think any more. Too many things just don't add up," he said, at last. "She can't be... I can't even say it. Just can't be. She's just too full of life. She'll be fine. Wherever she is. She'll be okay. She's strong."

"I'm sure," I replied, with all the confidence of a kitten making its way through the exercise yard at Battersea Dogs Home.

We ate in silence. I didn't really taste the food. I wasn't particularly hungry, but I was keen to make sure Danny had something. He looked similarly uninterested. His mind was clearly and understandably elsewhere.

"Do you have that list?" he asked after a while.

"List?"

"The one you made earlier. We've got to be missing something."

I fetched my notebook and recapped the earlier discussion.

"Serraillier, Ravenscroft, March. London bloke maybe. Car break-in, arriving late at work. That's it so far." I passed it over.

"I'm just trying to think of anyone else. Anyone she'd upset or who'd benefit from her disappearance."

I thought for a moment, and then said: "There's nobody at work, is there?"

"At the Echo? No, I don't think so."

"No jealous rivals, someone she beat to a story?"

"No... Actually yes! Not at the Echo, but yeah, there was a guy from another paper who gave me hell at an awards do. Said Clare was overrated, shallow, a fraud and she was using me. Ooh, what was his name? Haldane. Something Haldane. Mark? Mickey? Something."

"And he just came up to you?"

"Yes, in the toilets. Sean! Yes, Sean Haldane. I can't remember where he was from. The Express or the Mail or somewhere.

67

I think he's gone freelance now. He virtually pinned me to the wall and just went off on one. Seemed very, very bitter. I mentioned it to Clare when I got back to the table but she just said to ignore him. That he was old school, typical hack, drank too much, couldn't trust a word he said. Or wrote."

"Sounds like a knob. Add to the list?"

"May as well. Can't do any harm." Danny took the pen and wrote 'Sean Haldane?' at the bottom of the page. The pen hovered, waiting for inspiration to strike. Eventually he put it down and turned back to me.

"It's weird," he started. "She always criticised the press - not just newspapers but all news really - for employing people like Haldane. It's like living up to the stereotype. And for being too morbid. It's always stories of famine, wars, riots, murders, explosions, earthquakes, plane crashes. She hated all of that. She said it was too depressing. She'd become a writer to do good. Maybe not for the people she wrote about, but to make a positive difference."

I realised how little I really knew about Clare outside of her work. Of course I heard stories, occasionally, but she just seemed like this enigmatic figure, not to be messed with.

"Had she always wanted to write?" I asked.

"I think so. She had a couple of other jobs first, but she was looking after her mother who was ill, so that was the main focus. She didn't really talk about family much, but she did say how hard it was when her mum died. And how frustrating it was that she'd died before Clare had the chance to make her proud."

"I know. It's just such a shame. God, shame isn't the right word but I don't know what is. Tragedy, I suppose. There's no justice."

Danny nodded.

"She said she was there the night her mother died. It was at a hospice. It sounded horrible. She was getting worse by the day. The night she died, Clare sat up with her, holding her hand as her breathing got slower and slower until eventually it stopped. Her mother's skin had gone yellow with the jaundice. She looked terrible, yet somehow she looked at peace. Clare used to reminisce about the good times they'd shared together and how her mother had been the entire focus of her life from the age of eleven when her father died. She used to say how she hoped she was watching her from the other side."

"And do you think she was? Looking from the other side?"

"Oh God, I hope so for Clare's sake. I could see how much it hurt her. I could see how lonely she felt even though she tried her best not to show it. It was subtle things that set her off - Christmas without the annual trip home, other people getting birthday cards from their parents, having nobody she could talk to. There's no substitute for the maternal touch."

"What else did she talk about?"

"About work really." If Danny felt like he was being interviewed, it didn't show. "She used to say how happy she was in some ways, but not in others. She would say how vital the work was. And yet..." He paused as though lost in thought.

I gave him a moment. I can be quite thoughtful when I put my mind to it. He'd continue when he was ready.

"And yet," he said eventually, "on the morning she disappeared, she spoke about a daydream of leaving one day. She said she was tired and not to pay any attention. But I don't know if it was a premonition in some way. I'd give anything to be back in that room at that moment. If only I'd got to the phone first and answered the call."

"Assuming it was the call that prompted her to leave."

"It must have been. She'd not long been in. Said it was freezing outside and she wasn't going anywhere. And next minute... Gone."

"But the weird thing is that, from the state of the flat, it looks like she'd been gone for a couple of weeks at least before she actually went missing."

"I know. I don't understand it. Unless..."

"Unless?"

"Well, unless she's been hiding from someone. It's like we've been getting these letters from Ravenscroft. She always seemed to laugh them off. But what if she was spooked? What if she didn't dare go home? Because she was scared. I just don't know. I just don't know if that makes it more or less likely she's been taken. Part of me is convinced she's hiding out somewhere, but she'd know I'd be worried witless, so surely she'd get in touch."

"Of course she would."

"But that means that wherever she is, she either can't make contact or... "

Danny shook his head. He didn't need to finish the sentence. We both knew what he was thinking and it wasn't good.

"So what else did she talk about? Outside of work."

"Not a lot. I feel like I've got to know her really well and yet there are big parts that are just a mystery. I remember one night she said she had this vision of opening a global restaurant, like four kitchens in one place - one French, one Italian, one Chinese, and one Indian. Then you could go out as a group and order whatever you liked from any of the four menus. So everybody could go to the same restaurant without any arguments, and yet eat exactly what they wanted."

"Not a bad idea."

"I know, it's good. I can't imagine her ever doing it, though."

"Did she have any hobbies? Go to the cinema? Boyfriends?" Worth a try. I'm a bad person.

"No idea really. I know she had a fascination with the sea. Yes, she loved that. I think it comes from growing up on the coast because I feel much the same. And she'd talk about taking fictional dogs to a deserted beach as an expression of freedom, shouting at the waves to vent frustration. It's the power and sound of the ocean. It's soothing."

"I can imagine."

"At the beach you're standing at the very edge of a country, or a continent maybe. If you look out to sea, everything is behind you - all the great people, industries, works of art, and problems you can face in your life. She was getting into art as well towards the end. I suppose that's what that catalogue was about at the flat."

"Did she have many friends?"

"I don't think so. She always kept herself to herself. I went out with her a few times for awards dinners or functions, and she seemed to get on well with everybody, apart from the odd idiot from other papers, but she never really talked about friends. She rarely had personal calls at the office. She had no living relatives that I know of."

"It sounds lonely."

"It probably was."

"Which is where you come in?"

"Haha. Destined to be her soulmate. No, we got on really well, or at least I thought we did. She'd know that I'd be out there looking for her now. I suppose I can take strength from that. She trusted me, I know that."

"Oh Danny, it's hard." I reached for his hand and gave it a squeeze. "She sounds like a lovely person but she's had some tough times."

"I know. But I think that's what gives her the drive." He put his plate down on the table, and sat back, head tilted towards the ceiling as though looking for inspiration.

"I'll tell you one thing," he said. "She had two notices stuck to the wall by her desk. They're quotations. One was, 'Your body is a book and I can't look beyond the cover. Beauty is a flower that time will devour.' The other was, 'When she was born she was as pure as snow, but like the snow she drifted.'"

CHAPTER EIGHT

Friday, February 12th, 1993

ONCE in bed, Danny tossed and turned but finally dropped off. When he awoke the next morning, he checked the doormat, hoping for a sign - an anonymous note made up of letters cut from newspapers, or a ransom demand. But there was none.

He quietly had a shower, trying not to wake Anna, and was in the process of getting dressed when he heard something being pushed through the letterbox. He rushed to the doorway.

Anna had one letter which offered her a clothing catalogue and a choice of free gifts. Yet more junk mail. Yet more wasted paper.

The only letter addressed to Danny was in a large white envelope, slightly larger than A4. The address was handwritten, and the stamp was French. It looked strangely familiar but Danny struggled to place it, given the fog of fatigue.

He carefully opened it and withdrew a catalogue from an art gallery and a compliments slip, signed simply "as requested, Dominique". It was the same as the one he had found at Clare's flat the day before. He looked through the brochure, which was full of prints of the best works on display. La Galerie du Châtelet was in Paris, on the banks of the Seine, but had sales offices in other countries.

Danny looked at it and scanned the envelope for any further messages, but there were none. Dominique. Dominique who? And the R on the silver key. R who, or what? None of it made sense. He took a deep breath, wrote a note for Anna, finished getting dressed, skipped breakfast and headed to the Echo.

It seemed strange being back in the office, almost as though it was a crime scene. He half expected to find it cordoned off with police tape, but from what he could tell from the far end of the open-plan news floor, it was exactly the same as he'd left it the day before. He kept his head down as he passed Mike Walker's office, trying not to attract attention, but stopped when he heard the editor shout his name through the open door. The tone was brusque.

He turned back and stood at the doorway, but Walker gestured him inside.

"Danny, what's going on?" he asked without any opening pleasantries.

"In terms of?"

Walker's head jerked back, as though in surprise at the question. Either that, or the impudence of asking it.

"In terms of I'm relying on Clare to deliver a front page lead on police corruption and she's gone away on business to fuck knows where. I need it yesterday. Now is not the time to go swanning off."

"I'm sorry... It was er, unavoidable."

"It had better have been. When is she back?"

"I'm not sure, sorry."

"Jesus." Walker paused. Then he sighed and shook his head. "The deadline remains. I'm not happy about this, just in case you were in any doubt."

"No, I appreciate. But I thought we had until the end of next week."

"No. That's when she suggested. I didn't agree to it. I need something. From Clare, from you, or from the fucking post boy. I don't actually care. But I need it today. Understood?"

Before Danny had a chance to answer, the paper's sports editor entered the room, and Walker's attention was diverted. Danny just nodded, turned, and made his way back to his own office in the far corner. As if things weren't already stressful enough.

He spent an hour copying all of the Easter Bunny files, laboriously photocopying paper and backing up floppy disks to protect their research into DCI March. It didn't seem wise to keep things at home. He taped everything into two manila folders and found a hiding place under the plinth of the office bookcase. It wasn't perfect but it would have to do.

Once he was convinced everything was as safe as possible, he picked up the phone and dialled the code for France followed by the number on the front page of the art gallery catalogue. The call was answered by the third ring.

"Bonjour, La Galerie du Châtelet."

"Ah, good morning, I'm calling from England. Do you speak English?"

"Un moment s'il vous plaît."

Danny waited and finally spoke to a woman who introduced herself as Michelle. He asked if he could speak to Dominique, but Michelle assured him that nobody with that name worked at the gallery apart from one of the cleaners and he was away on holiday. It was possible, but unlikely, that he was the man. After a few minutes of further enquiries, which drew a similarly blank response, Danny hung up and looked at the brochure again.

The gallery was small but had an impressive list of exhibits, together with a similarly impressive list of addresses in France, Switzerland and the USA. The name rang a bell - Danny was sure he had heard it spoken recently, but where and by whom?

He took a piece of paper from his desk. At the top he wrote CLARE: THE FACTS, and then underneath all of the clues he had gathered so far and the leads he could pursue:

Mowbray Hall Hotel.
The ring.
Serraillier.
The dark blue sports car. What could that be?
The phone call from a man with an east London accent, asking Clare to meet him.
La Galerie du Châtelet, and Dominique.
The key, and the letter R.
The Lotus, and the M25.
The hours between leaving the hotel and finding the car.
The middle of the night phone call that never was.

Was that all there was? He scanned his notebook, desperately searching for clues that he may have missed. He ran through his movements from the moment he'd returned from Brannigan's. He ran through a list of the calls he'd made and how he'd called Clare's flat and left a message on the answering machine. How he'd... Hold on, the answering machine. He'd called twice and heard Clare's message both times, but only left a message once. Yet when he'd looked round Clare's flat the machine was set to "at home" and the tape had been removed. Who had been there? It must have been the police. And they would have heard his message, so at least that gave him some form of alibi. Some sort of confirmation that he was telling the truth. But why hadn't they left the machine to answer any incoming calls?

Unless they had.

Unless someone else had been there since. Or first, and removed the tape altogether.

It suddenly seemed obvious, but just raised more questions. Somebody had been to Clare's flat before him and maybe even before the police. But who and why? Why had they removed the tape? What other messages were on there?

Somebody else must have called. Somebody else who was somehow connected, who knew Clare's home number. And why had they not put another tape into the machine? What else had been changed before he arrived? Maybe before the police could search and find nothing at all.

He made a note of all those questions, and began a search through the Yellow Pages for any company with the distinctive R in its logo. He looked at Central London first, then South-East and South-West. Every so often, when his eyes grew tired of looking at the yellow paper, he turned to the London L-R white pages directory.

Danny worked all morning without success. Every so often the phone would ring and he'd stop to answer it, but it was just routine enquiries and nothing to do with the case. He worked through lunch, fighting eyestrain, and becoming ever more desperate for success. But it eluded him. He decided to leave the office early, risking more wrath from his editor, and head for home before the onslaught of a heavy Friday rush hour. The weekend was beckoning and with it would come time to collect his thoughts. Maybe he should trust DCI March. Maybe he should tell him about the ring, the key, the catalogue. But it went against every fibre of his instinct. He gave himself a deadline. If there was no progress by Monday, he'd tell the police everything.

By 2.30pm he'd checked all the directories without success. He packed up and headed back to the flat, via a key-cutting shop on Camden High Street. The steady rain was turning to sleet. The afternoon was already getting dark. It matched his mood.

"Don't know," said the locksmith once he'd looked at the key. "It's nothing too special, but it's not something we carry blanks for. Why are you asking?"

"No reason, really, it's just part of a puzzle I'm trying to solve. Sort of an initiative test, if you like," said Danny.

"It's a security key, which means you can't get spares cut easily. Any idea where it comes from?"

Danny shook his head.

"Then I think your best bet is to find out what the R stands for. It looks vaguely familiar, although it doesn't ring any bells with lock manufacturers that I know. Sorry I can't be any more help to you."

Danny pocketed the key and expressed his gratitude.

As he headed back to the car he had a sudden overwhelming need for food. He walked into a cafe offering all-day breakfasts and sat down to think. As he waited for his food to arrive, he picked up a copy of the early edition of the Evening Standard that someone had left on the table before him. But as he looked at the front page lead, his appetite vanished: his entire world seemed to stop on its axis.

CHAPTER NINE

I WAS a bit of a waif when I first moved to London, although I like to think I make up what I lack in height and physical presence with an effervescent, sparkling wit, haha. Remarkably I had no shortage of admirers. (Although I admit I was bit confused. I dressed like a goth but had big, curly eighties hair. Work that out.) But none had the depth of personality I was looking for.

Danny is different. Okay, so normally I like them taller (he's around 5'10") and he can come across a bit geeky at times, but he's in good shape for someone who spends a lot of time at a keyboard, and he dresses well. More important than physicality, though, we just seem to naturally understand each other. And when Danny is troubled I'm right there, feeling every moment of anguish beside him.

I didn't know how long he'd need me, but I knew I wanted to be there for him, whatever it took, and in my opinion that's more important than photographing fashion. So I spent the first part of Friday morning rearranging the shoots I'd planned for the following week, and then finalised the transparencies I'd already been working on so I could drop them off at the magazine's offices in Soho. I don't like sending things on bikes. They make me nervous. I think it's something to do with relinquishing control to strange men in black leather, but let's not even begin to ponder the implications of that.

I emerged from the magazine's building into the afternoon gloom and walked through the seedy backstreets, past neon signs of the strip joints and peep shows in the direction of Soho Square and then back onto the Underground at Tottenham Court Road. I don't like the tube at the best of times, either - it's claustrophobic, crowded, you're at the mercy of the staff and you never go exactly where you'd want to - but parking in Soho can be a nightmare so I'd left the car at home.

Pausing only to buy a copy of the afternoon edition of the Evening Standard, I headed down to the Northern Line. I was looking forward to seeing if Danny had made any progress, and trying to formulate the next stage of our nascent plan. My journey was spoilt slightly by an annoying youth with a Walkman producing an irritatingly tinny "tss tss tss" sound. It's the sort of thing that causes more stress to more passengers on a daily basis than the vague, omnipresent threat of an IRA bomb.

Mind you, talking of bombs... The Standard's headline told of yet another blast - the latest in a wave that was attempting to shake the city out of its complacency. I did the standard commuter thing of sitting with my legs crossed, attempting to stop other passengers reading my paper while being horrified by the story.

"NINE HURT IN HOTEL BLAST," shouted the headline beside a scene of utter destruction. "Nine people were seriously injured this morning when a bomb ripped through a south London hotel.

"The explosion happened shortly after 11.15 at the Mowbray

Hall Hotel in Silver Street, Streatham.

"As yet no group has come forward to claim responsibility, although it is believed that the attack bears all the hallmarks of the IRA."

The carriage seemed to be closing in on me, suspending me in a daze of shocked inertia. I had to get off but I couldn't move. I felt trapped in an ever-growing nightmare. My first thought was for Danny. Then Clare.

And then, what the fuck was actually going on?

I sprinted from the tube station up Camden Road and back to the flat in Rochester Square. I say sprinted. That was the initial plan, but it was pretty much a jog long before I reached Camden Road train station, and a fast walk by the end of it. Nevertheless, I wanted to get home as soon as I could.

Danny was on the phone when I arrived. He was holding the Standard and making enquiries about the condition of the victims. I don't know if he was calling the hospital or colleagues at the Echo, but either way he didn't seem to be getting very far.

There was a stunned silence between us as he ended the call, and we both acknowledged the terrible news from Streatham. Finally Danny spoke, and I listened as he told me of his fears for Julia and Carol.

"It's got to be connected to Clare," he said at last. "Got to be. Why else would somebody bomb a hotel down in Streatham?"

"But why?"

"I don't know. To hide something?"

"What have they got to hide?" I was hoping he wouldn't say her name. He didn't.

"I don't know. Something that links them to her disappearance. Or else... God. What if they thought she was going to be there?"

The thought was too horrifying to contemplate.

"So what's next?" I only just managed to stop myself calling him Poirot.

"Wait and see what happens, talk to the hotel people as soon as possible, and in the meantime work on the other leads."

"Are there many other leads to work on?"

"Well, that's the thing. Not really, no."

I picked up the paper and read the story again. As Danny got up to walk around, I flicked through the other pages. Until one of the advertisements shook me into action.

"Danny, where's the key?" I asked with urgency. "The key with the R on it."

Danny reached into his pocket, pulled out the bunch and passed it to me.

"Here, look at this."

I pointed out a small display advertisement at the bottom corner of the page.

Beside the wording was a tinted logo exactly the same as the R on the key.

"Wearside?"

"Sunderland," said Danny. "Clare's got a house there. She rents it out, although she keeps a flat to escape to. It all makes sense. Sort of."

It didn't make any sense at all, but suddenly Danny was animated. Why was a Wearside company advertising in the London Evening Standard? It was time to move first and ask questions later.

"What are you doing this weekend?" he asked.

"Nothing, apart from looking after you. Why?"

"Do you fancy a trip to the North-East?"

"I thought you were going to say that." I hadn't been back north for ages, and to be fair that was only Manchester. Sunderland was a good deal further again. Almost in Scotland. I was tempted to ask if we'd get duty frees. I didn't have a clue what I was getting into, but I set off to pack an overnight bag.

We were on the road by 6.30pm, entering the evening rush, fighting the weather, and trying to make small talk to allay the nagging sense of unease. I offered to drive. I don't like being a passenger. From Camden it's relatively easy to get on the A1 at Archway, but we were faced with more than two hundred and fifty miles of long slog after that. I couldn't wait to get away. To put as much distance as possible between us and whatever was going on in London. I just wanted to hide.

And then as the miles piled up, and the traffic got worse through the inevitable roadworks, Danny fell asleep, leaving me with just the radio for company. I didn't try to wake him. It was just miles and miles of headlights shining in my face. Unfamiliar towns, rivers, more roadworks. The repetitive, hypnotic sweep of the wiper blades working to keep the worst of the weather at bay.

I'm a photographer, for God's sake. The greatest dangers I ever face come from safety pins or overloaded extension cables. This was a whole new world and I was completely fucking terrified.

CHAPTER TEN

D ANNY wasn't asleep. He was just lost in thought, eyes closed, silently trying to process the latest shock.

They didn't seem to be getting any closer to Clare. If anything, it was looking increasingly less likely they'd ever find her. And now things were getting deadly.

Could it be DCI March? Really? Bombing a hotel? It seemed unlikely but Danny had reviewed the files and he knew that once they were in the public domain March would be finished. More than finished. He'd be inside, and life behind bars wouldn't be a holiday for a former DCI. Especially a corrupt one. So yes, it was conceivable March would stop at nothing - at all - to suppress the Echo's investigation. But that assumed he even knew about it. And if he did, then he'd need to put Danny out of action too, and preferably sooner rather than later.

But was March behind the death threat letters? That didn't seem likely. They were Ravenscroft, surely. So maybe March was in the clear and Ravenscroft was behind everything. He'd sought his revenge and now he was covering his tracks. But

Ravenscroft was already inside, so who was working on his behalf?

Was it Serraillier? Or was he Clare's lover? Or someone else she'd been getting close to in order to expose? He was European, possibly French, and the art gallery was in Paris, but Serraillier hadn't sent the catalogue. That was someone called Dominique. But he didn't seem to even exist, so who on earth was he? Was that Serraillier's real name? And why would Serraillier write a letter on the hotel's headed paper? And who had been to Clare's flat to take the tape from the answering machine? Was that the police or someone else entirely?

None of it made any sense. None of it seemed to be leading anywhere.

Now things seemed to be escalating and that could mean very real danger. He wasn't so concerned about his own welfare. He'd learned risk management from his time with Clare. But what was he getting Anna involved in? If things were getting dangerous, he needed to isolate her from any threat, and urgently. That's why he'd asked her to come with him now. Yes, he valued her insight and he loved her company, but he couldn't leave her alone in the flat in London while he went away. He didn't want to vocalise his fear, but if he was a target then he didn't want Anna getting hurt in the crossfire. Without knowing the enemy, he couldn't anticipate their next move.

***

In London, two men sat in a largely deserted bar, watching the news from a distance, on a screen at the end of the room. The sound was turned down so it was hard to hear, but they could just about make out the voices. There was extensive coverage of the bombing at the Mowbray Hall Hotel, showing the aftermath, with eyewitness interviews and a police spokesperson talking to camera.

The IRA seemed to be getting the blame, but the attack was unusual. The normal coded warning had not been received. The police were appealing for information. Asking for anyone who may know anything to get in touch.

The two men returned to their drinks. Getting in touch was the last thing they intended to do.

***

I thought Danny was waking up as we passed signs to Doncaster, but he just stirred and then seemed to go again. I'd been driving for hours and yet according to the milometer there was still about a hundred miles to go. Eventually, he did come round, and then asked me where we were, as if I'd have any idea. Which, of course, I didn't. He answered his own question by announcing Selby Fork, which meant nothing to me even though I'm proud of my northern heritage. This was an alien land. He said we were getting close. It didn't seem that way to me, but I'm not one to hold a grudge.

We weren't planning on going to Rougemont until the morning. He'd arranged for us to stay at a friend's house, and I was getting concerned that we'd be waking them up in the middle of the night. But at around 11pm we finally turned off the A1 and headed through the bright lights of industrial Teesside. The rain had turned to sleet and then snow, which seemed to be trying to settle. I was just getting concerned about getting stranded when we finally saw signs to Sunderland. And then, just past midnight, we turned up at the house belonging to Danny's friends, Simon and Rebecca.

Rebecca was already in bed but Simon was awake and let us in, opening the gate to his backyard so I could park my car in relative safety. I was grateful but shattered in equal measure. When I'd parked I made small talk for a bit, but then concentrated on the offered biscuits while Danny and Simon caught up with developments in each other's lives. Simon was soon going to be a father. It's an exciting time. But at that moment I just wanted to go to bed to rest my eyes and hope that everything would be sorted by the morning. Not that I expected it would be.

"Grab your bags and I'll show you to your room," Simon said eventually, taking my bag in a welcome display of chivalry. "I've made the bed up, and there's an alarm clock for the morning. If you get up before us help yourself to anything you like for breakfast."

Room singular, bed singular. I looked at Danny who looked sheepishly back at me. He clearly hadn't explained that we weren't a couple. I was too tired to complain; in any other circumstances, I'd have been delighted.

Simon opened the door. The bedroom was large, and dominated by a double bed against one wall. Opposite it was an open fireplace and two fitted wardrobes.

"The bathroom's upstairs. Feel free to use the shower if you want to," Simon continued.

Danny decided to try to save my blushes.

"Simon, I don't mean to be funny but we're not..." he began.

"Shhh! Say no more. Nudge nudge, wink wink, and all of that! See you tomorrow, sweet dreams, and don't do anything to mark the sheets!" Simon left us with a smile and disappeared into the master bedroom next door.

I looked at Danny. He looked at me.

"You have the bed, I'll have the floor..." he started.

"Don't be stupid. It's fine. We're grown adults." I gave him an encouraging smile. Bordering on a pout. "We know each other well enough to be able to share a bed. Just bear in mind, if you snore, I can be quite aggressive."

Within ten minutes we were lying in bed together. We said our goodnights and I turned to face the window. I know it was completely inappropriate in the circumstances but I did try to sneak a little bit closer than was strictly necessary, just to feel the warmth of his skin. Told you, I'm a bad person.

And then, just as I was drifting off, Danny put his arm around me, and kissed me lightly on the shoulder.

"Thanks for coming," he said.

I didn't dare turn around but reached out to give his hand a squeeze.

"That's all right. Think of it as a favour for a friend."

He could have made a move, for heaven's sake. The problem, I think, is that we have too much respect for each other. It's probably for the best, though, all things considered, and we have a lifetime ahead of us. Hopefully.

The following morning, I awoke Danny with a cup of tea and four slices of toast. I'd already been in the shower so took a certain joy in his slightly dishevelled appearance. He looked at the clock through sleep-troubled eyes but didn't seem able to focus, coming to terms with the unfamiliar surroundings. It was just after eight. There was just the merest hint of daylight filtering through the curtains, but spring still seemed a long way away.

He thanked me for the toast and I settled into one of the large wicker chairs beside the window, pulling back the curtains slightly so I could see the view out to sea. There was a ship far out on the horizon, slowly moving south. It looked like a tanker, although I confess maritime definitions are beyond my normal frame of reference.

I picked up the copy of the Evening Standard from the day before and looked again at the Rougemont advertisement. Why advertise in London? Was somebody deliberately leaving a trail of clues? In the drama of the previous day, I'd done little more than glance at the stories inside. I started now, reading much of the news from home and abroad while Danny ate his breakfast. I like to keep up on world events. It helps me feel in control of my life - if I know what's going on in some obscure African republic, then logic dictates I'm bound to know what's going on in my own little part of London NW1. That's the theory, anyway.

And then I saw a story that changed everything.

"Listen to this, Danny," I said, suddenly excited but struggling to process the words in front of me.

"Page fourteen, same as the Rougemont ad: Police search for hit and run killer. 'Police are looking for the driver of a distinctive Italian sports car after it was used in a brutal hit and run in a central London car park yesterday afternoon. The incident took place at the NCP multi-storey car park in Saffron Hill, Farringdon, shortly after 4.30pm. Police have released CCTV footage that shows the driver of the car - a dark blue or black Maserati 430 - drop off a passenger on the second floor, before immediately accelerating towards him.'"

"Jesus," Danny began.

"No, hold on, there's more. 'The car was then seen speeding away. The victim was pronounced dead at the scene and has now been identified as French art dealer Dominique Chernin.'"

I stressed that bit.

"'As yet there seems to be no motive for the attack. Police are appealing for witnesses or for anybody who has seen the car, registration number K586EFG, to come forward with any information but have stressed that the driver should not be approached.'"

"Bloody hell," said Danny, propping himself up in bed.

"I know. Do you think that's our Dominique?"

"Show me." I passed him the paper and he read the story again.

"It's got to be," he said at last. "I mean, it doesn't have to be, but bloody hell. And the car..."

"The car?"

"Maserati 430. Dark blue or black. They said at the Mowbray

that Clare and Serraillier had left in a dark blue sports car but didn't recognise the make."

It was worse than I thought. Two more pieces of the jigsaw had fallen into place, but we still had no idea of the bigger picture.

"That was Thursday afternoon." Danny thought for a bit. "That was about, what, half an hour, forty-five minutes after I left the Mowbray? I'd have virtually driven past. So bloody close. This is driving me mad."

Danny started to get out of bed.

"So what now?" I asked. I was way out of my depth.

"I'll get up and get dressed. We go to Rougemont, and find out what our key opens and then we find out as much as we can about Chernin and where he fits into all of this. May not be our Dominique, but I think it's got to be."

"Good plan."

"And then if he is the gallery man, we'll need to find this car. Half of the Met's going to be looking for it but I expect it's not going to be easy. Unless it's found burned out and abandoned somewhere."

I was tempted to say that with the quality of Italian electrics, burned out was most likely, but it wasn't the time for jokes.

"But what's the connection with the gallery?"

"His or Clare's?"

"Both."

"Presumably if he's a dealer he works with lots of them, so that would explain why he's sending catalogues but doesn't work there. But the connection with Clare... No idea. We still don't know if this was a story she was working on, or something else. Where the fuck is she?"

"Come on, quick shower and we'll get going."

"Yeah, okay. It's just... She said this was the biggest story ever. Art can be big business, but is it bigger than some of the stuff she's already done? Bigger than government and police corruption? Unless..."

"Unless?"

"Unless Clare knew different."

Danny thought for a moment.

"Can you do me a favour?" he asked. "I'm getting up, but can you pop downstairs and get the phone if it's a cordless one. I think it is. I'm sure Simon wouldn't mind. I have to make a phone call."

I jumped to it, glad to be able to help. When I returned Danny was out of bed, wrapped in a towel, nearly ready to head to the bathroom. I left him while he rang a number and spoke for a couple of minutes. Then he shouted down the stairs for me to return.

"It wasn't Rougemont who placed the ad," he said, as I came up the stairs. "I just called them. Pretended to be from a business in London and enquired about the sort of service I could expect to receive. The bloke asked how I'd heard of the company. He said he'd had a lot of calls from London and couldn't understand why. He denied ever placing the ad."

"So what sort of company is it?"

"Just a kind of safety deposit box place meets Mail Boxes Etc. They've got safes but it's not the sort of place you'd stick a Van Gogh."

"But it pays to advertise."

"Apparently."

"So who put the ad in?"

"No idea."

"And yet it's like we were supposed to see it."

"Exactly. Somebody must know I've got the key. And if they're connected with the bombing and the Maserati, they'll know we're going to see the connection, too."

"Oh, Danny."

"It's just... Do you ever get the feeling that somebody's watching you and that they know a lot more about what's going on? Only you can't see them because you don't know what they look like and you don't know where they're hiding?"

"A bit like hide and seek with blindfolds on?"

"Exactly."

"It's eerie."

"It could be dangerous. Whoever it is has bombed a hotel and killed an art dealer so far, and I don't suppose they'd think too long and hard about stopping us if we got too close."

"So why don't they just demand a ransom for Clare, or do away with her permanently?"

I could see Danny thinking.

"Because if they asked for a ransom it would identify them, and even if the ransom was paid, the story would still exist as soon as Clare was released. And if they killed her, there's no guarantee that somebody else wouldn't have a second copy."

"Namely you."

"Namely me. Oh my God. They're probably looking for me now, as we speak. Sorry, I'm getting paranoid. And there's something else."

"Yes?"

"The answering tape. They've got that with my voice on it. They know me by name. I really am getting paranoid."

"I don't blame you. I am too."

We both looked at the newspaper again. Danny spoke first.

"Time to get up," he said. "If it's hide and seek, we may have blindfolds on, but they sure as hell haven't."

CHAPTER ELEVEN

Saturday, February 13th, 1993

UNDERSTANDABLY, I think, we were both extremely nervous when we left the house. What if we were being watched? We could be gunned down in the street.

I fetched the car and Danny ran to get inside, minimising time in the open, partly due to fear of being shot and partly because it was freezing cold with sleety rain. I was tempted to floor it as if I was in an American cop show, but there were speed humps in the street so it wouldn't have achieved much apart from light bruising and suspension damage.

Danny gave directions and I navigated the city streets. Eventually we reached the roundabout that led towards the Rougemont Securities building. We turned left and took the road towards the river. The business park - in earlier years it would have been called an industrial estate - was nearly deserted. A few cars were parked outside some of the units but there were no people to be seen. Which was probably just as well, because we were feeling increasingly paranoid.

The Rougemont building was at the far end of the park. The company occupied the ground floor of one of the units nearest the river. The windows were heavily barred, but that was the only outside indication that there may be valuables stored inside. I parked the car at the front, and we made our way to the reception. I felt like an under-rehearsed actor on opening night. And yet I had to fight the fear. This could be a breakthrough moment. Whatever the key opened could solve everything.

The reception area was plush. It had a marble floor, on which stood huge plant pots, filled with overflowing greenery. The uniformed security receptionist sat at a large limed oak desk. Behind him on the wall was a frosted copy of the familiar R logo, set into a mirror.

With fingers crossed, metaphorically and physically, I went up to the desk and attempted my best Hollywood smile.

"Hello," I said, preparing to deliver the lines we'd rehearsed in the car. "My name's Clare Woodbrook - that's Clare without an i. I've just come to see if there's anything for me."

I took the key from my purse and handed it to the security man, whose name tag said "Barry".

"Have you been here before?" he asked.

I crossed my fingers tighter.

"Only once," I lied. "When I first opened the box."

Right answer.

"Have you got your card with you?"

"Card? Er, yes." Er, no. Shit. I made a show of searching my pockets and bag, but came up blank. I deserved a BAFTA. "Oh God, I'm sorry. I haven't." Oh, genius. "But I've got identification."

I produced an impressive-looking identification card from the inside pocket of my bag.

"There you go - Clare Woodbrook, journalist. And I've got

the key."

Barry examined the card. It certainly looked professional. He wasn't to know I'd made it six months earlier, in my darkroom, to blag my way into a sold out Pet Shop Boys concert. Even Danny didn't know about that. Told you already, I'm bad.

"I shouldn't let you through without your card. Just this once, though. Sign the book please."

I signed Clare's name. So far so good. Nearly there.

"If you'd like to take a seat, I'll get somebody to show you through," said the guard. "And look after the key, you'll need it. Oh, and one last thing - if you could bring the card with you next time..."

"Certainly," I said, moving away. Danny had taken a seat on one of the two leather sofas. I winked as I approached him.

The guard picked up the phone, but his voice was inaudible. It seemed to take an eternity before another uniformed guard arrived and beckoned me towards him.

"Mrs Woodbrook?"

Mrs? I nodded.

"This way please."

Danny stood up to follow, but the guard was having none of it.

"Sorry, key holders only this side of reception."

Danny sat down again and picked up a magazine, holding up a hand in deference. The guard and I disappeared through heavy double doors. I was shown down a series of corridors until I entered a large, brightly lit room, with rows of stainless steel lockers. It looked like the changing room in an upmarket swimming pool. Without the puddles of water or smell of chlorine.

"What's your number?" asked the guard.

"1196," I replied, quickly glancing at the key, just to be sure.

The guard led me between two rows of lockers before finally stopping and pointing to one on the third row. It looked like a mini mailbox, doubling as safe deposit and mail drop. He stood back and leaned against the stainless steel wall, leaving me free to turn the key.

This is it, I thought, as I put the key into the lock. The door was surprisingly stiff. I opened it with considerable caution and looked inside. The locker was empty. I reached inside and felt all of the walls, the back, the roof, and the base, but still there was nothing. I couldn't disguise the look of disappointment on my face. Reluctantly I shut the door.

"Are you sure that's the right one?" I asked the guard. "I was sure there should be something in there."

"That's definitely it," he replied, "but your fella was here yesterday and he took something."

"My fella?"

"Yeah, French bloke? Didn't he tell you? Came round late yesterday afternoon. Come to think of it, he said something about you coming today. There's a message for you I think. Did you ask on reception?"

"Er, no, I didn't. I didn't realise he was coming."

"Come on, I'll take you back."

Who was coming today? The real Clare? If so, she must be all right. And a French bloke? That would be Serraillier again I presumed. We still didn't know if he was friend or foe, or, let's be brutally honest, hopefully boyfriend. What was he doing all the way up here? Or did he know that Danny and I were on the trail, and if so, how? I didn't like it. Too many things didn't add up. I followed the guard back to reception, where he looked in a large leather-bound book and found Serraillier's message.

"Here it is. 'Got here first. Meet me at yours, 11.30 Sat.'"

"Is that all?"

"'Fraid so."

"Hmmm, you didn't see his car by any chance?"

"His car? No, sorry."

"Not to worry. Well, thank you very much, I'll go and see

what he wants." I shook him by the hand. I'm not sure why. It just seemed like the right thing to do.

I went back into the main reception, beckoned to Danny and whispered to him, "Outside." He followed me. When we were in the privacy of the car park, I told him what had happened.

"11.30 am or pm?" asked Danny.

"It didn't say."

"And there was nothing else?"

"Nothing. I suppose it's straight back to London and camp round Clare's until one of them shows up."

"No." Danny stopped to collect his thoughts. "Let's look at the facts. Serraillier was who she met at the hotel, so he's definitely involved. He drives a Maserati, and that ties in with the car park, which ties in with the art catalogues. My guess is that he knows we're here. And if so, he must know we've got a key for Rougemont."

"That's scary."

"Yes, but that would mean the message is for us. If it's for Clare it wouldn't make sense. How's she going to get here when her car is in a police lockup? Unless she's being forced to come here by someone to collect whatever was in the locker, to hand it over."

"But that doesn't make sense, because they've already got whatever was in there. Serraillier took it."

"Exactly. But we know he likes to play games because of the fan letter on the Mowbray paper. So that could mean..."

"She could be on her way here now."

"Exactly. Or he is."

We both paused for a moment.

"But that doesn't make sense, because we know she's already met him several times and if he's arranging to meet again then presumably he's a good guy, or at least thinks he is," I said.

"That's just what I was thinking. Which is hard to believe,

under the circumstances."

"So what now, do we go to meet him? If so, let's hope it is 11.30pm because we'll never get to London this morning. Perhaps he thought we'd come straight here last night."

"Perhaps, but not necessarily. Clare's got another house up here. We'll go there for 11.30 this morning, and if we're no further forward, head back to London to get to her flat for 11.30 tonight."

We got into the car. I started the engine and reversed out of the parking bay. Danny was on guard, checking to see if anyone followed us, but we seemed to be in the clear.

***

It was Association Time in the tough B Wing of London's oldest prison, at Brixton. One of the inmates was standing in a bleak corridor, using a phone card to make an outside call.

"Listen to me, good progress. But I need this finished."

"But Jimmy..."

"There's no 'but Jimmy'. No excuses. Unacceptable. Finished. Get me?"

"Yeah, but..."

"What did I just tell you?"

"No buts."

"Exactly. Finish it off. Clean it up. Now."

"And we're looking for...?"

"Fuck me. You know what you're looking for."

"Just checking."

"Stop dicking about."

"Sorry, Jimmy. Just making sure. And the sidekick? The photographer?"

"If you need to. Just do it quickly. I've got to go."

He put the phone down as a brass bell sounded to signal time to return to his cell. He hated relying on others when there was important business to attend to. But it hopefully wouldn't be for much longer.

***

Clare's house stood in a small private road in a district of Sunderland called Ashbrooke. It was a seven-bedroom Victorian terraced townhouse with large rooms and high ceilings, right in the middle of student bedsit land. Apparently she'd bought it as an investment property and never had any trouble renting out the rooms, as that side of it was managed by the university. But she kept a separate flat at the back of the house which she could use as a base whenever she was back in the North-East.

It transpired that Danny had stayed there a couple of times when he and Clare had been back in the area at the same time, which I wasn't altogether happy about if I'm being strictly honest. He'd kept that rather quiet. I'm going to have to watch him much more closely when this is all over.

On our arrival, Danny knocked on the front door and asked one of the students if she'd seen Clare or had anyone calling round asking for her. The answer was negative on both counts. He asked if she'd noticed any movement from the flat behind, but she hadn't - with the exception of a noise that sounded like a door slamming an hour or so ago, but that could have been from upstairs.

It was nearly 11am. We were deliberately early because we wanted to see Serraillier arrive - if, indeed, he was going to. We also had little else to do. We drove round to the back of the house, parked in the back lane between two garages and switched off the engine. We waited. Nobody arrived. At precisely half past eleven, Danny got out of the car and walked up to the solid, full-height double gate which was the entrance to Clare's backyard and flat. I followed closely behind, wanting to hold on to him for lots of reasons, only some of which were romantic. He knocked, but there was no answer so he tried again, harder. Again, nothing. He pushed gently on the large red gate and it swung open, catching on the concrete floor as it did so.

We stepped through and my heart nearly stopped. Facing us, front-on, was a midnight blue Maserati with damage to the front bumper. Registration number K586EFG. There was a man behind the wheel. He had dark hair and was dressed in an expensive-looking suit, but the suit was now ruined with blood. My first instinct was to run, second to be violently sick. But I resisted both. We moved closer and saw his eyes were still open. He had been shot in the chest. Probably once but maybe more. There was no sign of any gun, but the blood looked wet. "A noise that sounded like a door slamming."

I felt dizzy. Danny looked very pale and kicked the front tyre - I'm not sure whether in fear or frustration. We looked around, but there was nobody in the yard. The Maserati was a mess. Everything had been emptied from the glove compartment and was now strewn across the passenger seat and the floor. I looked inside the car while Danny checked the flat. There was an identity card with a photograph of the dead man. His name was Benjamin Serraillier. I was scared. Shit scared. It was no longer a game of hide and seek.

CHAPTER TWELVE

IN the basement of a massage parlour near Euston station in London, DCI Graham March was indulging in a half hour of relaxation, on the house. It was one of the perks of being a sleeping partner. That and the tax-free cash that he collected every week as his share of the proceeds. And for turning a professional blind eye.

Of all of his extracurricular activities this was one of his favourites, which made the thought of having to give it up even less palatable. He wasn't going to think about that today, though. For now he was enjoying the touch of Aurelia, his Polish masseuse. He'd personally overseen her arrival into the UK and provided accommodation in exchange for the safekeeping of her passport. She was now working extra hours to buy it back, but it was going to take a very long time. He'd make sure of that.

As she rubbed oil into his naked torso, his mind wandered. He'd heard the news from Sunderland about the discovery of the missing Maserati. That was one less on his patch to worry about. The Northerners could take over now. Give them some real policing to worry about rather than pissheads in the Bigg Market who wanted to fight each other.

And yet something was troubling him. The car was found at a house belonging to Clare Woodbrook, and Danny Churchill had shown up again. What was he doing there? Time for another chat.

***

In flat 35 on the third floor of a concrete tower block in Southwark, south London, a man took a mobile phone out of a drawer, followed by the three notebooks that were beneath it. It was time to study the notebooks in more depth. To the untutored eye, the writing looked like another language. Arabic, maybe, or Egyptian hieroglyphics. But he recognised the Teeline shorthand and read it as easily as if it had been plain English.

He went through the notebooks in detail, but was frustrated by their contents. He'd expected more. He swore to himself, cursing Clare and everything she stood for. Bitch. Still, she'd be less of a problem once he was finished with her. It was time to get rid of the mobile, though.

He put the notebooks back in the drawer, picked up the phone and grabbed his jacket. Maybe time for a couple of quick ones and then he'd find somewhere to lose it. It wasn't like she'd be needing it. He left the flat, and walked out through the main front door, through the car park, and past his black Ford Sierra.

***

We phoned 999 from the student house to report the body. An ambulance turned up within five minutes, but it was clearly a bit late for that. Two police cars arrived a few minutes later, and the yard was cordoned off as a crime scene.

We both had lots of questions to answer. What were we doing there? Had we touched anything? Did we know the victim? I followed Danny's lead until we were taken off to answer questions separately. I tried to be as helpful as possible without giving anything away. I said we'd been to the house to look for Clare as she'd gone missing, but didn't mention Rougemont or the Mowbray Hall bombing. They could work all that out for themselves if they wanted to. I just wanted to get out of there. To think I'd been pleased to come north, thinking I was getting away from danger, and now I was face to contorted face with my first actual murder victim. But the way things were going, maybe not my last. I shuddered.

After an hour giving our statements, we were allowed to leave on the understanding that we may be called again with further questions or to give evidence in court. We called into the student house on the way out, to give them an update on what was happening. The students were understandably shocked. It's not often you come so close to tragedy, never mind an actual murder. It was a lot to take in. Then the police came knocking to take statements from them too, so Danny left our phone number in case they heard anything more, and we got out of there as fast as we could.

I don't remember much about the journey home. Just that it seemed to take ages. We stopped briefly at a service station to fill up with petrol, but neither of us seemed in a particularly talkative mood. I felt safe with Danny, though. I was glad he was with me.

When we finally pulled off the A1 at Archway, I was struck by how I'd done the whole thing on autopilot. I was looking forward to getting back to the relative sanctuary of home, but I didn't know what to expect when we got there.

What we found was a police car and a woman standing next to it. Danny introduced her to me as DC Amy

Cranston. Apparently she was working with March on Clare's disappearance. I wondered whose side she was really on. But I was tired. I just wanted to get in, lie down and try to forget about everything I'd seen.

"March wants another word," she said. "At the station."

I offered to go with him but she refused. Said it was Danny on his own without any helpers, which I took to be a touch condescending. He set off and I headed inside with both of our bags, hoping for an uneventful evening. How little I knew.

***

"Danny, I would like to start with an apology," March began. "My esteemed colleague here thinks I may have been a bit unfair in our earlier discussion when I mentioned my disenchantment with jumped-up, so-called journalists. I was not, of course, referring to you."

"Thank you."

"Stop you there. Because while I think you probably could tell the difference, at a push, between Colonel Mustard and Professor fucking Plum, God help me, I'm not sure what you've actually written. Which makes you what? A glorified tea boy? And that's ten times fucking worse."

So it was going to be like that. Danny sat on one side of the now familiar Formica desk, refusing to be intimidated by DCI March and his growing belligerence.

"So maybe you'd like to tell me what the fuck you were doing in Sunderland? Unless you're going to be one of those 'no comment' fuckwits, in which case I'll have to see if we can arrange a nice little room for you. Can't promise the breakfast's up to much, though."

"I'm happy to answer questions if they're relevant. But as for travelling, I thought it was a free country," Danny replied, inwardly fuming.

"Free country? That's a common misconception. Yes, for your average man in the street, but you're hardly that are you. First you've got no alibi for the time Clare disappeared. No alibi for the rest of the night. Then your prints are in her car. And now you turn up at her flat with a dead body. And you've got no alibi for that because you were fucking there."

"Not when the actual shooting..."

"So I'll ask you one more time. Where is Clare?"

Danny just felt desperate. He always thought he'd be only too willing to help the police with their enquiries if he was ever faced with this situation, but all his instincts were telling him to say as little as possible. And definitely not mention the connection with the hotel or Rougemont because they'd almost certainly see him get formally arrested.

"I don't know. If I knew that, I'd go and get her. I have no idea. I'm looking for her. You're supposed to be too, unless you already know and you're just calling me in to mess with me. I do not know."

"Mess with you?"

"Yeah. Do you know where she is?"

"I'll tell you the way this works, Danny. I'm the one who asks the questions. You supply the answers. If I don't think you're answering properly or I don't like the answers that you're giving, I lock you up until you realise the waywardness of your actions. And in the meantime, I gather evidence I can stick in front of a judge so that when we do find Clare and I can prove you're responsible, you'll be going on a little holiday somewhere, where little is defined as somewhere north of twenty years, depending on what's left of her when we get there."

"Jesus. Can you please just understand. I have nothing to do with this. I'm the one who actually wants to find her."

"Are you saying I don't?"

"No, I..."

"I used to like you, Danny. I thought you were a bit, shall we say, effeminate. Not really a man's man. But my colleague here, the lovely DC Cranston, reckons you're the kind of boy who'd be nice to his mum. You're lucky she likes you, though I've no fucking idea why. Because if she didn't I suspect you'd see what I like to call the less patient side of my demeanour. So why were you in Sunderland?"

"I was looking for Clare."

"That's better. Did you find her?"

"No, of course not."

"So you decided to just off the first person you met in a wanky sports car?"

"No! Jesus. You know that didn't have anything to do with me. I drove up last night with my friend. This morning we went to the flat. And when we got there, we found the car."

"And you have someone who can vouch for your whereabouts in the hours leading up to the alleged discovery?"

"There's nothing alleged about it. And I was with Anna. Ask Northumbria Police. They'll confirm they were happy it had nothing to do with either of us, except we found the body."

"Danny, no disrespect to our colleagues from the frozen north, but we're not talking stolen sheep or somebody carving their name into a park bench here. This is your actual class A gangland shooting. And I'll be the judge of whether I believe you or not. Now you wait here with the delicious DC Cranston for a couple of minutes, not that she's your type I imagine. I need to check something and I will be back." And with that he left the room.

Danny turned to the DC.

"Is he always like this?" he asked.

"No comment," she whispered after a moment. But her eyes betrayed a hidden message, flicking briefly in the direction of the two-way mirror. The subtext was clear: he's still out there. He's still listening.

105

"I just don't get it," he continued, eventually. "I don't know what's happened. I wish I did."

"I understand. Don't worry. If she's out there, we'll find her."

"How's it going? The investigation?"

"It's, well... We're being very thorough. It can take time. Normally, in these kinds of cases, the most progress comes in the first twenty-four hours, but it can take longer. We're working on a few theories."

"But is anything actually leading anywhere?"

"Look, we know that Serraillier killed the French guy - Chernin. What we don't know is why. And how it connects to Clare, which we assume it does because of where he ended up. I've had Chernin looked into. He was a dealer - made lots of money supplying works of art to a select band of very rich clients. It was a bit like dial-a-pizza. They called him up, told him what they were looking for, and he found it for them at an agreed price."

"Okay."

"Indeed. And sometimes he'd locate galleries that had a specific range of exhibits and send out information packs to his most respected customers, suggesting what they should buy."

"La Galerie du Châtelet," thought Danny aloud.

"You what?"

"La Galerie du Châtelet. Small gallery in Paris - I saw a catalogue from it at Clare's flat."

"Doesn't ring a bell, but I'll have it looked into. Could you write it down for me? The problem we have is that there's so much money involved, the buyers are hard to track down. Money may not be able to buy love, but it sure as hell gets privacy. Chernin's client list is a mystery. We've found a list of transactions and checked out his bank account, but everything's been coded."

"Do you think Clare was a client?"

"I don't know. Could she afford it?"

"It depends how big you're talking. She did all right but I don't think she was in the super league. She made lots of money from books and syndication. But it wasn't millions."

"You said she was working on a story when she disappeared."

Danny nodded.

"I'll run this by you - perhaps she was doing a story on Serraillier. We still don't know much about him. Now, let's suppose he was a Mr Big in something dodgy and collected art as a hobby. Clare was on his trail and found Chernin. He opened his mouth, told her a few things he should have kept quiet and bang! He gets dealt with at the multi-storey."

"Sounds feasible. Except Serraillier's been shot, so who did that?"

"Maybe Serraillier was a middleman, or a member of some organisation. Perhaps he'd brought shame on the organisation by being found out and he paid the price."

"In Clare's backyard?"

"He could have been there to try and steal the evidence - cover his own tracks. Maybe the location of his shooting was irrelevant. They'd have got to him wherever. Maybe he'd gone there to hide. We don't know."

"So where does that leave Clare? Why not either a ransom demand or a body? She can't just have vanished."

"I don't know." DC Cranston leaned forward in her chair, put her elbows on the desk and rested her chin on her hands. She let out a sigh.

Danny wasn't convinced by the theory. It sounded good, but it didn't explain the bombing or the chain of clues that had led him to Sunderland.

He still didn't understand the Rougemont connection. Was the message for Clare? And if not, why had Serraillier wanted to meet him and Anna at Clare's flat? He still didn't know who had called in the middle of the night, or why he'd also been sent a catalogue from the gallery. Then there was the ring he'd found

107

at the hotel, the phone call from the Scotsman, the abandoned Lotus and the missing hours before finding it. No, he decided, there were too many loose ends to be tied up yet. And they were still no nearer to finding Clare.

"What else do we know about Serraillier?" he asked.

"Not much. The car was stolen. There's nothing about him on our files. No known address. All the ID he had was false. The chances are he had a different name for every day of the week and a few left over for when it rained."

"Where was he from?"

"It's hard to tell. He certainly looked and dressed European. France maybe? Or Switzerland. I quite fancy Switzerland myself. It's impossible to tell unless we find where he was staying. He may have been English for all we know. We've taken photographs from his ID cards and we'll ask around, but nobody seems to recognise him so far."

She paused, sensing Danny was about to speak. When he didn't she continued, probing.

"Tell me," she said. "What do you think is happening?"

Danny spent a moment in deep concentration before replying.

"I think the story Clare was working on is key," he said eventually. "Whatever it was has upset somebody. There's always risk, but normally we manage to avoid it. Don't ask me how - it's just an instinct you develop. For Clare to get caught out, she was either careless or she was out of her depth. Either way, it was out of character."

"No clues on what it was about?"

"No, like I said, none whatsoever. And the strange thing is, there doesn't seem to be any record of it. Normally she'd have tapes of conversations and files full of transparencies. There'd be notepads full of information and some semblance of a story written down. She was going to unveil it at lunch. She normally wouldn't do that unless she had something written down to show me."

"Where would she hide it?"

Danny was suddenly back on alert. Maybe this was part of the act. Lull him into a false sense of security with the softly softly approach. DC Cranston could be as corrupt as March for all he knew.

"You tell me. I've searched the office to try to find something - even before she went missing I was curious about what she was up to. But no, I haven't found anything. And you've had a good look round her flat, I assume?"

"London yes, but not Sunderland. Northumbria are going through there and they'll let us know if anything comes up."

Suddenly the door opened. DCI March walked in.

"Danny, you're in luck," he announced. "The guest rooms are full this evening and I'm frankly fucking bored of the sight of you so we'll end it here for now. But don't think I won't be watching you. Make your way to reception and I've even arranged a lovely DC to give you a lift home." He looked at DC Cranston. "No, not this one. She's coming with me. I'll speak to you again very, very soon. Interview suspended, blah blah."

March held the door open. Danny rose, said goodbye to DC Cranston, who smiled at him, and a curt goodbye to March. He made his exit and went through to the front of the station to wait for his driver.

Almost immediately she arrived. He went to open the front passenger door but she indicated he should get in the back.

"That was quick," he said as he got inside. She pulled away quickly and asked for his address in a soft Scottish accent. It was hard to tell from the back, but from what he could see in the rear-view mirror she looked to be in her early thirties, with short dark hair, attractively cut, leaving one side slightly longer over her face. She wore glasses and was wrapped up warm against the cold with a padded, down-filled jacket and scarf.

"Are you working on the Woodbrook case?" she asked as they stopped at traffic lights.

"And the Serraillier, and the Chernin," Danny replied with a sigh.

"What about the Mowbray Hall bombing, Daniel, are you involved in that?"

"The what?"

"You heard."

It was enough to throw Danny off guard.

"How do you know about that?"

The policewoman avoided the question.

"And Rougemont, Daniel, does that mean anything to you?"

Danny started to feel uncomfortable. The way she repeated his name made him feel uneasy. The lights changed and they set off, slowly.

"What do you know? Have you been watching me?" asked Danny.

"Only in the line of duty."

"Nobody else knows about that. Or at least they didn't."

"Don't worry. I haven't told anybody. But tell me. Why didn't you mention it to Graham?"

"DCI March? I... I didn't think it was relevant."

"Oh, come on! How are we supposed to help if you don't tell us everything you know, Daniel?"

He didn't know what to say. He could hardly explain about his suspicions that DCI March was actually responsible at worst - and at the very least deeply corrupt.

"I've just given up a Saturday evening helping the police, and now I'm knackered and I want to go home."

"Isn't that a bit selfish, though, keeping things to yourself? Wouldn't we all find Clare quicker if we all worked together?"

"Possibly."

"More than likely, Daniel. You do want to find Clare, don't you?"

"Well, obviously, I..."

"Then why not tell us what you know?"

"Because I don't know what's going on. Everything is weird. I don't know who I can trust. Let's put it that way."

"But you've just told me."

"I've told you nothing." Danny was defiant.

"Oh yes you have. You've told me that you've been keeping facts to yourself. Relevant facts, Daniel. Facts that could get this whole thing wrapped up much more quickly. And you've confirmed the connection with the Mowbray bomb and Rougemont. I've been wondering about those."

"I... Oh, for heaven's sake."

"You shouldn't keep secrets Daniel."

"I'm not. I'm doing what I think is right."

"And was it right to go to Clare's flat on Thursday night? Did you have a good look round?"

"What?"

"Oh come on, Daniel. You're not going to deny that are you?"

"No, of course not. But how do you know?"

"I've told you - it's all in the line of duty."

"So what do you think then? Do you know the connection?"

"Daniel, I've only just had several of my suspicions confirmed. It's a bit early for theories." She laughed. But it was the hollow, humourless kind of laughter.

Danny was getting exasperated. He was tired. It had been a long day. He wasn't in the mood for playing games. As the car turned into Rochester Square, his mind was more on a good night's sleep than this sort of cross-examination.

"Don't worry, Daniel," said the policewoman as she approached the house. "I won't tell anybody. This little chat is just between us. But it would be in your interests to start trusting me."

"How can I? I don't even know your name," he said.

111

"Do you know the World's End pub in Camden?"

"By the station? Of course."

"Meet me there tomorrow, 6pm, unless you've got yourself into more trouble by then. I think we need to talk. I may be able to help you. And it's Lisa, by the way, or Detective Constable Miller if you want to be official."

"Good night then, Detective Constable Miller," said Danny as he opened the car door.

"Lisa."

"Good night then, Lisa," he said, still trying to work her out.

"6pm. Be there."

"I'll be there." Danny turned towards the house. Pausing at the gate, he turned round to thank Lisa for the lift, but she was already driving away.

***

Back at the station, DCI March was worried.

"He was here a minute ago," he said to his colleague. The one with the car keys in her hand. The one he had summoned.

"Perhaps he's decided to walk home, or his girlfriend came to meet him - what's her name? Anna something?" The young detective constable tapped her fingers impatiently on the main desk at the front of the station. "Well, if he doesn't need me, I'm going back through," she said. "There's plenty of paperwork. It's been a busy night."

"Yes, well, I'm sorry about that. Not to worry - thanks for coming round anyway."

DCI March went back up to his office. The young policewoman returned to hers.

March frowned and picked up his phone. He tapped in Danny's number, but couldn't make a connection. A bittersweet voice from British Telecom told him there was a fault on the line and perhaps he should try later. He made a note to do that, and rang instead for a cup of coffee.

Back in Camden, Danny slept fitfully, unaware that his phone was out of order. He'd crept in quietly so as not to disturb Anna, and headed to bed in a state of confusion and exhaustion. He was intrigued about Lisa. He would have been more intrigued had his phone not been out of order. DCI March was not the only person trying to call him that night.

CHAPTER THIRTEEN

Sunday, February 14th, 1993

DANNY awoke just before 9am to the sound of a 2
Unlimited record played at high volume in the house
next door. He hadn't set an alarm as he just wanted
to catch up on sleep, but trying to doze off was futile with the
bass beat of Eurodance blasting through his bedroom wall. The
song changed to Charles and Eddie's Would I Lie To You?. It
still wasn't the best way to be woken up on a Sunday morning,
but musically at least it was a slight improvement.

He lay in bed for a few moments readjusting to the shape of
his own room. He'd only spent one night away, but it seemed
like an eternity. There was still much work to be done, but
where on earth to start?

He pulled on a bathrobe and wandered down to the kitchen
to make a cup of tea. There was no post to look forward to
on a Sunday, but he checked the doormat just in case. It was
bare. Once in the kitchen he filled the kettle, switched it on,

and got a mug, tea bag and milk at the ready. The first cup of tea was a morning ritual in the Churchill household. It always had been, as far back as he could remember. He was keeping a family tradition. Now that he'd got out of bed, it seemed the only logical thing to do.

He checked on Anna to see if she was awake and, if so, whether she was interested in a morning cup. Her bedroom door was open so he looked inside, but she wasn't there. It seemed strange - she didn't often have to go out on a Sunday, especially this early, but he supposed she'd gone to the studio to catch up on work she'd missed by taking the trip to Sunderland.

Once the tea was made, he picked up the phone to call the studio to see if she was there, but the line was dead.

"Bloody British Telecom," he muttered under his breath. "Dial 151 to report a fault. How the hell are you supposed to do that if your phone's knackered?"

A wave of premature concern washed over him. There was no note to say where she'd gone. He'd assumed she was in bed when he got home the night before, but what if she wasn't? Where was she? With a full-scale panic attack looming, he started to look round the house for any sign that Anna was safe. He found none. He looked at her room again. The bag she'd taken to Sunderland was on the floor, unopened. He looked inside and found her toiletries and make-up bag. They both seemed untouched.

He went to the phone again, but it was still dead. He cursed in frustration, desperation overcoming rational thought. He ran to the window and looked outside. There was no white Honda.

At least that was something, Danny reassured himself. If she had her car, then she was probably safe. Then he remembered Clare's Lotus abandoned on the M25. It hadn't done her much good.

He rushed towards the bedroom to get dressed, to get to the

studio as quickly as possible. He needed to find her. He needed to know she was safe. But as he ran through to the hallway, he saw the outer door swing open and two shadowy figures behind the glass. He retreated to the kitchen, ready to grab the nearest implement to use as a weapon.

***

We opened the door to find Danny looking particularly manly in a dressing gown, holding a plastic potato masher. I didn't want to ask. Boys will be boys.

"Oh, thank God," he said, looking shaken. And then his eyes turned to my companion, Megan, who looked as gorgeous as ever with her shoulder-length blonde hair, short leather jacket and jeans. I was a little bit jealous.

"You're safe," he said. "I'm so glad you're back. I was so worried."

I gave Danny a hug, then Megan and I went through to the kitchen and collapsed into two of the wooden chairs.

"Sorry, Danny," I said at last. "I tried to call but the phone was out. I should have left a note but I thought I'd be back last night. Oh, and by the way, meet Megan, one of my favourite models."

Danny and Megan said hello and shook hands. He did look pale.

"Where were you?"

I took a deep breath.

"Is the kettle hot? You couldn't do us a favour, could you... Tea or coffee, Megan?"

"Coffee, please. White, no sugar."

Danny refilled the kettle as I began to recount the events of the previous night.

"Well, it was only supposed to be a quick trip to the studio. There were a few things I wanted to check and I had a couple of films to sort out for processing. I thought I'd do it while you were with the police. No more than an hour, tops."

"So what happened?"

"God. Full on drama. I got there and saw a smashed window and a light on in the back. I was all for running to the nearest phone box when I saw Megan."

"I'd been trying to call Anna to discuss an idea," Megan continued, "but the phone was off so I tried popping up to the studio. Anyway, she wasn't there, but when I got home there was a knock at the door and there were these two giant geezers. I hadn't even taken my jacket off, which was a blessing frankly. Scared the living daylights. They told me to go with them, but didn't say where, and when I asked where and why, one pulled a gun and told me to shut up and just go. I thought fuck..."

"Bloody hell." That was Danny. "Are you okay?"

"I am now. The biggest bastard got in the driver's seat and the one with the gun got into the back with me. I was shitting myself. I had no idea what the fuck was happening. I just thought I'd do what they asked and try to escape at the first opportunity. So when we stopped at traffic lights I managed to get my hand in my pocket for a can of pepper spray and give him a face-full. Then made a run for it."

"Jesus. You're brave. What on earth is going on? The pair of you. I'm so sorry. Did you recognise them, or the car? Have you called the police?"

"No, no idea. The car was big but it was dark and I didn't see the number."

"So then what?"

"The bloke with the gun jumped out and ran after me, and the other tried but he was struggling. I jumped a couple of fences, crossed a couple of roads, and hid for a while. And I got a bloody big bruise for the privilege. I saw the car again as it passed further on, and the other guy was back inside. Then I realised where I was, and I was back just down the road from the studio. So I made a dash for it and broke in. I didn't think Anna would mind. I tried to call the police, but the phone was still out of order."

"The phone in the studio?"

"Yeah, I picked it up and the line was completely dead. Then I saw headlights outside, and heard an engine stop. I heard footsteps coming to the door, so I tried to hide. I was beyond being scared by then. Then I saw it was Anna and I just breathed a huge sigh of relief."

"And you've got no idea who they were or what they wanted?"

"No, none at all."

"I mended the window with a bit of wood and then we went down to the police station," I continued.

"Then we both gave statements, and drove back here," added Megan.

"Who did you see at the station?"

"A woman - Lisa something. DC Miller."

"Lisa Miller?"

"Yeah. D'you know her?"

"Only in passing. I'll tell you about her. Anyway, what happened then? I can't take all this in."

"Well, the plan was to stay here," said Megan. "I hope you wouldn't have minded..."

"No, of course not."

"... but then just before we got here I thought I saw the car again. I was on a knife edge. Still shitting it. It may not have been, but it definitely looked like their car."

"Where was this?"

"At the top of Pergammon Street," I replied, with the benefit of knowledge of local geography. "They were going in the opposite direction, but they stopped and started doing a U-turn. It was like something out of the movies then. We just legged it - I drove like a madwoman, cutting up cars, jumping

118

lights, going the wrong way down one-way systems. Eventually we lost them. Then I remembered I still had the keys to Clare's flat in the car, so we headed there. We parked in the garage and spent the night crashed out on the sofas. Do you think she'd have minded?"

"Of course not. Best thing you could have done."

"And then," said Megan excitedly, remembering, "the phone rang!"

"Clare's phone?"

"Yes," I replied. "I didn't want to answer it, but then I thought what the hell! I picked it up and there was a bloke on the other end asking to speak to Clare. I said she'd gone away for a while, and he said he thought so, because he'd rung the office a few times and she was never at work. He said he'd spoken to her assistant, which I took to be you, on Wednesday morning and that it wasn't important."

"Who was he? What did he sound like?"

"I don't know. Quite rough I suppose. Bit of a London geezer. He wouldn't leave a message but he left a name - Richard something."

I fished around in my shirt pocket and withdrew a scrap of paper on which I'd written his name.

"Here you go. Richard Kirk. Ring a bell? Sorry there's no number."

Danny looked uneasy.

"Name's not familiar. I couldn't ring him anyway. The phone's off."

"Here as well?"

There was an awkward silence. Danny broke it.

"I don't like this," he said. "There's something bloody weird going on."

He looked at his watch. It was nearly 11.15.

"So what are you two doing now?" he asked.

"Having a rest, probably. I can't cope with all of this

119

excitement," I said. "And I don't know about Megan, but I didn't have the best night's sleep."

"No, me neither."

Danny thought for a moment. Finally he spoke.

"Look, this isn't good. What happened last night may or may not have been connected to what's being going on over the last few days, but either way I'd feel happier if you two were safe somewhere, away from it all."

"But I thought I was Hastings to your Hercule Poirot," I protested.

"You're the best assistant I could have," he replied, "but I'm not having you in danger. Listen, I've got some friends in Reigate. They've got a huge farmhouse kind of place. I'm sure you could stay with them for a bit. I'll give you the address and I'll call them from a phone box and tell them you're on your way. Please, just go there for a few days, till we know what's going on."

"Whatever you say, Captain," I said, and saluted. I have no idea why. "But I'm not leaving you behind. What are you doing? You should come with us."

"I've got an appointment at six," he said. "With the only person who seems to know what's happening. I'll come to Reigate tonight and we'll make a plan of action for next week. Fair deal?"

He explained about DC Lisa Miller and her suggestion that she might be able to help. We all stood up.

"Thanks, Danny," said Megan. "Anna said you were a great guy. I'm feeling safer already, just having spoken to you."

"A friend in need is a friend indeed, and all of that," said Danny. "Just look after Anna for me, and make sure she doesn't come to any harm. And vice versa."

And at that, Danny disappeared to the bathroom to have a shower. We went to my bedroom to pack enough clothes for a few days away. In my top drawer was the Valentine's card I'd bought for Danny. I'd written it out and was going to leave it on the doormat this morning, but that hadn't gone to plan. Nothing ever does. One day, maybe.

CHAPTER FOURTEEN

AT just before 6pm Danny arrived at the World's End. The pub had a colourful history. Built in 1817 on the site of a cottage owned by Old Mother Red Cap (a notorious 17th-century woman suspected of witchcraft and the poisoning of her many husbands), it claimed to be the world's largest pub. Charles Dickens had been a regular in his younger, Camden years. Today it was filled with low wooden tables and chairs. The bar itself was dark oak, with peeling varnish. Green antique lamps gave a warm glow that served to highlight the cigarette smoke.

Danny ordered a pint of Courage Director's Bitter from a barmaid dressed in a black Castlemaine XXXX T-shirt and retired to wait for DC Lisa Miller at a table with a good view of the entrance. He checked his watch. Drank. Checked again. Still no sign. He looked around. Maybe she was already here. The pub was busy with a mix of students, tourists and locals, but no, he couldn't see her anywhere. A 134 bus destined for North Finchley went past the window. He checked his watch again. Maybe he'd got the time wrong. Maybe the venue. Maybe she just wasn't going to show at all. By 6.30pm he was feeling stirrings of anxiety. What if something had happened? What if he was a target?

And then, just as he was beginning to give in to the apparent futility of his situation, the door opened and from a distance he saw her arrive, wearing the same padded jacket and scarf as the night before, together with jeans and low black ankle boots.

She looked at him. Made eye contact. And then immediately turned to leave.

This wasn't the plan. He left his drink and made a dash for the door. Somebody tried to stop him to ask for the time, but he just pushed past. He didn't want to lose her now.

He emerged onto Camden Road. It was dark, but traffic was heavy and he looked both ways. Where was she? There was no sign. And then he saw her, in the distance, walking in the direction of Camden Road rail station. He set off to follow, but her pace seemed to quicken.

Before the station, she turned right onto Lyme Terrace. He started to run. The gap closed.

"Lisa," he called, his breath fogging the cold night air. But he got no response. Then, as though checking he was still there, she glanced over her shoulder before starting to descend the steps to the Regent's Canal towpath on the corner of Baynes Street. She turned right, and then stopped, underneath a bridge. And waited.

Danny came running down the stairs, looked both ways, and saw her, standing in the darkness.

"Lisa?"

Again she didn't respond. But she didn't move either. Slightly out of breath, he finally caught up with her. It was dark. And deserted. He suddenly felt a spike of fear shooting through his brain.

"Lisa?" he said for a third time.

"Hello Daniel," she replied, in her soft Scottish accent. "I'm pleased you followed."

"What's up?" he asked. "What's going on? Why the drama?"

She turned away slightly as she lit a cigarette, and flicked the spent match into the canal.

"Oh Daniel. How little you know."

He felt the onset of panic. Was it a trap? It had to be. He backed off. And turned. He wanted to get out of here. Now.

"Don't think of leaving, Daniel," she said, calmly. "I can see what you're thinking. But believe me, you're safer down here. I recommend you stay. We need to talk."

He was in two minds. He stopped. Turned back.

"Come on," he said. "Please. Just tell me what's going on."

"That's what I was hoping you were going to tell me."

"I... but that's the point. I don't know."

"Oh, but I think you do. I've told you. No secrets. And you need to learn to trust me. You're in a lot of danger. Do you trust me, Daniel?"

"I... I don't know."

"Seems like you don't know much. Or at least that's what you keep telling me. So listen. Cut the crap. Calm down. And let's see what we can do for each other."

"But... Why here? I'm getting freaked out."

"I can't be seen talking to you. I thought I could, but I can't. Hence our little nature walk. We should be okay down here. But we may not have long."

"Okay. But... Jesus."

She took a drag on the cigarette, and flicked ash toward the canal. The orange tip gave a faint, brief glow of illumination, reflected in the lenses of her glasses, but it wasn't much comfort.

"I'll start," she said. "Does the name Richard Kirk mean anything to you, Daniel?"

Danny was instantly back on guard.

"Yes," he said. "And please, call me Danny."

"Okay then, Danny. What do you know about him?"

"Just that he was presumably a friend of Clare's and he called the office the morning she disappeared."

"How do you know his name? From your statement at the time you said the caller hadn't left a message."

Danny decided not to tell her about last night's adventures. She wasn't to know where Anna and Megan had gone when they left the station. He thought she knew enough already.

"He, er, he called again. He left a message on the switchboard. He said he'd called a few times," he lied.

"But you didn't let us know."

"I only just found out myself."

"Have you checked him out?"

"No, not yet, but presumably you have or you wouldn't be asking me about him."

"No, it's just a name that cropped up."

"You met two of my friends last night," said Danny, taking the initiative.

"Did I?"

"Yes, Anna Burgin and Megan - I don't know her surname."

"She can't be much of a friend if you don't know her surname."

"I only just met her."

"Even more so, then. The name rings a bell. But tell me what else you know about Clare's disappearance. What else have you been keeping from us?" she asked, changing the subject.

"Nothing you don't already know."

Danny watched as she took a final drag on her cigarette and flicked it into the canal as well. Lisa moved closer to him so that he could smell the smoke on her breath. Her voice lowered.

"Did you find anything at the Mowbray Hall Hotel linking it with Clare?"

"No, I just took a picture down and the staff there recognised her."

"But you didn't actually find anything?"

"No."

"Not even a ring?"

There was no way she could have known that.

"There is no way you could have known that," he said.

"Come on Danny. I've told you, I've been watching you. Or at least, making sure you come to no harm. Think of me as your guardian angel. One of the main problems in my job is members of the public who've read a few Agatha Christies or seen a P. D. James mystery on the television and they fancy themselves as some sort of crack detective."

She was beginning to sound like DCI March.

"No offence, of course. Sometimes they do more harm than good. But you seem to have been doing very well so I've left you alone. I've just been there in the background in case you run into any trouble. Which it appears you have."

Danny felt uncomfortable.

"Clare was good at her job, wasn't she?" DC Miller continued.

"Yeah, she was the best. And for what it's worth I know how to conduct investigations because I've worked with the best in the business for the past year and a half. She taught me a lot, and if I've been 'doing very well' as you say, then it's all credit to her."

"You obviously think very highly of her."

"Absolutely."

"And yet you're holding back information that could help us find her."

"I'm not, I'm just..."

"What, Danny?"

"Oh, just she was a hero of mine long before I met her. I never dreamed I'd actually meet her, never mind end up working for her. And yet here I am. Or at least I was, and soon I hope we'll be back working together again. And in the meantime, while

126

she's away, I'll stick to the principles she taught me."

She let out another hollow laugh.

"Did you love her?"

"What?"

"You heard. Did you love her? As a friend? Or were you in love with her?"

"What's that got to do with anything?"

"Daniel. Sorry, Danny. I know I keep saying this, but believe me, it will be better for you if you just answer every question. You must, repeat, must, trust me. I ask, you answer. I'm not DCI March. I'm on your side here. He thinks you did it. You've got no alibis. The evidence is stacking up. He likes an easy conclusion. And he's not looking much further than you at this moment. I don't think you did anything, so I'm looking out for you. But if you lie to me, or hold back on me, I can give up, swap sides, and you're in it on your own. And that won't end well. So, for the final time, did you love her?"

"You say 'did I'. It's not a question of 'did I'. I still do."

"As a friend, or...?"

"God. Everything. You know what, nothing was ever going to come of it. I'm not naive and stupid. But yes, I loved her. I admired her. She was beautiful, clever, tough. And dealt with an awful lot of shit. So yeah, fancied first, from afar. I didn't ever think I'd meet her. And then I did and I was awestruck. And then I got to know her and admiration kind of took over because I realised she was way out of my league. So yes, loved sums it up, but on lots of levels. I've never met anyone like her."

"And do you honestly think she'll come back?"

"Oh God I hope so. Yes, of course. What else can possibly happen? We don't know where she is or why she disappeared. All we know is that she was on the verge of breaking a big story when she went. She'll be back. She can be bloody tough when she has to be."

"What do you know about Geneva?"

"Geneva?"

"Yes."

"Nothing. Why?"

"Sure?"

"Yeah... Actually maybe. The catalogue from the art gallery that Chernin sent. That had an office in Switzerland - it may have been Geneva. I'm not sure."

"Okay, very good. Tell me about Rougemont. How did you find out about that?"

"Clare always kept a spare set of keys in the office. There was this one key I couldn't identify, but eventually I traced it through an advert in the Standard."

"The Standard?"

"Yeah. It was in the one with the Mowbray bomb on the front."

"Convenient. So you decided to go up there?"

"Yes. But when we got there the locker was empty, so there was nothing to report anyway."

"You say 'we'. Who's 'we'?"

"Anna Burgin, my flatmate, and myself."

"Where's Anna now?"

"She's gone away for a few days. Staying with friends."

"With Megan?"

"Yes."

"Okay, what happened then?"

"When?"

"At Rougemont."

"I may as well tell you. You probably know all this anyway. There was a message, for Clare. It was from Serraillier asking her to meet him at her house in Sunderland. We went round instead and that's when I found his body."

"This message, you said it was for Clare?"

"Yes. Although it didn't actually have her name on it."

"So it may have been for you?"

128

"I suppose. Which means that either he knew where Clare was or he didn't know she'd gone missing, or..."

"... Or he knew you were going to Rougemont and he wanted you to find the message and meet him at the house."

"Exactly."

"But you don't know why?"

"No."

"It doesn't make much sense, does it?"

"None of it makes any sense."

DC Miller paused for a moment, lost in thought.

"Have you got any theories?" she asked.

"Lots, but none amount to anything."

"Tell me."

"Well... Serraillier seems important, but that could be nothing. We know she was meeting him, but he's now dead so he's out. And Chernin was a possibility but he's dead too."

"Killed by Serraillier."

"Exactly. It's a mess."

"So..."

"Well, that means it's probably one of three things. Either something to do with that story, whatever it was. Or it's revenge, so possibly Jimmy Ravenscroft. Or, most likely, someone else who wants to stop something else going into print."

"Like who?"

"Well..."

"Wait."

In the distance they heard the sound of a motorbike engine. DC Miller paused, motionless. It seemed to be getting louder.

"Come with me," she said, starting to walk back towards the steps. Danny followed.

"Listen, Daniel, Danny. You are in big, big danger. Whoever took Clare may be coming for you. We don't know. You have to be extremely careful. Do not, under any circumstances, tell DCI March about this conversation. He cannot be trusted."

The motorbike was getting louder. They could see a single headlight approaching along the towpath.

"Danny, come on." She took his hand and started up the steps, gathering pace. The motorbike got louder still. The headlamp illuminated the space they'd just vacated and seemed to be getting brighter. They were almost at the top when the bike stopped at the foot of the stairs. They turned to see the rider pointing a gun in their direction. He fired. The shot narrowly missed. They dived for cover. He shot again.

"Danny, run!" DC Miller shouted. "Split. I'll find you. Soon." They both sprinted away, in opposite directions. The bike started again, echoing through the cold night air. Danny ran back to Camden Road, his ears ringing. He turned right towards Rochester Square but was immediately struck by indecision. He wanted to go back to find DC Miller, but she'd gone in a different direction. Nothing would be gained except possibly putting them both at risk. He was in a state of shock. She'd warned of danger and it now seemed terrifyingly real.

She said she'd find him. He wasn't to know she was lying.

***

That night several callers rang 999 reporting the sound of gunshots by the Regents Canal. One, who lived in a flat overlooking the steps on Baynes Street, had been returning home just as it happened. She got a good look at Danny as he sprinted away and was able to give a clear description. The reports were filed. They would find their way to the desk of DCI March by the end of the night.

130

CHAPTER FIFTEEN

I'D never been to Reigate before, and to be strictly honest I had little idea where it even was. But given the risks I seemed to be facing everywhere else, I was delighted to be able to luxuriate in the sanctuary of anonymity on the outskirts of suburbia.

Danny's friends were called Claudia and Philip Regnard. I was grateful (and bemused) that he seemed to have a network of acquaintances up and down the country, able to supply accommodation at short notice. It certainly beat staying in a hotel. Claudia had done the "any friend of Danny's is a friend of mine" routine and we received a warm welcome. Sunday was a traditional day of rest. Having two guests at short notice seemed like a considerable disruption, but if so then neither let it show.

The house was big enough to accommodate up to six guests at any time, and there was a separate granny flat at the back for us, with its own entrance, kitchen and lounge. To her credit, Claudia didn't ask too many questions, but said we could stay as long as we wanted. And then, better still, she invited us to dinner in the main house in the evening. I went through the whole charade of saying we couldn't possibly, but thankfully she was insistent and we gladly accepted. It was either that or finding a petrol station somewhere with pre-packed sandwiches.

Before it got too dark, we wandered outside to explore some of the outbuildings, but it was freezing cold so that didn't last long. We found an old barn that was now used as a garage and workshop, with odd-looking bits of vintage machinery in the corner, well rusted into obsolescence.

At half past six, as directed, we returned to the main house for dinner. I felt terribly guilty turning up without at least a bottle of wine, and offered my apologies, but Claudia and Philip seemed to genuinely not mind. Still, I offered to replace anything we drank, as soon as I could find a shop that was open, but they said not to worry. It was a pleasure to have the company.

It transpired that Philip was the main cook, so Claudia poured wine - a beautiful glass of Château Mayne-Boyer 1986 - and showed us round the house. A huge living room led to an orangery with a full-size snooker table.

"This is amazing," I said. "It's such a beautiful house."

She laughed.

"Thank you. It's been hard work but worth it. You should have a game while Phil's cooking." She indicated to the table.

Telling you, I was pretty sure I could get used to this. I'd played a fair bit of pool at college, but found it hard to adjust to the much larger table. To the surprise of both of us, Megan, a snooker novice, won the frame easily, mainly thanks to the large number of fouls I conceded. Claudia stayed with us, and explained she used to be one of Danny's colleagues from the Daily Echo, in picture research. She'd just got engaged to Philip when he joined the newspaper and the wedding took place six months later, after which she'd left. I remember Danny being invited; I'd felt a bit miffed he hadn't asked me to go along as well. I love a wedding. And you never know what might have happened if we'd spent the day in an atmosphere of loved-up romance.

By 10pm we'd finished a third bottle of wine between the four of us and I was feeling decidedly squiffy. And then there was a knock at the door. Immediately I was on red alert, drawn back to reality. But clearly still very tiddled.

"Danny! This is a surprise." Philip led him into the room. I was so pleased to see him that I jumped up to give him a hug, which may have been rash because I was a little bit wobbly. It suddenly occurred to me that I might be looking a little bit flushed, given the wine, and the heat from the open fire, but I don't think Danny noticed. Megan moved along the sofa so he could come and sit next to me. He looked pale and terrified. Something was clearly on his mind, but it was equally clear he couldn't talk about it in front of Claudia and Philip. There was a complete blackout on news of Clare's disappearance, and it had to stay that way.

Philip went to get another bottle and Claudia excused herself to go to the bathroom. We had a moment together.

"Are you okay?" I asked, as quietly as I could, aware that alcohol can have an alarming impact on one's ability to whisper.

Danny shook his head. He looked terrible. Although all things are relative and I'm biased.

"No. It's not good."

"News about Clare?"

"No, not yet, just.... I'll tell you in a moment."

He was cut short as Philip returned, offering Danny a glass of wine from the newly opened fourth bottle. I wasn't sure if he was planning to stay the night but he looked like he could do with a drink and I was pleased to see that he accepted.

We could do the bed share thing again. We're adults.

Claudia returned, and Danny did his best to engage in the conversation, but I could see he was desperate to talk and the laughter was washing over him. I was equally keen to find out what was happening. I suggested taking him next door to show him our accommodation, and he gladly accepted.

As soon as we got outside, he turned towards me.

"Shit, I was nearly killed."

"What?"

"I was shot at. God knows how he missed."

"Danny, you're not making any sense. Are you okay? What happened?"

"I don't know. I was supposed to meet the policewoman, Lisa, at the World's End. She didn't show. Eventually she arrived but didn't come in. I saw her at the door and she went straight back out again."

"Sounds weird."

"It gets far worse."

"Jesus."

"She was halfway up the street when I got outside to look for her, so I ran to catch up, but she went down on the towpath by the canal. Said she couldn't be seen talking to me. She seemed to know everything. The ring. Rougemont. Everything I hadn't told March. And then a motorbike came and... Fuck."

"Ooh, Danny, is she okay? What on earth...?"

"Yeah, she seemed on edge. Said we couldn't trust March. Then we heard this motorbike engine and she led me back to the stairs. The bike got closer and she started running. We got to the top and I looked down and he had a gun, pointing at us. There were two shots. Maybe more. I don't know. We just ran."

"Together?"

"No, she said we should split and she'd be in touch. I've never been so scared. An actual fucking gun."

"Did he try to follow?"

134

"The bike man? No, he was stuck at the bottom of the stairs. I heard the bike start up again but I was running by then. I just went straight home, packed a few things as quickly as I could and got out of there."

"So what about the policewoman?"

"I don't know. She was okay, I think. She wasn't hit. But Jesus. What on earth is going on?"

"Danny, we've got to tell the police."

"But we can't, can we? I mean, she's the police. And she was adamant we shouldn't say another word to March. He's bent. He's behind all this. Got to be."

Suddenly I really rather regretted not being sober.

"Danny, we are way out of our depth here."

"I know. And yet what can we do?"

"I don't know."

I just wanted to stay here forever, but I knew that wasn't an option. We'd just have to find Clare. But the thought of the near miss and how close I'd come to losing him was terrifying. It gave me a glimpse into the anguish he must be feeling about Clare.

We'd arrived at the entrance to the flat. I opened the door and we went inside.

"Oh Danny, you gorgeous man," I said, and immediately regretted it, but still gave him the biggest hug I could muster. Neither of us was interested in the guided tour, but we had a quick look in case he was asked his opinion. And then we headed back.

"Listen, let's get to bed," he said as we approached the main house. "Tomorrow you can stay here with Megan. I'll go into the office and have another look. I'm missing something. Got to be."

"I'm coming with you."

"You can't."

"I'm coming."

135

"Anna..."

"Danny. Shut up and listen. I'm coming. You know what? I may be a bit pissed but I'm being very sensible here. I may even be useful. We need each other. And I'm not letting you out of my sight."

"But..."

"But nothing. Come on. Let's go in, finish your glass and we'll call it a night."

He paused by the door.

"Thanks Anna," he said.

I reached up to kiss his cheek. It was quite a distance. I'm only little. We opened the door and went inside.

There were knowing looks as we re-entered the living room and we both tried hard to put on a brave face, as though nothing had happened. Nothing had happened, at least not of the kind the other three were clearly assuming. I did my best to blend in but the jovial mood in the room suddenly seemed as alien to me as a comedy club on Mars.

Danny tried too, but apologised. Said he just felt exhausted after a long day, which the others seemed to accept.

The fire was dying down in the hearth, and Philip announced he had to be up in the morning, to be in the office by 7am ahead of a business trip later in the day. He was heading to Frankfurt and Claudia was going with him. She said not to worry - she'd leave us a key for the flat and we could come and go as we pleased while they were away. I think they were glad that someone was going to be around while the house was empty. You can never be too careful with security, as I was beginning to discover only too well.

Both Megan and I expressed our deep gratitude for their hospitality and for the meal and all of the wine. It had been a truly lovely evening up until Danny told me what had happened. We said goodnight and Danny, Megan and I made our way back across the courtyard to the flat.

Something seemed to be troubling Megan.

"Are you two...?" she began, with a grin. "Sorry, I hadn't realised."

"Just good friends, Megan," I replied, although it pained me to say it.

"Ah, okay." She didn't look convinced. "It's just we've only got two bedrooms."

"It's fine, honestly. We're past masters at it," I said. But didn't elaborate.

We briefly told her our plan for the morning, and said we'd try not to wake her up. But I think her mind was working overtime.

"And will you try not to wake me up in the morning either?" she said with a wink. We said farewell, and I took Danny into the bedroom.

"Becoming a bit of a habit, this," I said.

"I'm sorry, I should have thought..."

"Shhh, it's fine. I said before. We're adults. And you know now I don't bite. But the snoring warning remains."

He smiled for the first time that evening. We got ready for bed and within a few minutes were both beneath the duvet. Again I tried to edge closer than was strictly necessary.

"There is one thing you should know," I said, once the light was out and we were facing in opposite directions.

"What's that?" he asked.

"I'm an honourable girl," I said. "A kiss is the limit on a second date, even if I'm the worse for drink."

I turned to face him, just as he turned towards me. I gave him the briefest peck on the lips, and then turned back the other way, laughing to myself. This time he reached round to give my hand a squeeze. I didn't want to let go. I was determined

137

to stay awake and enjoy the moment. But not for the first time, and I doubt the last, the alcohol did for me, and the next thing I knew it was the start of another dramatic day.

CHAPTER SIXTEEN

Monday, February 15th, 1993

THE following morning Megan rose first, and made tea and toast for the three of us. I heard the knock at the door and tried to ignore it, wanting to luxuriate for a moment in my surroundings, but she didn't wait for an answer.

"Morning lovebirds," she said with a grin.

"What on earth time is it?" I asked, sitting up. And then a ripping headache hit, and I immediately regretted the sudden movement. Danny, sensibly, sank further beneath the duvet. And he'd only had one glass.

"Seven o'clock. I've made breakfast."

I said thanks but fear it just came out as a groan. Thankfully she left us to it. Danny resurfaced, and I got out of bed to retrieve the plate.

"How are you feeling?" he asked.

"Slight headache, I'm not going to lie," I lied. "But I'm still coming with you."

"What about Megan?"

"She'll be okay here on her own. It's you that needs looking after."

"Come on then," he said. "Quick shower and we'll get going. But please promise me you'll be careful."

I did the salute thing again. I'll have to watch that, it's becoming an annoying habit.

An hour later we were in my car, heading back into London and the Echo offices. Danny directed me to the underground car park and after signing me in at reception we took the lift to editorial on the third floor.

I'd only been to the Echo building once before, but I found it fascinating. I wondered if the novelty ever wore off for those who worked there, although I felt like a 20-a-day girl just breathing the smoke-filled air. The double glazing cut most of the noise from outside, but I couldn't help but be impressed by the sheer buzz of the place.

Danny led the way. He seemed curiously keen to keep a low profile but was stopped by a man he introduced as Derek Hughes, one the newspaper's sub-editors.

"Hello Danny, howyadoin? How's Clare these days? Sunning herself on some sun-soaked holiday paradise isle?"

"Something like that," Danny replied with a forced smile. I said nothing, but looked away uncomfortably. One day the story would be public. Or the paper would be employing investigative reporters to find out its own investigative reporters.

"Listen, word to the wise. Mike's looking for you," Derek continued. "Didn't look happy. Never does, obviously. You know what he's like. But he looked bloody furious this morning."

"God. When was this?"

"First thing. Eightish. Which is why it seemed a bit ominous."

140

"Fuck. Is he here now?"

"It's conference at the moment. What's going on, Danny?"

"Ah, you don't want to know. It's just a deadline. He's pissed off that Clare's not here and he's taking it out on me. Was he bad?"

"Well, I've been a sub twenty years and even I learned some new swear words. Just be careful Danny."

"I will. Cheers, Derek. Thanks for the warning."

I'm not an expert in office politics but that didn't sound good. We speeded up and made it to the office at the far end that Danny shared with Clare. Special Investigations Unit read the door sign, and underneath: Miss C. Woodbrook, Mr D. Churchill. I was impressed.

"Is everything all right?" I asked.

Danny just shook his head.

"Come on, we've got to be quick and get out of here."

There was a pile of post on Clare's desk but not too much on Danny's. While he waded through both, I studied the large Collins dictionary on his desk.

"The first time I saw a dictionary I thought it was a poem about everything," I said, more to myself than Danny.

"What was that?" asked Danny, with a hint of impatience.

"Nothing, it was just me getting philosophical."

"Look at this."

He passed me a sheet of computer paper. It read: "Justice comes to those who seek to destroy for their own selfish ends."

"What's that?"

"It's another of the hate letters."

"Jesus. It sounds scary."

"I know. But it's just... Is it a warning? Or a statement? A confession?"

I didn't have time to answer before the silence was punctuated by the sharp shrill of the telephone. Danny answered with his extension number.

"2247."

"Hello, Danny? DCI Graham March here. Long time no speak."

"Yeah, sorry about that. The phone's been out of order - I'll get on to them today."

"And there was me thinking you were just hiding from me. You're an elusive man. I thought you'd left the country, and I could understand why, in your position. Any developments we should know about?"

Danny thought about his conversation with DC Lisa Miller and was instantly conflicted.

"No, nothing," he replied. "Yourself?"

"Funny you should say that. I had a very interesting report land on my desk. Apparently there were gunshots in Camden last night. That's round your way, I believe. You didn't hear anything?"

Danny was immediately on the defensive.

"No, nothing. What happened?"

"Are you sure?"

"Yeah, definitely."

"That's strange. Because I've got an eyewitness report and somebody has described a man seen running from the scene. And I can't see the point of making a photofit when I could just use a picture of you."

"Me?"

"Yes, Danny. And I don't need to remind you that lying to me or withholding information is very much what I like to call, not in your best interests."

"Well if I knew anything, I'd..."

"I'm watching you, Danny. I've clearly not been watching you closely enough."

"Honestly, I don't..."

"Save it for the judge. Oh, and here's a bit of information for you. We've run some checks on La Galerie du Châtelet and it appears it's mixed up with some kind of organised crime gang."

"Is that what you think Clare was working on?"

"You're the expert, Danny, you tell me. But it all fits. Hell of a story. The Mystery of the Mona Lisa. And talking of Lisa, how did you get home the other night? Our young DC Miller turned up to give you a lift but it seems you'd already gone."

"No, she was waiting for me in the car when I went outside. I got a lift all the way home."

"Are you sure?"

"Yeah, definitely. DC Lisa Miller. Early thirties, dark hair, glasses."

"No, it couldn't be. Lisa's about twenty-four and a redhead. I prefer blondes myself but I'd make an exception."

"That's what she told me she was called."

"Well, it wasn't her. It was Lisa who came to reception. Then she spoke to me. When she couldn't find you, she went back to do some paperwork - something about a couple of models in a car chase."

Danny couldn't reply. His mind was in a whirl. If that wasn't Lisa, who the hell was it?

CHAPTER SEVENTEEN

I'D only heard Danny's half of the conversation but I could tell it hadn't gone well.

"That was March," he said.

"I gathered. Any news?"

"Yeah. It's just going to take me a minute to get my head round this."

"What's up?"

"It's Lisa."

"Is she all right?"

"I've got no idea. You said you'd met her when you took Marie down to make a statement."

"Yeah, that's right."

"What did she look like?"

"Ooh, now you're asking. Tallish, red hair."

"Uniform?"

"Yes."

"Shit. And definitely not dark hair with glasses?"

"No, definitely red."

"Fuck..."

"What's up?"

"It wasn't her then. Whoever I met. Whoever gave me a lift. Whoever I met last night. It wasn't her."

Danny gave me a synopsis of his conversation with March. Told me about the gallery, which was big enough news in itself, and at least maybe explained something of the background. But then when he explained about Lisa...

"We'll have to find her," he said by way of a positive suggestion. "Whoever she was, she knew a hell of a lot about the case. More than I've told the police. She kept saying she'd been watching me."

A light switched on in my mind.

"You don't think she had anything to do with the hotel bombing, do you?"

"How do you mean?"

"Well, you know what we said up in Sunderland? About somebody leaving a trail of clues and how it felt like somebody was watching us and it was like playing a game of hide and seek with blindfolds on? Maybe they've just taken the blindfolds off."

"You mean Lisa, or whoever she is, was behind the trail of clues?"

"Makes sense."

Danny thought about it for a moment.

"Perhaps," he said. "Maybe we're right, and she's working for whoever's got Clare. But if so, why identify herself? And on top of that she must have known exactly where Clare was being held. Oh my God! So close. But why run the risk of being discovered?"

"Unless she wasn't working for whoever's got Clare. Maybe there's somebody else trying to find her as well - for whatever reason - and they wanted to compare notes."

"Could be."

"They obviously couldn't just come right out and ask us, so they hatched their little plan."

"It was a hell of a plan. She seemed to know more than I did."

"Perhaps she just wanted it confirming."

"Do you reckon that they're the ones who blew up the hotel?"

"If they were, I'd assume their interest in finding Clare is less than friendly. Oh God."

We took a moment to think. Then Danny swore again. He was looking through the office window towards a group of people emerging from a conference room. Some dispersed quickly while others chatted in smaller groups. Several looked in our direction.

"Shit. We've got to be quick," he said. "We need to get out of here. Hold on. No, we're okay for a minute. He's gone into his office."

"Who? Mike?"

"Yeah. He's going to kill me."

"Okay. Right, one minute then. Let's just work this out. Clare met Serraillier. We know that. And he killed Chernin and is now dead himself. It could be March. It could be whoever is sending you the letters."

"Ravenscroft."

"So, who killed Serraillier? And why? Who's Lisa? And who tried to shoot the pair of you yesterday? Because that to me implies Lisa's not necessarily one of the bad guys, unless there's two lots of them."

"Oh good God. That's all we need."

"We still don't know for certain that Clare was investigating Serraillier. He could have been a boyfriend. Maybe she just goes for bad boys." I just thought I'd put it out there.

"No, I can't see it." Bugger.

"And we've still got the issue of the car being broken into

146

and the phone being stolen. There was Haldane, the jealous journo, but he seems to have disappeared. And Richard Kirk or whatever his name was. The East End geezer."

"Right," said Danny. "I'll run this by you. Serraillier's dodgy, running a scam with Chernin. And maybe March is involved."

"March? Is that his kind of thing?"

"God knows. He's into all sorts. Okay, so there's two factions. March and Serraillier. They fall out. Maybe because Clare's uncovered something, which would fit because we've been investigating March, so that would explain how she got onto it."

"Okay."

"So March, somehow, is involved in Clare disappearing. And he organises a hit on Serraillier. Lisa's on the other side, the Serraillier side, and she's trying to find out what I know so she can find out what's going on and who's responsible."

"Okay, that fits."

"But it doesn't, though, does it? Because if so, then why all the clues? And what about Jimmy?"

"Ravenscroft?"

"Yeah. How does he fit in? Unless he doesn't."

"Maybe Clare's in hiding for her own safety."

"I wish. But no, it doesn't all add up. She would have let me know she was safe before now."

"Hmm, I suppose so. But then it didn't look like she'd been at the flat for a while."

There was a knock at the door. It opened and a young woman walked in, maybe mid-twenties.

"Danny," she said. "Message from Mike. Can you come to his office please?"

"Now?"

"That's what he said."

"Can you say I'll be there in five?"

"He's not going to like that."

"I know, but... Please?"

"I'll try."

"Thanks, Emma."

"Who was that?" I asked as the door closed.

"Emma. Mike's secretary. I can't cope with him at the moment."

"Couldn't you just have a chat and say you're still working on whatever it is he's after?"

The look he gave me needed no further words.

"Okay, well we still don't know how, or even if, all this relates to what happened to Megan," I said after a moment.

"God, I'd forgotten about that. Is that really bad of me?"

"No, it's understandable. Let's assume it doesn't all tie up. But we need to find Lisa. Top priority."

"Well I know her car," said Danny. "Red Escort, registration number H768LSV. I wrote it down on the off chance and memorised it. I'll call the crime desk and ask them to pull a favour and get someone to trace it."

When the trace came back, we weren't much further forward.

"Marque One Rent-A-Car, Hammersmith," said Danny. "Come on. We're going to pay them a visit."

The traffic in west London was as heavy as expected. I parked up and we walked back towards King Street, past fast food outlets and a parade of smaller shops to the office of Marque One Rent-A-Car.

"How, exactly, are we going to do this?" I asked as we walked. I wasn't particularly sure we'd thought it through. They weren't likely to give out confidential client information to just any casual passer-by. "You can't say you had an accident and need her name and address, because if they've had the car back unmarked, they'd know that's not true. And it would be on their insurance anyway, rather than hers."

"Luckily I've got a plan," said Danny.

"Which is?"

"To be honest, a bit flimsy."

"Oh God."

"It'll be fine. We'll blag it. First thing you learn in journalism."

"I'm getting a bad feeling."

"Panic not. We go in. We explain that Lisa is an old friend. She came for dinner, but left something behind, like a watch or something, and we need to give it back but we don't have her address. She'd been telling us about the great deal she got on the hire car, so we thought we'd try on the off chance. And that's the beauty of it being the two of us. I won't look like a stalker."

"Danny."

"What?"

"Are you being serious?"

"Of course."

"That, my dear, is a shit plan."

"What?"

"They're just going to go, 'Sorry, can't help. Wait until she gets in touch and tell her then.' It's a rubbish plan."

"Cheers."

"Better that I tell you now before you go in and stuff things up. We get one crack at this."

"Okay. Let's hear yours then."

"I haven't got a plan."

"Brilliant."

"Well, let's look at it. Who are Marque One Rent-A-Car? I've never heard of them. Hertz, yes, Avis, yes. But this lot? No idea. It's not a big chain so the chances are they only have a few cars. Right? And why did Lisa go there? Is she from round here, or did they offer the best price? Or possibly because they're a bit dodgy, no questions asked?"

"Maybe."

"Okay. Lets assume the latter."

"It's a big assumption."

"It's all we've bloody got."

"Granted."

"So we go in, lean a bit, imply we know what they're up to, and if they want us to keep it quiet they're going have to pay up. In information."

Danny started laughing at me.

Actually started laughing at me.

"What's so funny?"

Eventually he stopped laughing at me, but it took a while.

"God you're sweet. Which I mean in a good way," he said. I wasn't sure if that was progress or not in bigger-picture terms. "We look about as threatening as a couple of baby lambs in the soft toys section of Hamleys. You know what we could do?"

"What?"

"Actually go in and just tell the truth."

"Yeah, that might work."

And so that's what we did.

And it was going well, up to the point where they denied any knowledge of anyone called Lisa Miller. Which was, admittedly, quite early in the proceedings.

"No, nobody of that name on the books here," said the man behind the counter, who I still think looked a bit dodgy if I'm honest.

"Is it possible to see who did rent the car?" I asked. "Maybe she used a different name."

He tapped at his computer for a bit.

"It came back yesterday. But it was a Charlotte Sadler according to this."

Danny and I looked at each other. Charlotte who?

"Do you have an address?" asked Danny

"I shouldn't really..."

"Ooh go, on. We'll owe you." That was me, accompanied by what I hoped was a flirty smile but may have come across as slightly unhinged. Either way, it worked. He wrote the name and address on a piece of paper, and handed it over.

"Thank you," I said.

"No problem. But you didn't get it from here. Okay?"

I stopped myself just in time to avoid another annoying saluting moment, while Danny assured him discretion was assured. We left the office and looked at the address: 11 Belvedere Terrace, Paddington. It felt like we were getting somewhere.

CHAPTER EIGHTEEN

BELVEDERE Terrace was a tree lined square of imposing white Victorian houses. Virtually all of them had been turned into cheap hotels, several of which offered rooms by the hour. Each property in the row had four or five storeys and most had pillars at the entrance. It was a seedy area, but nevertheless had a certain down-market charm.

The front door of number 11 was painted red, but the paint was old and had started peeling. A sign on the window said: Bed And Breakfast - Vacancies, £15 per night. I think we were both apprehensive as Danny rang the bell. And shivering in the cold.

The door was opened by an elderly woman in the kind of blue and white floral dress that somehow older people manage to buy, even though they're not sold in any shop that I've ever come across. It's one of life's mysteries. She had white curly hair and looked at us through tinted bifocal glasses.

"Can I help you?" she said in a shaky voice. A smell of cooked breakfasts came wafting through the door. I was still nursing a bit of a hangover and suddenly felt famished.

"We've come about a friend of ours, Charlotte Sadler. She was staying here," said Danny.

"Charlotte who?" The woman was hard of hearing.

"Sadler," I repeated, slightly louder.

"No, there's nobody called Charlotte Sadler staying here. Not now."

"Was she here? Within the last few days?"

"Eh?"

"*Charlotte Sadler.* Was she a resident here?"

"No, she's gone. Moved out."

"When was she here?"

"Who?"

"Charlotte Sadler."

"Oh. Moved out this morning. Sorry I can't help you." The woman moved to close the door. Danny intervened.

"Have you got any vacancies? We'd like a room."

The woman's eyes brightened.

"A room? How long for? We're busy, you know."

I doubted the legitimacy of that remark. London was hardly awash with tourists in February.

"Just a couple of nights. I wondered how much you charged."

"You better come inside. I'll get my husband."

We were shown through the door, and wiped our shoes before stepping onto the patterned, partially threadbare carpet. We were taken past a half-full English Tourist Board leaflet dispenser before arriving at a communal sitting room which was filled with furniture that, like the rest of the building, had seen more affluent days. The covers on the armchairs were wearing thin. The settee sloped dangerously at one end, and the aged television, which was tuned to BBC1, had a distinctly green cast.

"Come in, take a seat," the woman urged. "Make yourselves at home."

153

I looked at Danny. I think we both had doubts, but nonetheless we sat down and waited. A minute or two later, a portly man in a grubby shirt and ill-fitting trousers came into the room. He extended a hand towards us.

"Bill Osborne. Friends call me Billy. How you doing?"

We both shook his hand. He had a firm, manly grip, with the rough skin of a builder.

"You want a room then. How long will that be for?"

"Just a couple of nights," said Danny. "Actually, not tonight but Thursday and Friday if you've got room."

"Aye, we can fit you in. You two tourists?"

"Sort of. We've come down for the week, just to have a look really. I'm thinking of moving here to go to college and I wanted to get a feel for the place."

Billy nodded. "This your girlfriend?"

"Yes." Ooh, my heart did a little flip.

"What do you think about him moving to London? Are you coming too?" He was addressing me.

I said that I was, and answered further questions about the length of our relationship, where we'd met, and what courses we were going to be studying. Not a bad performance, I thought at the end, considering it was all nonsense.

"So how did you hear about this place, then?" Billy asked after a while. Danny seized the opportunity.

"It was recommended to us by our friend who stayed here recently."

"Who was that then?"

"Charlotte Sadler."

"Oh, you're friends of Charlotte, are you?" he said, taking the bait.

"Yeah. Do you know her?"

"Aye. Nice girl. She only moved out this morning. It was early, like. She didn't even stay for breakfast, but she paid her bills, and that's all that matters to me."

"This morning, eh? Have you tidied her room out yet? I was chatting to her yesterday and she said if we came here like she said, she'd leave a surprise for us."

"Well, no, I don't suppose it's been done yet. The wife's been busy with breakfasts this morning."

"Do you mind if we take a look? It'd be lovely to check a room out anyway," I said with a smile. Billy rose to the bait again.

"No, not if you want to. Hold on, I'll get the key and I'll show you up."

The room was on the second floor, up four flights of stairs. On the way up, Billy chatted about how visitors were normally surprised at the spaciousness of the rooms and the height of the ceilings. He explained that they'd been busy despite the time of year and the recession. At last we arrived and he unlocked the large, panelled Victorian door, showing us through.

The room was sparsely furnished, but looked almost comfortable. There were two single beds, one of which was made up while the other was a tangle of sheets, pillows, and a bedspread. The doors were hanging open on the fitted wardrobes but there was nothing inside except for a few empty hangers. Apart from that, there was a dressing table and stool, two old, battered armchairs and an overflowing wastepaper basket. The full-length curtains were half pulled, allowing just enough light into the room to see everything through a midday haze. The air was stale and heavy with the scent of cigarettes.

"Here you go, then," said Billy. "I don't know what you'll find, but I'll leave you on your own to have a look."

"Thanks," said Danny. "One last thing before you go. When did you say Charlotte moved in here?"

"Oh, it was a couple of weeks back. About the Tuesday. No, I tell a lie, it was Wednesday - late on Wednesday. I remember it because there was a fire in the place across the road and she couldn't get parked because the place was full of fire engines."

"And had she booked the room long before?"

"Oh aye. That was the strange thing. She must have booked it a good four or five months ago."

"Had she ever stayed here before?"

"No. Not as far as I can remember. We did have another Charlotte Sadler a couple of years ago, but it wasn't the same one. She was here for a few weeks, back in 1990, '91. I thought when this Charlotte booked that we'd be renewing acquaintances, but it wasn't to be."

Danny's curiosity was roused.

"This other Charlotte. What can you remember about her?"

"Not a lot now. I doubt I'd recognise her again. She always kept herself to herself - it was as though she wasn't here most of the time. I think she was here from work on some sort of project. Don't ask me who she worked for, though. Then one day she came in and said she was needed back at home and she was gone. Still, like I said, she paid her bills, so I didn't ask questions."

"Thanks, Billy," said Danny.

Billy turned to leave.

"I'll leave you to it, then," he said. "Come down when you've finished."

Once the door was closed I moved across to open the curtains. The room looked brighter but it was still as sparse. Danny started opening the drawers on the dressing table.

"It's not looking hopeful, is it?" he said.

I started looking through the wardrobes and amongst the sheets on the bed. I lifted the mattress up but found nothing. Danny helped me move the bed away from the wall and we looked underneath it, but there was nothing there either.

After ten minutes of thorough searching, there was only one place left to look.

"Come on then," I said. "Waste bin time."

I picked up the wastepaper basket and emptied the contents

156

on the dressing table. A pile of torn-up paper, cigarette butts, and used cotton wool appeared. It wasn't pleasant but the job had to be done. We sifted through the remains of her stay but there was nothing of any use at all.

We resigned ourselves to the futility of looking any further. After one last look around the room, we replaced everything as we'd found it, and headed back downstairs.

"Any luck then?" asked Billy with a smile when we reached the ground floor. But he could tell by our faces that the answer was negative.

"Here, you couldn't do me a favour, could you?" he asked.

"Yeah, no problem," said Danny.

"You haven't got a forwarding address for Charlotte, have you?"

"No, I'm sorry, I haven't." There was genuine disappointment in Danny's voice.

"It's just that this letter arrived for her this morning after she left," continued Billy, waving a handwritten white envelope at him, "and I don't know what to do with it."

I felt like giving him a big sloppy kiss, but obviously didn't. "I can take it and give it to her," I said. "I should be seeing her again later in the week so I can pass it on for you."

"Are you sure it's not too much trouble?"

"No, no trouble at all."

I took the envelope from the man's hand.

"Well, thank you very much," said Billy. "That's one less thing to worry about. Now about that room you wanted..."

We escaped as quickly as we could. Outside in the car, Danny couldn't wait to open the envelope. I handed it over and he carefully tore down its length.

There was only one enclosure - a leaflet from a pub called the Otter Tavern near Ely in Cambridgeshire, offering traditional accommodation in an apparently beautiful country setting. There was no covering letter. No explanation or acknowledgement. There was no name to say who'd sent it, but that didn't matter. It was a clue first and foremost, and far more than we could have hoped for when we left Charlotte's room empty-handed.

"M11?" I asked.

Danny nodded. "M11."

***

They hadn't noticed the person in the black Sierra taking photographs as they left the hotel. And they didn't notice the same car set out to follow them as they pulled out of the parking space, heading north to Cambridgeshire. They hadn't noticed it in Hammersmith either, nor the figure who'd shadowed them the length of King Street.

CHAPTER NINETEEN

THE landscape stretched endlessly to either side as we drove north through the Cambridge Fens. Danny read sections of the Otter Tavern leaflet aloud to help me stay awake.

"It has a reputation for Sunday lunches, apparently," he said, "and has recently started offering bed and breakfast accommodation. All this talk of breakfast is making me hungry. If I don't get something to eat soon I'm going to wither." I had to agree.

Within fifteen minutes, a sign for the pub appeared on the right. We followed a small road down to a yellow painted building set close to the riverbank.

Up until that point, we hadn't really discussed the consequences of this particular excursion. What if Charlotte, or Lisa or whatever she was really called, was actually staying there? She'd clearly moved out of the hotel, so it was logically possible, though unlikely, given that the leaflet had turned up after she'd left. But maybe she'd booked on the strength of a phone call. How would we confront her? What if it turned nasty? Worse still, what if the people who ran the pub had never heard of her?

I think we were both feeling apprehensive as I parked the car. We decided to simply go in, buy a drink, and ask to speak to the landlord. From there it would be a case of following our instincts and watching our backs.

We walked into the pub looking every inch the happy couple out for a late Monday afternoon drink, which was an image I was keen to nurture. I took a stool by the bar while Danny ordered the drinks. There was a beer garden outside with access to the riverside. It was unquestionably scenic but far too cold at this time of the year.

"Is the landlord in?" asked Danny as the barman returned with orange juice and lemonade twice.

"I'll find out for you. Who's asking?"

"Danny Churchill, a friend of a friend."

The man extended his hand.

"I'm the landlord. Mick Flynn. Pleased to meet you."

They shook hands.

"We've come looking for a couple of friends of ours, Charlotte Sadler, travelling with Lisa Miller. I thought they might have been staying here," said Danny, covering both options. I was suitably impressed. I sat quietly, playing the obedient companion. Bizarrely I fancied a cigarette even though I don't smoke. Can't work that out.

"No, they're not here. What makes you think they would be?"

"Oh, they just mentioned it and I saw one of your leaflets at Charlotte's place in London. I was on my way through and I thought I'd call in and say hello." I was always struck by how easily telling white lies came to a journalist.

"Ah, I thought I knew the name. She phoned a couple of days ago, Friday I think, and asked for a leaflet so I stuck one in the post, but she's not been back in touch. I was rather hoping she might have been, because it's been slow of late. We had one room taken last week, but there's nobody here at the moment."

"Bad time of the year?"

"Ah, you know how it is. Always slow between Christmas and Easter. We're busy during the summer, though."

It suddenly struck me that we were the only customers in the pub. I wondered whether it was worth keeping it open all day.

The three of us chatted generally about the pub trade, and the local area. I think Mick was glad of the company as much as the small profit on our drinks. Eventually the conversation came round to our occupations. I simply said I was a photographer. When Danny explained he was a journalist, Mick's curiosity was aroused.

"You should have been here last week," he said. "We had a journalist staying here. You would have enjoyed chatting to her. What was her name now? Clare something or other. I can't remember now, but she works on The Daily Echo on Fleet Street. She's an investigative reporter."

My ears nearly fell off, and my heart rate quickened. I can't speak for Danny but I expect he was much the same. He certainly looked on high alert.

"Clare Woodbrook?" he asked

"Yes, that was her. Lovely-looking woman. Sorry," he added, nodding at me. Don't rub it in, sunshine.

"No, go on," I urged. "Was she here working on a case or was it just a social visit?"

"She didn't say. But I'd say it was social. I was chatting to them in the bar, a bit like we are now."

"When was she here?"

"Let me think. Tuesday. Yes, last Tuesday."

The day before she went missing.

"You said 'them'. Was she was with somebody?" Danny

asked.

"Yes, now what was his name..." Mick was warming to his subject. He didn't often get such an attentive audience. "Benjamin something."

"Serraillier?"

"That's right. Foreign-looking chap. Very well dressed, but he didn't say much. Do you know them?"

Danny shook his head. I expect he was feeling an emotion close to jealousy but I was inwardly jumping for joy.

"Only of them," he said. "She's quite a legend. Did they say where they were going?"

"No, afraid not. I didn't do the breakfasts on Wednesday so I only spoke to them on the night. She said something about needing to be up early and having to be back in London by ten o'clock, but she didn't say what for."

Despite several more probing questions, the landlord was unable - or unwilling - to reveal any more details. But he'd already said enough to raise questions. Danny and I thanked him for his time and wished him well. He responded by showing us to the door and inviting us back for a drink the next time we were in the area.

I plipped the temperamental central locking and we got back into the car. Happily for Mick Flynn, another customer seemed to have turned up. There was a black Sierra at the far end of the car park. I was pretty sure it hadn't been there when we arrived. We set off back towards London to try to make sense of it all.

"A few things puzzle me," said Danny, as I drove back towards Cambridge. "Apart from the obvious, like what on earth was Clare doing, staying in a bed and breakfast with Serraillier? The main one is: why would would he write her a fan letter if they already knew each other?"

"I don't know. Maybe as a joke. Ooh, maybe it was a coded

message."

"You make it sound like she's a spy."

"Maybe she is."

"Ha... And there's a couple of other things. When Charlotte hired her car, she must have needed a driving licence. And it must have had the address in Paddington on it. How did she get it? They're not easily forged now they've got watermarks."

"Didn't Billy say there'd been another Charlotte a couple of years ago?"

"Yeah."

"So maybe she stole it. Or maybe the original Charlotte was an accomplice. She applied for it and waited every day for it to arrive. As soon as it did, she left."

"But that would mean this, whatever it is, has been planned for over two years."

"Wow." I couldn't think of anything more constructive.

Danny hadn't finished.

"There's one more thing that's been puzzling me for a while. Clare left the office shortly after ten o'clock. She met Serraillier at about half past eleven, and left shortly after. But her car wasn't found until some time in the middle of the night. What happened in between? Where did she go? What was she doing?"

"Perhaps that's the key to the whole thing."

"It must be. It was during that time that she disappeared, but nobody's seen her since she left the hotel."

"Except Serraillier, and he's dead. Perhaps he didn't know about the kidnapping. Maybe that's why he left the message to meet Clare at the house in Sunderland."

"Which would mean it was somebody else completely. Oh God, it gets worse. Although, having said that, whatever happened to Clare must have happened shortly after she left the hotel because she was supposed to meet me at half past one. Which would point to Serraillier. And she told me she'd be

163

able to explain everything when we met, which would suggest the story was near to completion. So why would she arrange to meet Serraillier in Sunderland, unless she was setting him up."

"Assuming he was one of the bad guys."

"But he must be, because he killed Chernin."

"Unless that was an act of self-defence."

"In a car park? It's not very likely."

Danny paused for thought.

"None of this explains Charlotte, or what happened to Megan. I'm beginning to think that that must be unconnected, but something at the back of my mind tells me it is linked, somehow."

"Do you know what puzzles me?" I asked. "When we were at Rougemont, the guard thought I was Clare and he said that Serraillier was my partner. Why would Clare go into partnership with Serraillier?"

"I don't know, but she was definitely with him at the Otter. It's all a mystery."

"You're an investigative journalist. You're supposed to like mysteries."

"I do normally, but I prefer it when I don't know the people involved. This one scares me. We don't seem to have any control over what's happening. I just don't know what to do next."

"Well, we've got the choice of going back to London or Reigate." I'd just joined the M11.

"London first. I ought to check if there are any messages, then I suppose back to Reigate to see how Megan's doing."

Halfway down the motorway, Danny confessed his darkest fear.

"I've got a bad feeling about this. The longer it goes on, the less chance there is of finding her alive. Especially as we haven't even had a word from the captors yet. I hate to say it, but I think they've..."

His words tailed off. I searched hard to find something of

comfort and reassurance. But the words wouldn't come.

***

Five days, thought Danny. Five days since she disappeared, and we're no nearer to finding her. It seemed like an age. It was the hardest case he'd ever worked on, and he was beginning to have doubts about his ability as an investigator.

He and Anna climbed the steps to their front door, and once inside Danny switched the answering machine to the "at home" position and pressed the "message play" button. It was as much to see if British Telecom had mended the fault on the line as to hear the actual messages. They had.

"Hello, this is a message for Anna Burgin," said the first voice. "Dennis Milne from the Four Keys photographic agency. I've been talking to a friend of yours who suggested you might be in need of an agent, and I thought we might meet some time to see if I could be of any help to you. Still, I'll call you again later. Goodbye."

"Bloody agents," said Anna, who had followed Danny to the answering machine. "Fifteen per cent of your earnings down the pan just so they can sell your pictures to some dodgy foreign magazine. Sod off."

The messages continued.

"Hi Danny, it's Derek. Sorry to be the messenger, buddy, but Mike is absolutely flaming. Just a word to the wise. I don't know what you're up to but he's a powerful man, mate. Speak to him. Urgently. Or if there's something you need to talk about, call me. Please?"

Danny swore. He didn't want to lose his job but now wasn't the time.

"Danny. Mike Walker. What the hell are you playing at? I need copy *now*. Emma told you to see me and you left the building. If you value your career, call me. *Immediately*."

Shit...

"Er, hello, I'm trying to contact Danny Churchill. It's Joanne Appleby from Sunderland. We met when you came round to the house. You asked me to call if I heard anything - well, this morning there was definite movement in the flat. I didn't see anybody, but I thought I'd better let you know. Call me when you get in. Bye."

That was more like it. Danny stopped the tape and played the message again. It was the last one on the tape. Danny found the number for Clare's house in Sunderland and made a call. Nobody answered. But then there was a knock on the door.

CHAPTER TWENTY

"**D**ANNY," said DCI March when the door was opened. "Are you going to welcome us inside and offer us both a nice cup of tea?"

Danny turned and walked back towards the kitchen, indicating that March and DC Amy Cranston should follow.

"Nice place you've got here, if we overlook the residual whiff of student. Are you on your own?"

"No, Anna's here. We've just got in. Are you here with news?" asked Danny.

"Ah, that's what you'd like, I suspect. Something to get you off the hook. But I fear we'll have a long and fruitless wait for that kind of development. No, Danny, I'm here because you intrigue me."

"Intrigue you?"

"Indeed. In fact I was only just saying exactly the same to the delectable Ms Cranston. We never seem to know what you're up to. So we thought we'd come over to find out."

Anna had already moved to the kitchen before they entered.

Danny gave her a look, part despair and part frustration. She got up to leave.

"No, no, my dear, there's no need to vacate on my account," said March. "Please, feel free to stay. You may be able to help us." She sat down again until Danny started to fill the kettle and then she got back up and took over.

"So, just to get this straight, is this a formal interview?" asked Danny.

"Do you mean are we recording it? No, not this time. But we will be taking notes." He nodded to DC Cranston, who had a pen and notebook at the ready, and then turned to Anna. "No sugar in either, my love, thank you."

"Okay, well how can I help?"

"So here, Danny, is the thing. You don't look a bad lad. Bit of a mummy's boy, as we've discussed, and you haven't got a girlfriend, or so you reckon, and I can't pretend to be astonished. But you don't look like the murderous type."

"Thank you."

"Ah, not so quick. See, in my line of work - your actual real investigation, if you will, not the pretend stuff you dabble in - you learn not to judge by appearances. Have you heard of the baby-faced assassin?"

"I've heard the phrase."

"Exactly. More of an abstract concept I believe, rather than pertaining to any particular junior hitman. But the principle applies. You can look all sweet and innocent, and yet behind the eyes lurks the disturbed mind of a killer."

"Right. And your point is?"

"Well. We've already established that you don't have an alibi for when Clare went missing. We've already got you unaccounted for on the whole of the rest of that day. And we've got your fingerprints all over the car. And then we have you at the scene somewhere in the frozen north where our esteemed French friend met his untimely demise."

"I've explained…"

"Shhh, Danny. There's a good boy. I'll tell you when it's your turn. Don't want to lose my track here. Where was I? Ah yes, so you're unaccounted for during the disappearance, and on the scene, by your own admission, shhh again, for the actual topping of the frog. And then I got an eyewitness report describing you down to the number of eyelashes about five minutes from here when guns started going off yesterday evening. Which could lead a suspicious mind to conclude you're in it up to your armpits. But I'm a fair man, as you know, so I like to give the benefit of the doubt."

"I've…"

"Danny, third time. Shut. The. Fuck. Up. The problem is that I then read the reports from a certain incident at a hotel down in Streatham, south of the river, can't get a taxi, and to be frank why the fuck would you want to? But anyway, I get the reports and there's an interview with the receptionist who tells of a visit from a young man the day before the bomb went off, who asked to be left alone in the very bar where it was detonated, who not only fitted your description down to the number of freckles as well as the number of eyelashes, but better still actually identified himself with your fucking name. So I'm thinking, maybe you've got a twin brother because I told you very clearly to keep me up to date on things, and if you were to forget to mention something as significant as that then it doesn't exactly look what I like to call favourable when it goes in front of a jury."

He turned to Anna.

"Lovely cup of tea, love. Maybe a biscuit? Small one won't hurt." Anna walked over to a cupboard and pulled out half a packet of Digestives, passing them over without a word.

"Anyway," March continued, turning back to Danny, "so just to summarise the tally so far, that's you in the right place, right time, with no alibis, and actual physical evidence for a

169

disappearance, an abandoned car, a shooting, an attempted shooting and an actual fucking bomb. Which you would think would be enough to raise a modicum of suspicion. And then I did a little bit of mathematics, and I plotted the route back from Streatham to here, given the time our witness says you left, and guess what? Bingo. You'd be in the vicinity of Farringdon around the exact moment our other esteemed French friend is meeting a similarly untimely demise in Saffron Hill. So we'll add that to the list too. And that, kind of, tips the balance into maybe me thinking you're not the naive innocent you like to pretend."

There was a silence in the room, only punctuated by the ticking of a clock.

"You may now speak," said March.

Danny sighed.

"I'm sorry, but that is all utter crap. And you must know it or you wouldn't be here. You'd have sent in an armed response unit."

"You don't know who's waiting outside, Danny."

Danny thought for a moment but dismissed the idea.

"No," he said. "I don't believe it. Yes, all right, that was me. Yes I was at the hotel. But I'm just going to repeat what I've said from the outset. Nobody - nobody - wants to find Clare more than me. Yes, I've been looking for her, and if I've got close a couple of times it's no real surprise that I'm not the only one. I've explained about the fingerprints in the car. The police in Sunderland were happy I had nothing to do with what went on up there. I just discovered it."

"Well, we did," said Anna.

"Yes, sorry. Anna and I. We discovered it together."

"So if you're suspicious about Danny, you should also be looking at me," said Anna. "I haven't got any alibis. I'm helping Danny, so if he's in the wrong place at the wrong time then I am too."

"And you're... Anna?"

"Yes, Anna Burgin."

"Ah, Anna Burgin. Would that be the same Anna Burgin who came into the station on Saturday just gone to report an attempted kidnapping of a young porn starlet?"

"Fashion model. But yes. That was me."

"Interesting." March paused for a moment. "And needless to say, Danny, do you have an alibi for that particular event or is that another for the list?"

"Ha! Yes I do. I was in with you getting fucking interviewed."

"Hmmm. Fair play. But watch your language in front of the ladies."

"Jesus."

"Can I just interject?" That was DC Cranston. "You've mentioned the hotel, which is helpful, but still haven't explained about the gunfire in Camden."

"God, sorry. No, that just freaked me out."

"So you're saying it was you, despite your earlier protestation of complete ignorance when we spoke this morning?" asked March.

"Yes, sorry, I..."

"I'll stop you there. That's a bit suspicious, isn't it? You're down by the canal, on a deserted towpath, late at night. Has it turned into a gay cruising spot all of a sudden? You dealing drugs Danny?"

"No, God no. I... Well..."

"You don't sound very sure. Wouldn't you be better off up on Hampstead Heath with the rest of them? Nice boy like you, be popular I'd imagine."

"Jesus. I'm not gay. But what if I was? Wouldn't make any difference. I just want to find Clare."

"So you say. So the canal then?"

"I was in the pub. The World's End. By the station. On my own. You can check with the bar staff. I had a drink. I left. I walked home."

"Via the towpath."

"No, not via the towpath. But along there, yes, on the street above. I heard a shout from the bottom of the steps which sounded like for a cry for help, so I started to go down, then I saw a man on a motorbike, with a gun. He pointed it at me and I ran. That's it. He fired but missed. So sorry, yes, but it scared the life out of me. I didn't see anything apart from a bloke in a crash helmet who could have been anyone, and it was dark so I couldn't even tell you what colour it was."

"Right. And you didn't tell me because?"

"Because I'm sick of being accused of things that I haven't done. And as far as I'm aware, it's got nothing to do with anything. It may have been a drug deal. I don't know. I was just wrong place, wrong time. I'm trying not to have nightmares about it."

"Does that sound feasible to you, DC Cranston?"

"It's possible. And Farringdon?"

"Coincidence," said Danny. "Pure coincidence. I was in my car. I didn't go anywhere near the car park and I didn't know anything about that until I read about it in the Standard."

"Okay." DCI March stood up. "I'll tell you what we're going to do. Have you got a passport?"

"Yes."

"Go and get it for me."

Danny got up and went to the bedroom to get his passport from his underwear drawer. He stopped for a moment, rested his head against the wall, eyes closed, body sagging in fatigue and despair. After a moment he took a deep breath, returned to the kitchen and handed the passport to DCI March, who passed it on to DC Cranston.

"Thank you," said March. "We'll look after that. We don't want you disappearing out of the country all of a sudden, do we? Now, I've said it before, but I'll say it again, one last

172

time with emphasis. I'll be watching you. And you have the delightful Amy to thank for not taking you in this instant and banging you up for the rest of your natural. I suggest, for your own safety, and my sanity, you stop pretending to be a detective. You stop trying to find Clare. You leave it to the professionals. If anything happens, you call me, personally. You do not keep anything from me, ever again. Because if you do, you're coming in, being charged with God knows whatever I fancy from a fucking long list of possibles. Understood?"

"Yes, understood."

"And Anna?"

"What?"

"Thank you for a lovely cup of tea, darling, although the biscuits were a bit damp if you don't mind me saying. But the same applies to you: this is our job. Leave it to us. We know what we're doing. It stops now."

"Okay," said Anna.

"We'll leave you to the rest of your evening. Do not go anywhere. I will know if you do. We'll show ourselves out."

And with that, the two detectives got up and went to the front door. When they'd heard it close behind them, Danny and Anna went to the front room window to watch them leave. Their car pulled out from between a red Ford Escort and a black Ford Sierra, and they drove away.

***

"What the fuck was that?" I asked, not particularly politely.

"He's a bastard. It's got to be him. Surely," said Danny.

"Are we going to stop?"

"What?"

"You heard what he said. We've got to stop looking or he's going to nick us. You at least, and me too, probably."

"No, that just means we're getting somewhere. We're getting

173

close. Must be. Of course he wants us to stop. If he's the one who's done it then he absolutely doesn't want us looking into it any more."

"So he's just trying to put the frighteners on?"

"Absolutely. I meant what I said. If he really thought I was responsible, he'd have sent in the big boys with guns. I'd be a multiple killer and terrorist. He's not stupid. Bent, but not that. He knows I've got nothing to do with any of it. He just wants us out of the picture."

"So we carry on?"

"I'm going to, but you shouldn't. I can't get you into any more trouble."

"Shut up, Danny," I said, with a hint of a sigh. How many times? "We're a team. If we go down we go down together." I meant every word. He smiled at me so I reached out and shook his hand. No real idea why I did that, but at least it wasn't another salute.

Later, before heading to bed, Danny tried calling Joanne again, but there was still no answer. We decided to leave it to morning and try then. I tried to call Megan in Reigate but there was no answer there, either. And then I remembered that Claudia and Philip had gone to Frankfurt and so there wouldn't be anyone in the main house. I just hoped she was okay.

It felt strange to be back in my own bed after a night in Sunderland, a night at Clare's apartment and then a night at Reigate. And it felt strange without Danny beside me. I could get used to having him there. But it wasn't just thoughts of romance. I felt safe when we were together, and I had a strong suspicion things were going to get a lot more dangerous yet.

CHAPTER TWENTY-ONE

Tuesday, February 16th, 1993

STUDENTS aren't renowned early risers, but Danny wanted to catch Joanne before she left for lectures, so he called the student house in Sunderland just after 8am. Finally the phone was answered, albeit by someone who only sounded half awake.

"Hi, sorry to bother you. Is Joanne there please?" he said, with a sense of relief. He'd had visions of them all lying in a blood bath.

"Just a moment."

Half a minute later he heard a young woman's voice.

"Hello."

"Hi, it's Danny Churchill. I'm just returning your call from yesterday."

"Danny who?"

"Danny Churchill, Clare's friend from London."

"Oh yes. I remember. You were up here when that guy got

175

shot. But I didn't call you."

"Yes you did. I got in last night and there was a message on the machine. You are Joanne Appleby?"

"Yes, that's me, but please, call me Jo. I hate Joanne. But no, I wasn't even in yesterday. We went straight from uni to the pub and then we went back to the Union because Sunscreem were playing. I didn't get back till gone midnight, so it wasn't me."

Danny was puzzled.

"So you haven't heard any noises from the flat out the back?"

"No, I haven't. I'll ask the others. Hold on a moment."

A minute later she came back on the line.

"Yes, apparently Chris heard something yesterday afternoon, like furniture being moved, apparently. I asked him if he'd called you and he said he hadn't given it any thought. Sorry. We should have done, I suppose, but I didn't know about it."

"None of the others would have called and used your name?"

"Not for any reason I can think of. There was only Chris here, and it wasn't him. Wait a minute - did you say the message was from Joanne Appleby?"

"Yes."

"Well, it definitely wasn't me. I haven't called myself Joanne since I was at primary school. Sorry."

"No, don't worry. I'm sorry to have disturbed you." Danny's confusion deepened. "Thanks anyway, Jo, you've been a big help. Keep in touch if you do hear anything."

"I will. Bye Danny."

"Goodbye."

Danny replaced the receiver. Anna had joined him and he looked at her in disbelief, shaking his head.

"You know, just once it would be nice if something happened that was actually straightforward," he said.

"What was that?"

"That was Joanne. Except she calls herself Jo and she says she didn't ring me and wasn't even in yesterday. Let's listen to the tape again."

Danny rewound the tape and hit the play button for yesterday's message.

"No. It's definitely a different voice. Oh for fuck's sake. Is anybody who they actually say they are?"

"Does it sound like Charlotte? I still can't get used to calling her Charlotte."

"No, not really. It could do, I suppose, but no I don't think so."

"Well, whoever it was, they wanted to draw your attention back to the flat."

"Which means something's happening."

"Exactly. Back to Sunderland then?"

"I'm sorry, Anna..."

"Don't worry. It's fine. I'll pack a bag. Just next time round could you lose someone who lives a little bit closer?"

***

Danny called Simon and asked if it would be all right for us to pop back again and stay another night. At least this time I knew I was going to get to share a bed. It still seemed like a bloody long way to go, mind.

I went to pack while Danny was in the shower. Knowing the sleeping arrangements, did I pack my best underwear? No. Seriously, what kind of a girl do you take me for? Deluded, possibly, but I'm not a floozy. Well, maybe just a little bit of a one. It all matched but that's as far as it goes.

I'm not claiming to be an expert in relationship matters (and indeed as you've seen, I'm largely clueless), but he's developed from being just a very good friend into somebody I genuinely couldn't imagine living without. And I can't imagine having that depth of connection with anyone else. Moreover, I can't imagine ever wanting to have it with anyone else, either. So while I'm not averse to the fripperies of lacy underwear, it really would be a giant step in the wrong direction to suddenly turn into some kind of seductive short-term vamp. I can do that happily if we ever get together. Got to keep things interesting. But I don't want to devalue the ultimate prize.

Danny was still getting ready when the phone rang. It was Megan, calling in from Reigate. All was well. In fact it sounded like she was having a lovely time in luxurious isolation, but she was a little bit lonely. I explained about the trip north and said we'd be in touch as soon as possible. I'd just made tea when Danny came back down, looking all freshly scrubbed and lovely.

"Are you sure you don't mind coming?" he asked. I assured him I wouldn't be anywhere else.

"I just feel bad. Should I drive? You must be worn out."

I gave him one of those looks. The one that says, "It's bad enough doing the best part of 600 miles without the added misery of being a passenger."

"It's fine. In any case your car will probably break down."

"Says the woman with the dodgy central locking."

Oooh, the cheek.

"No, Danny, it's fine," I said. "We'll split the petrol if it makes you feel better, but I'm happier driving. What about March, though? He specifically told us not to go anywhere."

"He did, but... Are you bothered?"

"Me? Not really."

"Me neither." And by just past 11am we were on the road.

"The more I think about it, the more Lisa - Charlotte - has got to be working with Serraillier," said Danny, just as we passed the Ram Jam Inn, north of Peterborough. "She knew too much."

"In what way?" I asked.

"It was just that night in the car she kept asking me about things that I hadn't told the police. She knew things. She knew about the Mowbray Hall Hotel. She knew about Rougemont. Long before anybody else. That could only be Serraillier because he was there at both of them. Nobody else made that connection until much later."

"That's a good point."

"She said something as well. She seemed pissed off that I was keeping things back, even though she already knew them. And then she said, 'Wouldn't we all find Clare quicker if we all worked together?'"

"Which means she's looking for Clare too."

"I think so. Doesn't it?"

"It makes sense."

"But we don't know why. I just want to believe that Clare's hiding out somewhere, but it doesn't add up. How would her car end up on the motorway? And how would she get anywhere from there? She'd be walking miles across fields in the middle of the night. It just doesn't make sense."

"Okay, so we assume she's definitely been taken, by someone. Let's say March. Maybe Ravenscroft. Doesn't matter. Either way, Charlotte, Lisa, whatever... Can we just choose a name, by the way, and stick to it?"

"Not a bad plan. Lisa?"

"Okay, Lisa. So either way, Lisa is working for Serraillier and looking for Clare. But why? Because she's worried? Or because she thinks Clare knows something about Serraillier getting killed and she's investigating that?"

"Or she's blaming her and wants revenge."

"Oh God, don't."

"We've got to face it. Whenever I've spoken to her it's like she's one step ahead and she's looking to me for verification. We've got to catch up. If Lisa finds Clare first then God knows what'll happen."

"But where's she now?"

"We don't know, do we? She said she'd be in touch. She won't necessarily know we've worked her out, so we've just got to hope she does something soon and then maybe we turn the tables, and we start interrogating her instead."

"Ooh Danny, you sound so masterful."

"Stop it! I'm being serious."

"I know. I just had this vision of you in knee-high boots going, 'Ve haf vays of making you talk.' Sorry. I'll try to be sensible."

Danny laughed. And reached across to squeeze my hand.

"Don't worry," he said. "You're keeping me sane."

We lapsed into silence. I concentrated on the road. And then suddenly Danny made my heart flip.

"You're brilliant, you know that?" he said.

"I'm sorry?"

"You're brilliant. I just... Oh I don't know. I just had to say it."

"Well you're not so bad yourself." I smiled. It's always nice to receive a compliment.

Where did that come from? Can't pretend I wasn't pleased. He'd been looking so lost, bless him. I just do what I can.

"Anyway I'm not so sure how brilliant I am, but I have been thinking," I said.

"Go on."

"Serraillier had keys to Clare's."

"Did he?"

"I think we can assume so. His car was in her backyard, so it makes sense. But let's go back a bit, to Ravenscroft." I was a bit anxious about how well this was going to go down, but I had to take the risk.

"What about him?"

"Well, what did you tell me about that? Clare was investigating him, and he seemed to think there was something more. It wasn't a case of a honeytrap, as such, but you did say he'd told her stuff because he was trying to get her kit off."

"Did I?"

"Yes, ages ago."

"Okay."

"Well you did. I'm not knocking Clare, don't get me wrong, but I think there's a pattern here." Deep breath. "I like Clare, I really do, but she seems, how can I put it, quite detached. I think there's an element of mystery there that men seem to be attracted to."

"In what way?"

I was getting into dangerous territory.

"She's gorgeous, yes, I get that. But she seems quite aloof, maybe. And men seem to think they've got a chance with her when they clearly haven't." Sorry Danny, but it had to be said. "And that's where Ravenscroft went wrong. He had his tongue hanging out and he's said too much and he's hung himself. Well, what if Serraillier's the same? She's investigating him. Just sounding out a story, which she's about to bring you in on, but he thinks there's something more. He thinks she wants him. Men can be a bit stupid like that." This last bit may not have been strictly necessary.

"Okay, I'm with you. So far."

"Right, so he does the same. He starts telling her stuff. She keeps it purely professional, obviously, but she needs to earn his trust so she, well, doesn't exactly discourage him. I'm not saying she led him on, but she'd be friendly and he's completely fallen for her. Thinks they're in a partnership when actually it's no more than it was with Jimmy."

"Which would explain why they've been meeting, but not staying the night together in Ely last Tuesday."

"But who says they stayed together?"

181

"Mick did. The landlord."

"Ah, but did he? He said he'd been chatting to them in the bar. And he said she'd booked a room. But it could have been a single. We don't know that he stayed too."

"Don't we?"

"No, think about what he said. 'I had a booking last week. It was that journalist.' Or something like that. He didn't actually say they'd both stayed, only that he was chatting to them both in the evening. Serraillier could have gone on somewhere. Mick didn't do the breakfasts so we don't know if they were both there next morning. But let's assume not." I could see Danny was delighted at the thought that she wasn't sleeping with the man, which was unfortunate, but I was on a roll.

"Okay, but why would he have a key then?"

"She's trying to earn his trust. We don't know exactly what he was trying to achieve, or her for that matter, but either way she gives him a key to the flat. We know they were meeting there. We don't know why, but it makes sense."

Danny was quiet for a moment, clearly thinking about things.

"I like it," he said at last. "I think you could be right. Told you you were brilliant."

I just smiled. There was more to come.

"Right, so let's go back again, to Lisa," I continued. "We're assuming she's working for Serraillier. So maybe she's got a key too."

"God. What if she's the one who shot him?"

That stopped me. I hadn't thought of that.

"Ah, that's not good," I said. "I was just coming to the actual theory but that's actually a good point. That would make a difference."

"Why? What's the theory?"

"Well, I was just going to say that if Lisa's got the key and there's something going on up in Sunderland, then maybe she's the one up there now, moving things about. Maybe searching for something. Or, better still, maybe staying there now she's left the hotel."

"But if she's the one who shot him..."

"... That would be bad. Substantially bad. Not completely sure she'll be pleased to see us."

We paused while I navigated the entrance to roadworks. Can't beat a contraflow for focusing the mind.

"But no!" said Danny after a moment. "That would make sense if one of the students had rung us and told us about the noises. But they didn't, did they? Whoever left that message pretended to be Jo, but it wasn't her. So someone's leading us here deliberately. They're expecting us."

He had a point. And they quite possibly had a gun.

"Something else Lisa said," he continued. "She said she'd been watching me. She said she was my guardian angel."

"That's encouraging," I replied. Anything that lessened the chances of us taking a bullet had to be a bonus.

"God, what on earth are we getting involved in?"

"No idea. But on the bright side, if there is one, we're still here, aren't we? Nobody's tried to kill us yet."

"Speak for yourself."

Ah yes, I'd forgotten about that.

"Okay. But nobody's actually managed it yet. We just have to be careful. Extra careful. If Lisa was behind the message, and she's the one who brought us up here, the chances are she's not going to shoot us, even if she did shoot Serraillier. And that was only a theory anyway. Let's work on the basis that she is what she says. That she is looking out for us, for whatever reason."

"She definitely was looking out for me on the towpath. If she hadn't dragged me up the steps, I'd be dead."

"Well there you go then."

We just had to be strong. But at that moment, a big part of

me wanted to be weak. To walk away and let everything sort itself out without involving either of us. I felt no braver than a goldfish innocently swimming around its bowl while peering over the rim was a tom-cat, claws extended, waiting to pounce.

CHAPTER TWENTY-TWO

WE finally arrived in Sunderland just before 6pm, having stopped for an early dinner somewhere north of Middlesbrough. Nobody attempted to shoot us. In fact everything seemed remarkably mundane and normal, if you consider two giant trips to the end of the world and back within four days normal.

We called briefly at Simon and Rebecca's house to drop off our bags and pick up a set of door keys.

"Leaving again so soon?" said Simon as we raced back out of the door.

"Important work to be done, mate. Back soon," said Danny.

"Hopefully," I added. And we were gone.

The thud of music we could hear on the street became louder as the students' door was opened by a thin young man with scruffy jeans, a baggy white T-shirt and glasses, holding a can of Double Maxim. The distinctive aroma of marijuana wafted out from the hallway.

"Jo? Yeah, I'll just get her," said the student when Danny introduced himself.

After a moment, Jo appeared, dressed in a baggy jumper and holding another can of beer and a roll-up cigarette.

"Oh, hello, it's you," she said by way of recognition. "Come on in and join the party."

"You're all right, thanks, it's just a flying visit. I just wondered if you'd heard any more."

"From the flat? No, not since I spoke to you."

"Not to worry, but if you do, let me know."

"I will."

"Thank you. Sorry to bother you. Have fun."

"I will," she said again as she closed the door. As I walked back to the car I wondered why, even in 1993, all students still played records by The Cure.

I drove round to the back of the row of houses and parked against the wall on Toward Road, adjacent to Clare's rear gates. We didn't have a key, obviously, but we were pretty sure it wasn't going to matter. Whoever had made us come back was hardly going to leave us abandoned on the street. That said, we were super-cautious. We didn't know what to expect, and I shuddered at the thought of what we'd found the last time.

We both got out of the car and Danny tried the gate while I kept watch on the street. A few cars passed but none paid us much attention. The gate was again unlocked, as we'd suspected. Danny eased it open, peeking through the crack between the doors, taking his time in case anyone, or anything, was on the far side.

But this time the yard was empty. The flat beyond looked empty too. It was dark and appeared deserted, although we weren't taking any chances.

I followed Danny into the backyard, and pulled the gate closed behind me. I was shaking, partly due to the cold, partly with the memory of the last time, and partly with a whole new dose of fear. I hadn't really considered the implications of stepping across this particular threshold until we were actually there. It was terrifying.

"What now?" I whispered, hoping Danny was feeling braver than me. He didn't reply. Just edged over to the flat's red front door. The door was ajar, and Danny only had to push it to gain entrance.

He gave me a look that I interpreted as encouragement, but maybe he was just being brave as well. He indicated for me to crouch down. I suppose the idea was to make ourselves smaller in case of attack, but in all honesty I'm a small enough target as it is. I did as directed, though. He pushed the door gently and waited. There was no sound. He pushed it some more. And then more again until it was open just enough to squeeze through.

"Wait here," he whispered. And slowly crept inside.

A few seconds later the light came on in the hall, making me jump. Then Danny appeared and beckoned me towards him. I went in and closed the door behind me.

The flat was as I remembered it - sparsely furnished, but well decorated and in good order, at least structurally. It had been cleaned up since the chaos of Saturday. By the police maybe? I thought it unlikely, but if not, then who? It only had four rooms. It was so different to Clare's place in London. So much less of a home. As well as the lounge there was a tiny kitchen, a bathroom, and a bedroom which just about had space for a double bed and a wardrobe. The bed was made, and the room was tidy. Nothing seemed out of place. We checked the wardrobe and under the bed, but if somebody was hiding they were doing an impeccable job.

Confident that we were alone, I followed Danny through to the kitchen. I flicked on the switch and the room was flooded with the harsh glare of a fluorescent strip light. Why do people always put fluorescent lights in kitchens? There seems no logical reason. One of the taps was dripping and had filled the washing-up bowl in the sink. I tightened it to stop the drip. Then, for reasons of safety, I moved the kettle away from its position perilously close to the edge of the worktop.

"Danny," I said, in an urgent whisper. "It's still warm." I instinctively reached for a kitchen knife from the block on the worktop. And then reached for another and passed it to Danny. If nothing else happened, we could at least have a sword fight.

Somebody had been in the flat - recently - but they didn't seem to be here now. That didn't mean they wouldn't return at any second. The tension was claustrophobic.

We returned to the front room. And then we noticed an envelope propped up on top of the gas fire that adorned one wall. Danny's name was written on the front.

He tore it open and pulled out a piece of typed paper. A key fell to the floor.

"Read it to me," I urged, picking up the key. He began:

> *Hello Danny. Sorry I had to go. I believe you've been looking for me.*

"Clare!" I gasped. My heart leapt. But he shook his head. "No. Lisa. Listen to this."

> *I'm sorry to have left you by the canal, but I told you it was getting dangerous. You cannot be too careful. I know you got away safely that time because I followed you home, but please let it serve as a warning. There are bad people out there. They will be looking for you.*

"Jesus." I sat on the arm of the sofa, suddenly feeling quite faint.

I've had to leave town, and I suppose by now you've guessed that I'm not DC Lisa Miller. I really didn't want to lead you on, but I had to speak to you to find out what you knew. I hope one day we will meet again and then I will have the chance to explain and make you understand. The truth is, I'm also looking for Clare, although I can't tell you why just now. But please rest assured that I wish her no harm. I would like to think that we can work together to find her.

I can't be seen to be working alongside you. It would put us both in enormous danger. It was enough of a risk to meet up with you the first time, and now I have had to leave town because of it. I can't tell you where I am, but I will contact you when I need to speak to you.

"That's big of her," I said. Danny nodded and joined me on the sofa.

I'll tell you what I know so far, as I think it might help you. Clare had hooked up with Benjamin Serraillier. I don't know why, but yes, I know about her job, so I suspect she may have been investigating him. I was Benjamin's assistant for a while and I know that he occasionally pushed the limits. That's why I got out.

Benjamin had a bodyguard called Richard Kirk. I introduced them as he was someone I knew could handle himself, but Richard doesn't like me. I think he took my departure as a betrayal and he's worried about who I may talk to. Richard is still out there. I don't know where he is. He'll be trying to find out who shot Benjamin and be warned he'll stop at nothing. It may have been Richard on the motorbike, but for obvious reasons I didn't hang around to find out.

Richard may be working alongside DCI Graham March. I've seen them talking to each other. Certainly do not trust DCI March under any circumstances.

There are some things I do not yet understand. I do not know who broke into Clare's car, or what happened at the Mowbray Hall Hotel, but I think it is connected. Be careful of a black Sierra car. I don't know who that belongs to, but it seems to be following you around. I don't know why Benjamin killed Dominique Chernin, but it appears that he did, unless that was Richard Kirk. I am trying to find out, but whoever killed Benjamin may well be trying to kill me too.

We must be careful, but you can trust me, and it is imperative that you do. We have to work together, and I need you to do a job for me. There's a nightclub in Sunderland called Bentleys. It will be open tonight (Tuesday) for a special promotion. I need you to go there and meet somebody for me. He will give you some information.

Go with your photographer friend Anna and take photographs throughout the evening. If anybody asks, tell them they're for the entertainment supplement of the local newspaper. The man will then recognise you and pass on the information we need.

Tomorrow morning bring the prints and negatives back to this flat and leave them under the pillow on the bed. I may need them later. Please also *leave a copy of anything you're given in the same place. I'm sorry this has to be so secretive, but I'm sure given the circumstances you will understand. Still, though, be careful.*

I had Benjamin's key to this flat, but I don't know who else had a copy. I have changed the lock and there's a spare key enclosed in this envelope. Please feel free to take it and use it when you return here. From now on we need to keep the doors locked. I don't think the gates lock properly, you just need to push those hard enough, but we must secure the flat.

Have a good time at the nightclub. Your name is on the door, and I'm sure if you ask them nicely they will give you free drinks. I will contact you again soon.

Lisa.

I just made a blowing-out noise. Danny passed me the letter.

"What do you think? Do you believe a word of it?" I asked after a moment.

"It's long enough, but no idea," said Danny. "I'd like to, but... Just no idea. You?"

"Well, she's a bit up herself. But at least it clears up a few things."

"If any of it's true."

"But surely. I mean, why else write it?"

"Because she's playing us? Or playing me, specifically. Right from the start she said she was asking me questions to check whether or not what she believed was actually right. And it's still going on."

"And yet, if it's genuine, she's doing the same as us. We're on the same side."

"If it's genuine."

"I'll tell you what, though, I did see a black Sierra.",
"Where?"

"In Ely, when we left the Otter Tavern. There was a black Sierra in the car park when we left. I remember being pleased because I felt sorry for Mick as he didn't have many customers. It wasn't there when we got there but it was when we left. I definitely remember that."

"Could just be a coincidence."

"Maybe." I wasn't so sure.

"And at least we now know who Richard Kirk is," said Danny.

"Do you reckon it was him in Camden? And if so, why's he trying to shoot you? I mean, what do they think you know?"

"Unless he's working for March, as she said. If March knows we've been investigating him then I'm definitely a target as much as Clare was, if that's what this is all about."

"Wait here a moment," I said, and got up and went back to the kitchen.

"What are you doing?" Danny called from the living room.

"Making a cup of tea," I called back.

I returned a few minutes later with two cups, and put them down on the floor beside Danny, and then joined him back on the sofa.

"Sorry," I said. "Where were we?"

"Tonight. This nightclub thing. Are we going? Have we even got a camera? What on earth is that all about?"

"I've definitely got a camera. There's always one in the car. Bloody good job we brought mine, mind."

"Excellent. I still think it's weird, though. If she can't go herself there's obviously something going on. And we're going to walk right into it."

"But if we don't go, we don't get whatever it is we're supposed to be picking up."

"God."

"It depends, I suppose, on how much we trust her. She said we should be okay. And so far she does genuinely seem to have been looking out for you. Like on the canal. I reckon we've got to go. Do you know the club?"

"Yeah, I know it. What's the time now?"

"Seven-ish."

"Okay. We'll have the tea then go back to Simon's. Freshen up and risk it. If you're sure."

"I'm sure. I don't think we've got an option."

When we'd finished the drinks I washed up the cups and put them back where I'd found them. We switched off the lights and left the flat, making sure the door was locked behind us. Danny added the key to his keyring. Why do men have such big keyrings? I suspect it's something Freudian, but I'll work that out one day too.

We emerged onto the street and Danny pulled the gates closed behind us. And then instinctively I grabbed his arm and froze.

"Danny, look!" I whispered with a growing sense of panic.

He turned. About fifty yards away, between two street lights, a black Sierra was parked at the side of the road. Its sidelights were on and the engine was running. I could see the exhaust fumes clouding the icy air.

My first thought was to get back inside the gates as quickly as possible. And then all the pressure of the week caught up with me. I don't know why, but I'd had enough. I didn't want to be scared any more.

"I'm going over," I said, and set off before Danny could stop me. I heard him calling, but it was too late. But as I started to cross the road, the Sierra's driver dropped his clutch and powered towards me. I jumped out of the way just in time as he went roaring past me and then through the traffic lights at the top of the street.

Danny came running towards me.

"Jesus, are you all right?" he asked, full of concern. Physically I was fine, but I couldn't say more than that. I'd looked into the eyes of the driver as he bore down upon me. And I couldn't shake the feeling that they could well be the eyes of a killer.

CHAPTER TWENTY-THREE

BENTLEYS held happy memories for Danny, of youthful years spent chasing girls, discovering beer, and dancing until the early hours under a pulsating light show. It didn't quite measure up to some of the clubs he'd been to in London or abroad, but it felt like home. There were two dance floors and a separate quiet area with a bar. The main dance floor also boasted a stage where rising pop stars would occasionally pretend to sing along to their latest record in the name of live performance.

They hadn't, however, packed for a night out, so at Simon and Rebecca's house there was considerable debate about what to wear. Danny wished he'd brought his favourite Nik Boll suit, but his current outfit would suffice. Anna wished she'd brought anything other than the jeans and sweatshirt she'd travelled in.

Rebecca came to the rescue with the loan of a figure-hugging black dress. It wasn't getting any wear now she was pregnant and she doubted she'd ever be able to fit into it again. It was figure-hugging for Rebecca but far from it on Anna.

However, with the additional offer of a red belt and black tights it started to take on the semblance of acceptability. The shoes, though, were a problem. Rebecca was a six to Anna's four and Anna only had the black Dr Martens boots she'd been wearing all day. The black tights were ditched in favour of borrowed fishnets, which in any case were more adaptable for size. For Anna it was a reluctant return to the goth look of her youth, but with enough hairspray, a bit of back-combing, a spritz of Poison and lots of make-up, she was ready.

***

"What the fuck are you laughing at?" I walked into the front room where Danny was waiting, having made precisely zero effort, and he collapsed into fits of laughter.

"No, I'm sorry, you look lovely," he said, trying to regain control without much success. "You're an absolute vision."

"Stuff it, I'm putting the jeans back on." I turned immediately towards the door.

"No, seriously. You look brilliant. It was just a shock."

I turned back.

"A shock?"

"Yeah, it's just... The hair, the outfit, everything. It's, well, striking." He started laughing again. "It's just that it reminds me of what you used to look like when I first met you."

"It's not through choice."

"No, I like it. You look... cute."

"Cute?" I repeated, with considerable venom. Of all the four-letter words beginning with C, it was perhaps my least favourite. "I don't want to look cute. I want to look tough and dangerous."

"I think you look amazing," said Rebecca, who'd followed me into the room. I turned to her.

"Do you think I look cute?" I asked.

196

"No," she said, "far from it. You look like a super cool ninja assassin."

"Which is the right answer." I'd not long known Rebecca but she'd already won me over.

"Honestly," she continued. "You look brilliant. Ignore Danny. If I was a man I'd be deeply flattered to have you anywhere near me."

Yes, I liked Rebecca a lot. Danny was trying to control himself, with limited success.

"I'm sorry, I agree," he said at last, trying to repair the damage. "You look gorgeous. And Rebecca's right. I'll be proud to be seen with you."

"Are you just saying that?"

"No, it's true. It was just like a time warp. I like it though. It's sexy."

I may have stuck two fingers up at that point. I turned to Simon who was in an armchair by the TV.

"Simon, you look like an intelligent man, of which there are precious few in the vicinity. Do I look okay, ridiculous or... cute?"

"I'm with Rebecca," he said. "You look amazing."

"Ninja?"

"Absolutely."

"Right, well that'll do then. Thank you." I turned back to Danny. "You are going to be on your best behaviour and will be responsible for getting the drinks in. Do that and I may - may - forgive you."

He just smiled at me and stood up and came to give me a hug. Secretly I was quite pleased he'd called me sexy, but I wasn't going to let it show.

I have to admit, it did feel quite cool when we sailed past the queue at the entrance, and then, when Danny said the magic words "guest list", the doormen stood aside. I felt strangely important. I removed my jacket and handed it in at the cloakroom, leaving me with just my Nikon F90 which I carried by the neck strap. I gave Danny five spare rolls of film to look after as I didn't have anywhere to store them.

We seemed to attract quite a bit of attention as we walked through to the bar. I wasn't sure if it was the camera or just that everyone was scared of my make-up. In retrospect I probably should have toned it down a bit. After all, Lisa said we should be careful, and yet how are you supposed to go unnoticed when you're standing in front of everyone asking them if you can take a picture?

"Southern Comfort and lemonade, please," I said, before Danny had a chance to ask the question. He asked for a double, and a can of Red Stripe for himself. I'd never taken pictures in a nightclub before, and had no idea what was going to happen, so the least I could do was try to enjoy myself.

The club manager came over to make introductions and check that we were okay. I mentioned taking pictures for the local newspaper, but he seemed to know all about it. He spoke to the bar staff and then announced that whatever we wanted, all night, was on the house. He seemed like a decent man.

After the first drink in the quiet bar area, we moved through to the main room with the big dance floor. I wanted to explore and get a feel for the place. The room was filling up. It was a big crowd for a chilly Tuesday evening, lured out, I suspect by a promotion for cheap Malibu and the opportunity to see a band called Heaven In Art mime to their latest record. A celebrity disc jockey from the local commercial radio station was playing dance records from the current top forty, and the strobe lighting was freezing the movement of the three hundred or so people who were already on the dance floor.

"Where do we start?" I asked, nervously holding my camera and making mildly suggestive movements with the zoom lens, adjusting it in and out. I hadn't brought a flashgun. I thought there'd be enough light bouncing around the place without it, and the coloured neon and strobes would look much more dramatic without being overpowered by a flash. I had to keep reminding myself that the pictures weren't for publication. In fact I had no idea what they were for. But no matter, it was a question of professional pride in doing the best possible job.

"There's no rush," said Danny. "We'll just start whenever you feel up for it. Have another drink and we'll have a wander."

That seemed like a very good idea.

After the second drink had taken the edge off, Heaven In Art took to the stage, performing a song called Making Love Hard. The band line-up was just a singer, keyboard player, and two female dancers. Danny nodded and I jumped up. We moved to the stairs at the side of the stage and I shot a few frames, trying to capture both the energy of the performance and the enthusiasm of the audience.

The problem with being little is that big people get in your way. But I actually started to relish the challenge. I moved onto the dance floor and fought my way through the throbbing mass of bodies to get some close-ups of the singer. Seeing the camera aimed at him, he smiled as he sang the chorus "You're making, you're making, you're making love hard".

The crowd went wild at the end of the song before the band moved effortlessly into another called Silently She Came. The deep synthesised bass boomed out of the speakers, soon followed by the relentless beat of a sampled bass drum.

I was beginning to enjoy myself immensely, settling into my role as a nightclub paparazzo. As the band played on, I started focusing on members of the crowd who were surprisingly more than happy to pose for me. It was a different style of photography to my usual, but once behind the viewfinder I felt at home.

The flashing disco lights played havoc with my camera's exposure meter, so I switched to manual and bracketed the exposures just in case. Before long I was crouching on the floor looking for an unusual angle, holding the camera in the air for group shots, and giving as good as I got as elbows were flying at the front of the stage.

Danny fought his way through to me and gave me a new film as the first ran out. Heaven In Art said their farewells at the end of their third song - Going Down To Heaven. The double entendre of the titles was largely lost on the crowd, who were swimming on a sea of cheap Malibu, but I allowed myself a smile of acknowledgement. They were good.

When the radio DJ took over, the crowd dispersed slightly, although the dance floor was still fairly full. We moved around the club, with Danny rounding up groups for photographs as I fired away.

"If I was single, this would be a brilliant way of chatting up men," I thought to myself. Then I remembered I was single, which came as quite a surprise. It felt very much like we were a couple, relaxed together and having a good time. I wondered if Danny felt the same. Fingers crossed. Sexy, he'd said. That was good, but I wasn't going to get carried away.

I took more pictures and loaded more rolls of film. We drank more Red Stripe and Southern Comfort. Too much, in all fairness. I had a strong suspicion I was going to be far less grateful for the free bar the following morning. The film ran out, which was probably just as well, as I'd lost the ability to focus, and the crowd started to disperse as the night wore on. And then we both seemed to remember what we were actually there for, and that the mystery person we'd come to meet had yet to show up. It wasn't like they could have missed us.

I asked Danny what we should do, as we finished off our final drinks, close to the exit.

"It wouldn't surprise me if this was a total wind up," he said.

"But why? Why bother?"

"To throw us off the scent."

"But why bother even putting us on the scent in the first place?"

"Perverse sense of humour?"

We waited until it was only ourselves and the staff left before deciding to leave. I retrieved my jacket and then we saw the club manager on the way out. He smiled at us and shook hands.

"I hope you had a good time," he said. "When can we expect to see the pictures in print?"

"Ooh, I don't know," I said, trying to remember what Lisa had written. "But we've got loads to choose from."

"Well, feel free to come back at any time, and don't forget to send us a copy."

"No problem," said Danny. "Before we go, I don't suppose anybody left any messages for us, did they?"

"Not so far as I know. Hold on, I'll just find out."

He disappeared to chat to members of his staff, leaving us on our own by the door. After a couple of minutes he returned with a smile as wide as a tie from the early seventies.

"Nobody left anything, but there was a phone call, apparently. Somebody from the paper."

"The paper?" I asked, confused for a moment.

"Yes. She said to remind you about dropping off the pictures tomorrow." Lisa then.

"Anything else?"

"Something about having a meeting but having to postpone it because somebody couldn't turn up."

"Did she leave a name?"

"No, she said you'd know who it was."

"Yes, I think we do." I turned back to Danny and we shrugged at each other.

We left the club and waited for a taxi to take us home.

"That last drink was a mistake," I said, as I leaned on the railings at the side of the road. "In fact I could probably say the same for any of the final four. I am completely pissed for the second time in three days and it's all your fault, Danny bloody wild goose chase Churchill."

"I'm completely knackered," said Danny, refusing to acknowledge my point.

"Where actually are we?"

"In terms of...?"

"In relation to somewhere to procure a Mars Bar."

"Ah," said Danny. "That could be difficult."

"And why is it so bloody cold?"

"Come here," he said. And opened his jacket to wrap around me, our bodies tight against each other.

"Danny," I said.

"Yes?"

"Can I tell you something?"

"Anything you like."

"I love you dearly."

"I love you too."

"But," I hadn't quite finished, "if you don't get me home immediately, put me to bed, and promise not to wake me up before lunchtime, I'm never talking to you again."

Danny smiled at me.

"Oh, and Danny."

"Yes?"

"Wipe that stupid grin off your face."

Ten minutes after getting into the taxi, we were home. Simon and Rebecca had presumably long since gone to sleep and I was determined to be as quiet as possible, albeit without a huge amount of success. I was glad of the DMs. If I'd been wearing heels I'd have been flat on my face in the garden.

"If I don't get to sleep in the next thirty seconds I shall die," I said as Danny opened the door.

"You need a glass of water," said Danny. "You'll feel better for it in the morning."

We stumbled through to the kitchen. I switched on the light and then thought much better of it. Bloody fluorescent strip lights again. I fiddled with the switches on the cooker hood until a much softer light came on there. Danny turned off the extractor fan and looked in the cupboards for glasses, filled two, and passed me one.

I drank as much as I could then collapsed onto a stool and put my head on the worktop. But before I could get to sleep he took my hand to help me stand up, and pointed me in the direction of the stairs towards the bathroom. He passed me my toothbrush and I made a bit of a foamy mess with it. The make-up was looking slightly less polished than it had done at the start of the night, but I didn't have the energy to remove it. I felt bad about the pillowcases, but not bad enough to actually do anything about it. I'd buy them some new ones. God I was tired.

Eventually we got under the duvet.

"We're making a bit of a habit of this - sleeping together," I said with as much of a wink as I could muster. I have no idea how he responded as I was already fast asleep.

CHAPTER TWENTY-FOUR

Wednesday, February 17th, 1993

WITH no alarm clock, it was gone 10am when I cautiously opened a single eye and reached for my watch. I was facing the window with my back to Danny. The curtains were closed but weak winter daylight was permeating the room. And then the horror of the headache hit.

I winced, vowing never to touch Southern Comfort again, but I had a bigger problem. I was going to look a complete state, and really didn't want Danny to see the remnants of last night's make-up smeared haphazardly over my face. And never mind the hair. I reached up to try to knock it into some semblance of shape, but it seemed to be pointing in all directions. Trying not to wake him, I edged my legs over the side of the bed, and attempted to move into a sitting position as the first stage of actually getting upright. This was going to hurt. I slowly levered myself up, and stood, albeit shakily. If I could just get to the bathroom before he saw me, everything would be okay.

Well, obviously not everything, but ibuprofen would help with the rest of it. With a deep breath I pulled on my sweatshirt and then turned towards the door.

Which was when Danny walked in, holding two cups of tea and a plate of toast.

"Good morning," he said, far too brightly. "How are you feeling?"

Thinking quickly, I pulled the sweatshirt up so it covered my face and hair.

"Nice pants," he said. You know that feeling when you're madly in love with someone but just for a moment you hate them? That.

With as much pride as I could muster, I attempted to cover my modesty and made for the door.

"Back in a minute," I said, with an entirely justified scowl, and then headed out towards the bathroom.

Fifteen minutes later I returned, wrapped in a lovely sage green towel, looking and feeling slightly better, and gave Danny the kind of look that left him in no doubt that further comments weren't required. The toast had gone but he offered to make more, so I sat on the bed and sipped the tea while I waited. By the time he returned, I was nearly dressed, and feeling vaguely human. And resigned to a life as a spinster.

"What's the plan today then?" I asked as he set the tray down on the bedside table beside me.

"We've got to get the films developed, I suppose. There are a couple of places in town that do a one hour service. Then we go round to the flat and wait for Lisa to come and pick them up in person."

"She won't do that," I said.

"Why not?"

"Because she's watching us, Danny, and she won't go round until we leave."

"In that case, we drop the pictures off and go away, but we

205

come back, hide and wait for her."

"Sounds good."

"And as soon as we see her, we'll go in and have a confrontation."

"What if she doesn't go round at all?"

"We have a long wait."

"But isn't that a waste of time? Wouldn't we be better off spending the time looking for Clare?"

"Probably, but Lisa's the only lead we have at the moment. And if she's messing with us I want to know why."

"Do you think she'll be dangerous?"

"As in armed?"

"Yeah. We just don't know, do we?"

"No. God. We'll be careful. Maybe we need to catch her before she goes in so she's not expecting us."

Half an hour later, we were in the car heading towards the city centre. I was fairly sure that the alcohol was out of my system, but I felt so delicate I was taking things extra carefully anyway. I parked in a multi-storey car park and we walked through to Boots, where I handed all six rolls of film to the assistant and asked for a one hour service with an extra set of prints. I winced at the bill - the best part of £70 - but nevertheless wrote out a cheque.

Once the films were developed we headed back to the car and opened the envelopes to look at the results.

"I don't know what the point of all this was," I said as I waded through picture after picture of drunken clubgoers beaming inanely at the camera, although I was quite pleased with the lighting. I passed them to Danny, who looked through them and then returned them to their envelopes. We agreed that we should head to the flat and then enact our plan.

But as it happened, we were too late. The flat looked exactly as we'd left it the night before, except there was another envelope on the mantelpiece. She'd been again.

Danny opened it and read the letter aloud.

> *Hello again.*
> *Hopefully be the time you read this you will have had the photographs developed. I'm sorry the rendezvous didn't come off last night, but don't worry, I've made alternative arrangements and I will let you know if anything relevant comes of it.*
> *You may ask why I asked you to take pictures last night. Don't worry, it wasn't just a whim. The chances are that there was somebody else there last night who was working for the other side. Obviously I couldn't turn up myself, but I may be able to recognise a face from the photographs.*
> *There's nothing else you can do for me at the moment so I suggest you return to London. I will call you soon. I think we are getting close now and I hope to have some good news for you imminently. Leave the pictures where I asked and have a safe journey.*
> *Yours in sincere cooperation,*
> *Lisa.*

There was a momentary silence, which I was the first to break.

"Why does she insist on calling herself Lisa when we all know that's not her name?"

"Because she's hiding her true identity."

"Do you trust her?"

Danny shook his head.

"Do you?"

"Not in the slightest. But I don't suppose we have much choice."

"Well, we can start by not obeying the instructions."

"About leaving the pictures?"

"No, I think we should leave them because it can't do any harm as long as we keep the spare set of prints and the negatives. But I don't think we should hurry back to London. I've had an idea."

"Go on."

"It's just while we're up here we should pop over to Rougemont and have another look in the box in case there's anything new. Then we come back here and see if Lisa's come back."

"Makes sense," I said, and then thought for a moment. "I can see a flaw, though. If she's watching us she'll see the car leave, and then it'd only take a minute to get the pictures and she'd be long gone by the time we get back."

"Do you think it was Lisa in the Sierra?"

I shook my head.

"No. It was definitely a man."

"I thought the same."

"I've got a better plan," I said. "I'll go to Rougemont on my own. I'll find it if you write directions. But then maybe she'll see the car leave, think the coast is clear, and come back. And you can be here waiting for her. With a rolling pin."

"No, no, can't do that," he said. "I'm not letting you out of my sight."

"I don't really want to let you out of my sight either, but it could work. You could hide here if you're worried. Actually, yes, definitely do that. At least you'll know if she's been back or not."

"I'm not worried about me, but I'm not having you disappearing off on your own."

"But Danny, it's a security company. It's what? Ten minutes away? I'll be back in half an hour. It'll be fine. We've got to."

"And what if the Sierra's out there?'

"It's fine. He's following us. God knows how long he's been

doing that for, but he seemed keen to get away last night. I don't think that's a problem."

Danny thought for a bit, but I could see he wasn't happy. So I made up his mind for him.

"Listen, I'm going. End of debate. Wait here. Hide. I'll be back before you know it, and if anything goes wrong and you have to make a run for it I'll meet you back at Simon's. But be careful. Please?"

He nodded, and started to draw the route to Rougemont with his finger on the table top.

***

DCI Graham March opened an internal mail envelope, and pulled out a report. The title page said Operation Tintoretto. He'd had to call in a favour to get hold of it, but nothing was more important. He got up and locked his office door.

It didn't make comfortable reading.

He read of art theft, forgery and fraud. He followed a flow chart of connections, scanning for anyone who looked familiar. Galleries, clients, dealers, victims, names from the criminal underworld in London, Paris and Geneva. Dominique Chernin and Benjamin Serraillier were there, both marked as deceased.

But there were gaps. Serraillier was suspected as the mastermind, but his London accomplice was a person or persons unknown. Progress was being made. Leads were being followed. Evidence was being gathered, but as yet there was nothing to indicate who else was involved.

March had to make sure it stayed that way, no matter what it cost.

***

I admit that I didn't feel anywhere near as brave as I'd tried to sound when I got back to the car. I checked the street in both directions for anyone who seemed to be watching me, but apart from a man walking a dog across the grass verge opposite, the street was largely empty. I saw a bus approaching in the distance, but if anything it gave me comfort. The passengers would be witnesses to anything that happened. I pressed the fob to open the door and it worked at the second attempt. Once behind the wheel, with the doors locked from the inside and the engine running, I felt slightly more confident. With one last look to make sure nobody was following, I set off towards Hylton Riverside.

When I got to Rougemont, the car park was largely deserted apart from a blue Vauxhall Cavalier, and an old, dark red Honda Accord. A distant cousin of my white Prelude. All seemed to be going very smoothly. I locked the car and started to walk across the car park when I heard the noise of an engine behind me. I turned. And my heart nearly stopped.

It was a black Sierra, and the driver was looking straight at me.

I panicked, trying to evaluate which was quicker - run to reception or back to my car. But the Sierra was still moving and was now blocking my route to reception, and if I made it to my car I'd never get away as I'd need to drive past the Sierra to leave the car park. And then the driver's door opened and a man emerged.

I was relieved to see he wasn't holding a gun. But he looked rough, dishevelled. As though he'd been sleeping in his car. I was terrified.

"Stop!" he shouted. I ignored him. My car was the only option. I sprinted back but he ran after me. I pressed the fob and was grateful the locks worked first time. But as I reached the handle I felt his hand on my shoulder, pulling me round. He was twice my size. It was an uneven contest. But I wasn't going to give up without a fight. I wrapped my fist around my keys and got ready to punch him. I didn't care where. But he dodged aside and then caught my arm and wrestled my keys from me. And then he wrenched my arm up behind my back before I could do anything more. I was trapped. I prayed someone from Rougemont would run to my rescue, but nobody came.

"Get off me!" I shouted, and his grip loosened, but only enough to turn me round, so I was facing him. He looked vaguely familiar from the night before, but in the daylight I had a clearer view of his beaten, unshaven features.

"Calm down," he ordered. "I'm not here to hurt you."

"Well you're doing a fucking good job of it," I spat back. His grip loosened.

"Sorry. I just need to talk to you. I'm just trying to stop you from hitting me."

He let go and I shook out my shoulder, rubbing my arm.

"Who the fuck are you?" I asked, getting ready to punch again if he made so much as a move on me. "And what on earth do you think you're playing at?"

"I'm so sorry," he said, voice thick with cigarettes. "I'll tell you who I am. I'm Sean. But I need to know who you are too."

"Me? None of your business, pal. Sean who?"

"Haldane. I'm a journalist."

"Oh God. What?"

"Seriously, Sean Haldane. Listen, I'm looking for Clare Woodbrook."

"Join the fucking club. She's not here."

"I know."

"So why are you attacking me then?"

"I'm not attacking you. I'm trying to stop you attacking me."

"Fuck's sake. Following me then."

"Look, can we just take a breath and I'll explain it to you?"

I did exactly that. His name was on our list. He hadn't disappeared after all.

"So who are you a journalist for?" I asked when I'd calmed

down.

"I'm freelance. Used to be at the Express but not now. I'm on my own. Whoever pays me."

"And why are you looking for Clare?"

"Because I know Clare, and Danny. I'm in a similar line of work. And I'm not following you. I've been following Danny because I'm trying to find Clare but I don't even know who you are."

"I'm Anna, a friend."

"Hi Anna," he said, offering me a handshake which I ignored.

"Why are you following Danny? Why not just ring him if you want to speak to him?" And then I suddenly remembered why he was on our list. The twisted hack who'd accosted Danny in the toilets at the awards event. Said Clare was a fraud and started mouthing off about her. At least this time he seemed reasonably sober.

"Listen, it's difficult, all right? I don't want to speak to Danny. He's just the assistant and I need the boss. I need to see Clare. We can do favours for each other. But I've been trying to get hold of her and she seems to have gone AWOL. I'm trying to find out what's going on. That's all."

"Because you want to find Clare or just want to speak to her?"

"Both."

"And you're happy to drive up and down the country and scare single women shitless in the process?"

"I've said I'm sorry."

"You should be."

"So, can you help me?"

"Can I help you?"

"Yeah, tell me where she is, or get a message to her? I'm getting desperate here."

And then I began to see something in him. Was it a look of

fear? I didn't know what he was scared of. Presumably not me. Maybe not fear, then, but something.

"What's the message?"

"I'd prefer to deliver it in person."

I was about to say that was going to be tricky, but then I stopped myself. If he didn't know the full story about Clare, it probably wasn't wise to tell him.

"The gist of it then."

"Do you know where she is?"

I ignored the question.

"Listen, Sean. I don't know who you are. But it's up to you. You can tell me the message and I'll do my very best to pass it on. Or you can fuck off, frankly, because I'm a busy person and I've got things to do."

"Okay. Just tell her I'm looking for her and it's in her interest to speak to me. And quickly."

"And why?"

"Because I know things she'd probably rather I didn't, okay? And if she wants me to keep it quiet she's going to need to speak to me."

"What things?"

"Just things?"

"What things, Sean?"

"Just things, all right? Things I've found out about how she gets her stories."

"Ah, right..."

"I'm trying to be fair here. I'm trying to give her a chance to speak to me. I don't want to have to tell anyone else. I'd much rather come to some sort of understanding. But it's getting urgent."

"So blackmail then?"

"No, not fucking blackmail. Just giving her the opportunity for us to help each other."

"And how can she contact you?"

"She's got my number."

"Sure?"

"Yeah."

"Give it to me anyway."

He got out a crumpled business card and passed it over. Just a name and number. No address.

"Okay and how long's she got to decide if she wants to speak to you?"

"End of the week."

"This week?"

"Yeah."

"Okay Sean," I said. "I'll pass the message on."

"She'll appreciate it," he said, handing me back my keys. I had my doubts. And I had no idea how on earth I was going to get the message across, but at least we now had one fewer suspect for the kidnapping. Unless it was an elaborate double bluff.

CHAPTER TWENTY-FIVE

ONCE Sean Haldane had left the car park, I relocked my car, second time of asking, and made my way to reception. I still didn't have my "card", whatever that was, but Barry, the security guard, recognised me and I gave him a smile of familiarity. I was allowed to sign in without too much interrogation and was shown through to the row of post lockers, where I inserted my key into 1196. I wasn't expecting anything, so had to do a double take when I opened the door and found a large manila envelope, sealed with tape.

I felt a tingle of excitement, knowing that the trip was entirely justified. Just as long as Danny wasn't in trouble back at the flat. In fact, despite the scare earlier, I felt I was making excellent progress. I knew he'd be proud of me.

I carefully removed the envelope and relocked the door, then thanked the security guard and made a hasty exit after checking to see if there were any messages, to no avail.

Once in my car, I started to peel back the tape when a presence at the window made me jump. Haldane again, I thought. But my heart nearly stopped when I turned and found myself looking down the barrel of a gun silencer, pointing straight in my face. The gun was held by a large man, clad in black leather, with his face hidden behind a crash helmet.

"Open the window," he shouted, although it came out muffled through the glass. There was a hard east London accent.

I did so, scared for my life. He indicated the envelope with the gun and I passed it through to him.

"Right then, bitch," he continued, "get out of the car."

I hated being called a bitch, almost as much as I hated being called cute, but for once I chose not to answer back. I opened the door and got out.

"Walk round the car and put your hands on the roof."

Again I did as I was asked. The biker fired a shot at the front drivers' side tyre, deflating it instantly, and proving to me that the gun was loaded.

Without another word, he got back on his bike, revved his engine and turned away from the car, pausing only to look at me, as though having second thoughts about leaving me alive, and then roared off into the distance. Shocked, I sank to the ground, paralysed by fear.

And then I heard footsteps running towards me. I looked up, dazed, with no idea what was going to happen next. Thankfully it was Barry, a look of deep concern on his face.

He said something like: "What happened, are you all right?"

I heard the words but my mind was a blur. I couldn't reply. I could only follow as he led me to the safety of reception.

"You wait here, I'll call the police," he said, sitting me down on one of the leather sofas.

That was the jolt I needed to find my voice.

"No! Not the police. Please. It was nothing, really."

"I hardly call what I saw nothing."

"No, believe me. Call National Breakdown or ATS or

somebody, but not the police. They wouldn't be able to help. Honestly."

Barry remained unconvinced, but seemed moved by the pleading look on my face.

"Listen, pet, a man with a gun just shot your tyre out. I've got to call the police. I wouldn't be doing my job... "

"I know, but trust me. It's a long story." I took a deep sigh and tilted my head back, looking at the ceiling. "You can call the police if you like but just do it after I've left. Please? I've got to get away from here. You've seen what he did. He doesn't want me to follow but I've got to."

"You've got to follow him?"

"Yeah."

"You mean you know who he was?"

"Kind of. But you know what, it's a long story. Please just get National Breakdown to come out with a tyre, and then once I've gone you can do anything you like."

"Wait there."

He went to talk to a colleague, and then the two came back to see me.

"You look shaken," said the new arrival, whose name tag said Phil.

"I'm fine, honestly. If you've got a cup of tea or something that'd be great, but really I just need to get away." The looked at each other, and then Phil nodded and went off, presumably to put the kettle on. Barry sat next to me, his face a picture of concern.

"I'll tell you what I'll do," he said. "Have you got a spare tyre?"

"I think so."

"And you're in National Breakdown?"

"Yeah, I never use it, but yes."

"I'll tell you what I'll do then. I'll give them a ring and see how long they'll take for a call out. If it's going to be too long,

217

I'll fit it for you. And then when you're sorted, we'll call it in. All right?"

"Perfect," I said, "you're a diamond."

He looked up the number, and made the call. He asked for my registration number and gave the address of the business park. Then he put the phone down and turned to me.

"Half an hour they reckon. Is that all right?"

"Brilliant."

"They said they'd need your membership card. Have you got it on you?"

"It's in the glove compartment."

"Give us your keys then and I'll get it for you." I handed him my keys and gave a warning about the faulty locks. He returned a minute later with my National Breakdown membership pack and put it down on the counter.

"I'll tell you what, he did a canny job," he said, as his colleague brought me a cup of tea. I took it with thanks and settled down to wait. I was beginning to worry about Danny. Worrying that he was okay, and concerned that he'd be worried about me.

Half an hour later, on the dot, a National Breakdown van pulled up, and the mechanic came in and asked me what the problem was. I took him out to the car and he started work, jacking up the front right corner so he could remove the old wheel and replace it with my spare. I went back inside to wait.

"Everything all right, Anna?" Barry asked when I returned, putting my membership pack back down on the counter. It looked like he'd been reading it. I didn't spot the danger until it was too late.

"Yeah, he's sorting it. Shouldn't be too long," I said.

"And is there anything else I can do for you while you wait?" He paused. "Anna."

At that moment I knew my cover was blown.

***

Back at the flat, Danny was experiencing the first pangs of a new attack of worry. An hour had passed. She should have been back by now. Nothing had happened at the flat. Nobody had arrived, and he hadn't found anything of interest when he'd undertaken another search. But she definitely should have been back by now. The feeling of panic grew more intense, as though he was standing in quicksand, watching the water level rise.

He thought he heard the gate creaking outside and was torn between going to look and the safe option of hiding in a wardrobe. He decided on the latter, but with his heart rate quickening, he could barely contain his excitement.

After five minutes in the wardrobe, there was still no further movement outside. Danny edged open the door and peered into the late afternoon semi-darkness of the bedroom. Gaining in confidence with every second, he crept out and moved along the wall towards the door. Again there was no sound. He moved through to the front room. Nobody was there. Ever so gingerly he edged towards the front door, which was still firmly closed. Finally, unable to bear the tension any longer, he looked out of the window.

The gate was slightly open, but there was still no sign of life. Then, from nowhere, a gust of February wind moved the gate even further ajar. Danny jumped but nobody appeared. A storm seemed to be brewing. The light was fading. Danny felt a shiver run down his spine.

And then the phone started ringing. Tentatively, he answered it.

"Hello, Danny," said a female voice with a soft Scottish accent.

CHAPTER TWENTY-SIX

I HAD some explaining to do. Apparently tricking your way past the reception of a security company with a fake ID was frowned upon.

"Ah," I said, when asked what I was up to. "Told you, it's a bit of a long story."

Barry didn't look pleased. I had a feeling I was going to find it difficult to protest my innocence. He'd taken me to a small office on the ground floor that only contained a light oak table and three vinyl-covered chairs. The window was barred. He was threatening to call the police again, and that could lead to any number of complications. What had started as a good idea had become a nightmare.

Through the door I heard the mechanic in reception dropping off my keys, saying that the car was ready. That was something. But I was no nearer to getting back on the road. I tried to give a brief summary, leaving out some of the details. Barry wasn't entirely convinced.

"So, to recap, you're working undercover on the trail of a

missing person?"

"Yes."

"But you won't tell me who."

"Well, it's not so much won't as can't."

"But you can't say why you can't."

"Again, difficult."

"So how do I know that you're not just trying to nick post from paying customers? Customers, I may add, who get things sent here for precisely the reason that they don't want them stolen."

"Yes, I can see why you might think that," I said, trying to come up with a plausible explanation.

"Look, Barry," I pleaded. "I know this doesn't look good. But you've got to believe me. Clare is a journalist. I don't know if you know her. She works for the Daily Echo."

"Which I've heard of, obviously. Go on."

"You know the thing about a journalist being legally bound to protect their sources?"

"No, but..."

"Well anyway, they are. She's working on a story and it's kind of proving a bit tricky."

"Uh-huh."

"So she gave me the key and asked me to come up here and check her box. It's basically that." I hoped my cheeky smile would work its magic, but it seemed to be missing the mark. There was a knock on the door. Phil came in with my keys and National Breakdown membership pack, placing them on the desk between us.

"Car's fixed," he said. And then left us to it.

"I wouldn't have the key, would I? If I was just a thief," I continued as the door closed. "But it is urgent. Because the bastard with the gun has just pinched the stuff I was supposed to be collecting and I've got to go and find him before the whole thing goes tits up."

I still wasn't sure if I was making progress. It was time to gamble.

"Tell you what. Ring her. She'll confirm it for you. You've got her number I assume?"

"We will have, somewhere." I just had to hope it was the number of the flat in Sunderland rather than London.

"Perfect. Get the number, and give her a call. If she's not there, ask for her husband, Danny." It pained me to say that. "He'll verify it. But if you could do it quite quickly it would be really much appreciated."

"Wait here," he said, and then left the room, locking the door behind him.

Barry came back, and I expected to be released.

"Did you ring her?" I asked.

"I did, but there was no answer. So we're no further forward."

"Shit."

"I'll tell you what I'm going to do. I'm going to call the police. I should have done it about the car anyway. When they get here, you can tell them what you've told me. And if they believe you it's up to them, but until then you're staying."

"God," I said, out of sheer frustration. And then I saw an opportunity and acted on it.

"Do you mind if I switch the light on?" I asked.

When Barry gave his consent I stood up and moved to the light switch, turning on the fluorescent strip in the centre of the ceiling. They do have their uses after all. Time to test the acting skills again.

"Ouch, you bastard!" I yelled as I did so, shaking my hand. "I just got a shock off the switch."

Barry stood up and moved towards me, full of concern. I wasn't proud of what I was about to do.

"Here, let me have a look," he said.

I extended my hand but withdrew it as he came close. Then,

222

with all of my strength, I clenched it into a fist and punched him hard in the stomach. He looked briefly stunned, and in his moment of hesitation I grabbed a chair and pushed it toward him, seizing my chance to open the door and run.

I ran straight through the reception, past Phil, who tried to stop me. And then out into the car park, hoping that the frigging key fob would work first time. It did. Barry and Phil weren't far behind.

"Sorry," I shouted, "but you should have believed me."

I just got the door closed and fired up the engine as they caught up with me. I floored the accelerator, dropped the clutch, and with a squeal of protest from the tyres I lurched forward. Then, with my foot to the floor, I powered away up the slip road, back to the roundabout, and as fast as I could towards the city centre.

I raced through a red light just before the Queen Alexandra Bridge, and narrowly avoided piling into the side of a Ford Escort. Other motorists flashed as I overtook them on the bridge, but I wasn't looking at them.

I hardly touched the brakes at all on the way back to Ashbrooke, and made the journey in record time. As I approached I saw a police car with its lights flashing and siren wailing. I pulled in to the side of the road and paused, heartbeat quickening, convinced I was in trouble, but was able to relax when it shot straight past me on the trail of somebody else.

When I arrived at the flat, I threw open the gates without a second thought and reversed the car inside, skidding to a halt on the gravel. It was only when I got out of the car that I wondered whether Danny had visitors. I hammered on the door and it opened. It was Danny. My relief was instant, but overwhelmed by a need to get out of there.

"Where have you been?" he asked, but I was too breathless to answer. "Are you all right? What's happened."

"Danny, we've got to go. I'll tell you on the way," I said, at speed. "Has anybody been here?"

"Not yet, but..."

"We've got to go. They've got the registration and they'll be setting up road blocks. We're going, now!"

Without a second thought, I got back into the car and edged it out onto the street. Danny closed the door and gate behind us, and jumped into the passenger's seat.

"What on earth's going on?" he asked.

I floored the throttle again and then took a breath and tried to calm down. I didn't want to draw any extra attention by driving erratically.

"Quickest way out of Sunderland?" I asked, urgently.

"Straight on, towards Ryhope."

"Guide me."

"Just tell me what's going on, you're worrying me."

And then, as I tried to relax into the flow of the traffic, it all came out. The gun. The motorbike. Sean Haldane and the message. The package. My escape. My display of uncharacteristic yet wanton violence.

"Jesus," said Danny. "Are you okay?" He directed me off the main road, onto a side road signposted Seaham.

"I am now. Just panicking that we're going to get stopped any minute. Sorry."

"Hey don't worry," he said. "You did brilliantly. I'm proud of you."

"Really?"

"Yes, really."

"But I had the package nicked and I've bloody assaulted an innocent man."

"You did what you had to do. You're safe. That's all that matters."

I reached out to do the hand squeeze thing.

"So what happened at the flat? No sign of Lisa, I assume?"

"God no, but she rang me."

"Rang you?'

"On the flat phone. The phone rang. I answered it."

"What did you say? Did you get the chance to ask her what on earth she's up to?"

"No, I'll tell you the full extent of it. I picked up the phone. She said, 'Hello Danny'. I said, 'Lisa!' And she said, 'Just a quick message, Danny, I'm not coming back today so there's no need to wait for me. I'll call you soon.' And she was gone."

"That was it?"

"Yup."

"Ooooh. Bastard. She's so frustrating!"

"Turn left here."

I did as directed, and turned into a deserted car park on a clifftop overlooking the grey mass of the North Sea. He directed me to a space at the far end of the car park and I stopped the engine.

"Come on," he said. "This'll help."

We got out of the car and Danny took my hand, led me to a footpath on the clifftop and then down towards a set of steps. We started to make our descent. The steps got steeper as they got nearer the beach. And then we were on the seafront, in the gathering gloom of the late afternoon, watching the waves crash in just in front of us. The beach was deserted. You couldn't fail to be impressed by the sheer size and noise of the sea.

"You remember when we were discussing Clare?" Danny shouted above the noise of sea and seagulls. "About going to a deserted beach and shouting at the waves? Getting rid of all your frustrations? Well, this is it."

We started to walk. It was unlike any beach I'd been to, but in a weird way it was beautiful. No palm trees. No bars and amusement arcades. Just miles of rugged coastline. Caves and rocks. Sand and pebbles. And a constant reminder of the power of nature to shape the world.

"What now then?" I shouted back, after a while, letting the wind and sea air take the stress away. "We can't go back to Sunderland because the police will be looking for me, but there's nothing to work on in London, and in any case they'll have traced the car to Rochester Square."

"Assuming they took the registration."

"They definitely did that. They phoned through to National Breakdown for me. I had to give them the reg number."

"We could hide the car and hire a new one."

"But they're watching us, Danny. Whoever was on the bike knew me and waited for me. That package must have been vital."

There was a moment's silence as we both paused for thought.

"We could go to Reigate," I suggested.

"But how will that help? It's supposed to be a safe haven. We don't want to take danger down there."

"There's danger everywhere." I sighed. I reached in my pocket for a bar of chocolate. Broke off a cube and gave it to Danny and then helped myself. "You decide."

Danny picked up a pebble and threw it into the advancing waves, then put his arm through mine.

"There's another way of looking at this. If it's getting this dangerous, it must mean we're getting close. If Clare was here she'd be in her element. She'd be telling me she's close to an excellent story. But she also said that no story was worth risking your life for."

"But this isn't a story. It's about people. It's about Clare, not some tabloid sensation."

"Which means we've got to hang in there."

"I think so."

Danny sighed. Then he looked at me as though struck by a new thought.

"How long have we lived in Rochester Square?"

"Since September."

"And how long have you had this car?"

"Since August."

"Have you ever changed the registration document?"

"No."

"Which means that even if they did trace the car, they wouldn't have the right address."

"Good point. So we'd be safe to go back to London?"

"For the moment... until they trace it another way. But even then it was only a bit of a punch-up." He looked at me, and then smiled and added "with a girl".

"Do you want me to demonstrate?" I asked.

He laughed.

"It wouldn't surprise me if they dropped the whole thing to avoid the publicity."

"If you ignore the other charges of burglary, falsification and the like." I smiled too. Coming down here put everything in perspective. We turned and started to walk back. It was cold. It was getting dark. The wind was getting stronger. But a part of me didn't want to leave.

"Do you think we need to worry about Haldane?" I asked as we started to climb back up the steps.

"What did he say?"

"He had a message for Clare. Wants to do mutual favours. Sounded like blackmail."

"I think the day Clare needs a favour from him will be the day the presses stop rolling and we all go home to witness the end of the world. No, he's a tosser. I think we can ignore him for now."

"But it sounded urgent."

"What's he going to do? He was sacked by the Express. He's trying it on."

"Okay. But at least it solves the Sierra mystery."

"Exactly. Did you manage to get a look at the bike, by the

227

way?"

"Not really. I don't know much about bikes. They all look a bit the same to me. I'd probably recognise the make, though, if you told me some."

"Kawasaki, Yamaha, Honda, Suzuki, Ducati, Moto Guzzi, BMW..."

I looked at him quizzically.

"How come you're the bike expert all of a sudden?"

"Top Trumps." He grinned.

"Definitely not a Honda, then. Yamaha I think. No idea of the model, though, sorry. And the number plate was plastered in mud, presumably deliberately, so I didn't get that. Do you think it was the same one you saw in London?"

"Most likely. Sounds like it anyway. Did you say he had an east London accent?"

"I think so. He didn't say much and it was through the helmet. But it sounded kind of geezer-ish. That was my first thought, anyway."

"That fits with Richard Kirk, then. So that's Serraillier's bodyguard. And that makes sense as well. You didn't see inside the envelope?"

"No, I didn't get a chance."

"I don't think it matters what it was. He'd just be trying to get hold of anything."

"But who put the envelope in the box if it was held in the names of Clare and Serraillier, bearing in mind neither could have done it?"

"It could have been something posted. He'd have been desperate to get hold of anything but he'd never get past reception, so he waited till you turned up and mugged you."

"Sounds logical."

We reached the top of the steps and started back towards the car.

"We're making progress, I think," I said. "We still don't know who attacked Megan but if we assume that was unconnected then it's looking like Kirk, possibly working for March."

"Although we've still got no idea where Clare is. Or what Lisa's playing at."

"True. Oh, Danny. It seems like we're getting there but maybe we're still as far as ever. We still don't know who shot Serraillier or bombed the hotel either."

"And don't forget Jimmy Ravenscroft."

"God, I had. Maybe they're all just in it together. So what now?"

"Back to London. If you're okay to drive."

"Very happy to. Come on, jump in."

And we set off. Slightly calmer but still confused. And completely unaware of the devastation that awaited us.

CHAPTER TWENTY-SEVEN

IT was now over a week since Clare disappeared. We'd been worried ever since, but tonight was something different. It was as though a cloud of hopelessness was beginning to descend, covering us in its fog, and showing no sign whatever of lifting.

Perhaps it was the frustration, combined with the tiredness, of a week spent searching fruitlessly without any real steps forward. Perhaps it was just the journey, and the hours of travelling that had preceded it, or just emotional and physical exhaustion brought on by everything that had happened. Whatever it was, the effect was growing and tightening its grip.

I was lost in thought on the final approach to London when Danny suddenly spoke.

"That envelope - I know you didn't open it, but what did it feel like? Was it thick? Thin? Heavy?" he asked.

"Not particularly heavy. It just seemed to have paper in it and something smaller maybe. I could feel something hard."

"Like a computer disk?"

"Maybe. Why?"

"I'm just thinking. Maybe it was a disk with Clare's story."

"Possibly."

"It would fit. That would explain why Kirk was so keen to get hold of it. If that was all of the evidence she'd uncovered, it would be as dangerous in somebody else's hands as it was in hers."

"Shit. I'm so sorry, Danny."

"Hey, don't worry. It's not your fault. But at least it seems to make some sort of sense."

"But how did it get there? When I looked on Saturday there was nothing there."

"But you were told that Serraillier had already been. What if he'd taken it, and then either put it back or sent it for safekeeping before he was shot?"

"He'd have had to have sent it. He wouldn't have had time to take it back. But are you saying the person who shot him did so for that reason - because he knew the story?"

"It fits. Then perhaps they were either looking for the disk or they were just trying to silence him. Either way, bang! End of problem."

"Which would mean Serraillier was one of the good guys again. I thought we'd decided he was a baddie?"

"Well, he's an honorary good guy for the moment."

"All right then, Danny, answer this. Where does that leave Lisa? And who was it we were supposed to meet in the nightclub? Maybe this was the package we were supposed to be picking up there."

"Ah, possibly. So that means one of two things. Lisa's trying to get hold of the disk to destroy it. And probably shot Serraillier. Or she's a good guy, but she's just got a strange way of showing it."

"And maybe the reason he didn't show up was because he couldn't get it from Rougemont."

"Perfect. You'd think there would be a copy somewhere, though."

"Yes, unless there was something in there that couldn't be copied."

"I like this. I think we're getting somewhere."

I turned the car into Rochester Square.

"We need to find that envelope," he said as we got out of the car and started walking up the path to our front door. "Whoever's got Clare would have less reason to keep her if the story got out anyway."

I inserted my key in the door. As I pushed it open I reached round for the light switch. But as the room filled with light I had the shock of my life. Danny, two paces behind, stopped, just as stunned.

The flat had been ransacked. I just stood, shocked, silent, violated, fighting a rising sensation of nausea. The mirror in the hallway was smashed. And through the open door to the living room I could just see chaos.

I turned to Danny, tears in my eyes. I'd had enough of this. I grabbed hold of him. It was all too much. And the worst of it was the blood.

There was a splatter on the wall, as though somebody standing in front of it had been shot. Not that I'm an expert. And below that a pool on the tiled floor. My first thought was to run. To never stop running. To never come back. But running wouldn't take away the horror of the sight in front of me. I had to confront it or be haunted evermore.

We held hands and led each other into the hallway. Stepping over broken glass, we reached the door to the living room. I turned on the light. Furniture was overturned, pictures and ornaments were smashed. The floor was covered in magazines and books, clothes and bed linen. The base station for the phone had been pulled from the wall and lay smashed on the floor next to a broken mirror and a table that seemed to have been kicked to pieces. It seemed that everything we owned was smashed apart.

"Oh my God!" I said in a hoarse whisper as I fell against the door.

Danny moved to support me. Moved to share my tears.

"Bastards," he said. "Filthy, fucking bastards."

We edged through the door. Where was the body? Clare. Slashed and mutilated. Never to return after all.

Gingerly we looked into the kitchen. Chaos ruled, but there were no signs of death. Even more carefully we moved through to the bedrooms. Again no body, just chaos, destruction, and despair. Danny led. I followed close behind, clutching his arm. There was no machismo. No gender stereotyping. Danny held me just as tightly. We were just two innocent people way out of our depth.

"Come on," he said. "Let's get out of here."

We led each other through the mess and back outside into the night air. We both breathed in deeply, trying to fight the overwhelming sensation of sickness and rising bile. And then a fresh wave of panic hit me hard again.

"The studio, Danny," I said, voice faint with fear. And then I ran to the car, with Danny by my side.

I gunned the engine and the wheels squealed again. I just wanted to be there. To know that in at least a small part of my world, everything was okay. But the sense of foreboding was overwhelming. Danny hung on while I blasted through side streets, over junctions, through the lights. And then held on again when I slammed on the brakes to turn into my street. The final approach was much more cautious.

A light was on downstairs. A Yamaha motorbike was parked outside. The number plate was covered with mud, just as it had been in Sunderland.

233

"Come on, Danny," I urged. "Let's get the bastard."

"Stop!" he shouted, holding my arm to restrain me. "He's got a fucking gun."

I was torn. I didn't care any more. I just wanted this to end. I was angry. More angry than I've ever been.

"I'm going in," I said. Voice supernaturally calm. I was too furious to feel fear. And yes, he had the weapon, but we had the element of surprise.

Danny looked at me. He could see there was no going back. He let go of my arm and we both got out of the car, closing the doors behind, as quietly as we could.

We stood apart. Dividing the target. And slowly we crept toward the building. My building. The flood of adrenaline was giving me a surge of clarity.

We reached the door. One on each side. It was slightly ajar. I could hear noises from inside. I could hear my world being destroyed. Slowly Danny pushed open the door. And then I could see him: a leather clad figure in the corner of the room, searching through my filing cabinet and throwing its contents to the floor.

And then we charged.

"Bastard!" I yelled as I flung myself at the figure, knocking him momentarily off balance. But he was far too big to tackle on my own. He fought back, landing a punch to my stomach, winding me. But Danny was behind me and launched a vicious attack. He punched hard. And then harder again. The biker kicked out, catching Danny in the knee. He cried out in pain.

Then I got a second breath. I picked up my desk lamp and swung it at him, ripping the cord from the wall. He dodged my attack. The lamp smashed against the wall, showering the floor in glass. He aimed another kick at Danny. Missed. I grabbed a tripod and swung that as well. It caught his arm and he cried out. But he was going to get away. He pushed the filing cabinet over so it fell between us. And I could see he was going to run.

Just as he did so, Danny, with all of his strength, grabbed his ankle. He fell, catching the edge of the desk. Studio lights went crashing to the ground. I jumped on top of him. Punching again. Aiming for the throat. And then Danny was up, beside me. He kicked him hard in the chest. And again. I heard something that sounded like ribs being broken. He cried out, a howl of pain. And then we had him. I picked up a metal camera case and was about to bring it down on his head, when Danny grabbed it off me. And did the same with every ounce of his strength. The man lay on the floor. Motionless. I thought we'd killed him. But then he moved. Just.

I ran to the other side of the room and grabbed two rolls of gaffer tape, and gave one to Danny. We wrapped it round him. Arms pinned behind his back. Legs pinned together. And then, just for good measure, we dragged him up against the edge of my desk and taped him to that. By the neck. He wasn't going anywhere.

He was conscious but beaten. Blood smeared his face. Danny searched his pockets. There was a gun, and a travelcard, with the name Richard Kirk. I found some rope and we bound him with that as well. He definitely wasn't going anywhere.

I leaned on the edge my desk to try to get my breath back. Danny stood with his hands on his knees, doing the same. Then he came toward me, and I realised he was limping.

"Are you okay?" he asked. I nodded.

"You?"

"I'll do."

***

Meanwhile, in Reigate, Megan was trying hard to hold her breath. The sound of smashed glass had penetrated the calm, the sound of furniture being destroyed rupturing it further. She hid under the bed. And then stopped breathing completely

235

as two men entered the bedroom. They picked up the mattress and threw it aside, and suddenly she was staring into their eyes.

CHAPTER TWENTY-EIGHT

AS Kirk came to, he struggled against his bindings, but to no avail. I got another of my studio lights - one he hadn't yet smashed - and shone the bright spotlight in his face. He winced, and blinked. He couldn't shade his eyes. The light was blinding.

And then for good measure, I got a cup of water and threw it in his face.

I pulled up two chairs. I sat on one, Danny on the other.

"We meet again," I said, when Kirk seemed up to listening. "So who the hell are you working for, and what the fuck are you doing here?" The level of fury rose with every word.

Kirk grunted and spat. Danny stood up and kicked him in the legs. I gestured to him to sit down again.

"We've got all night," I said.

Silence.

"Well?"

"Fuck off," he said, in his hard east London accent.

"Well, that's a start."

We waited. This was going nowhere. So I took the initiative.

"Okay, Richard," I began. "I'll tell you where we're up to. We know who you are. We know you were supposed to be looking after Benjamin Serraillier but he got shot. We don't know if you shot him, or whether you just fucked up and let somebody else do it on your watch. Either way, you've not done a very good job."

Still silence.

"I'll go on. We know you've got a motorbike. Obviously. And we know you were in Camden on Sunday because you turned up on your motorbike and took a shot at my friend here. Which wasn't very nice."

I waited.

"Okay. Never mind. I know you were up in Sunderland, today, because you attacked me in my car and shot my tyre out, which wasn't very nice either. And then you've come back down here, absolutely fucked over my flat and now you're making a mess of my studio. And I just want to know why."

And then he spoke. Just a single word.

"No."

"No what?" I was tempted to get my tripod again. It had vicious-looking spikes on the feet and I was tempted to see what would happen if I pushed them into his leg.

"No, I haven't touched your flat."

"You have."

"I haven't touched your fucking flat."

That came as a surprise. I looked at Danny. This wasn't necessarily good news.

"Who did, then?"

"No idea."

I couldn't even begin to compute that one.

"Okay. We'll try again. Who are you working for? Is it Lisa? Or Charlotte or whatever she's called?"

He just laughed.

Fuck it. I got the tripod. Danny tried to stop me but I wasn't in the mood. I extended the spikes, lifted it above his leg and then let it drop on his thigh.

"Ah, you bastard," he shouted, face contorted in pain. He tried again to escape from the bindings but to no effect.

I looked at Danny. He looked pale and particularly uncomfortable.

"We've got all night, Richard," I said. I lifted the tripod again.

"All right, all right, you bitch."

I dropped the tripod. Told you, I don't like being called that. He shouted out again, and swore at me. I didn't catch all the words. I sat back down.

"Last time, then: who are you working for?"

"Nobody."

"Oh for fuck's sake." I stood up again.

"I'm freelance," he spat.

"Freelancing for whom, Richard?"

"I don't know."

"Richard..."

"I don't know. Really, I don't. I just got hired."

"By whom?" I was getting frustrated.

"Some French geezer."

"Serraillier?"

"Aye."

"What did he hire you for?"

"To keep an eye on a woman. A journalist."

"Clare?"

He nodded.

"I had to follow her, find out what she was up to."

"And do you know where she is?"

He shook his head, as much as he could.

"Okay," I continued. "But Serraillier's dead, so now who are you working for?"

"Fuck off," he said. I sighed and lifted the tripod again.

239

Danny tried to stop me, but I wasn't in the mood. I asked him to go and make a cup of tea, but he ignored me.

"All right, I'm just trying to get my fucking money," Kirk said. I put the tripod down.

"Well it's not going to be in my filing cabinet. I'm losing patience here. In plain English, last chance. What are you doing here?"

"Jesus. I'm just trying to get paid. But there's this mental fucking Scottish bitch who fucked off with it, so I'm looking for her."

"Lisa?"

"No idea."

"Charlotte?"

"I've told you, no fucking idea."

"Okay, why did you try to shoot me?" said Danny.

"I didn't, it was her. I've no idea who the fuck you are." That was something.

"And you're here because?"

"It was suggested by someone."

"Who?"

"A copper."

"DCI March?"

"No idea, I don't ask names."

"Okay. And what about the package?" I asked.

"What package?"

"The one you stole from me this afternoon. And you owe me for a new tyre."

"I've no idea."

"Can you say anything other than you've got no idea? You're lying."

"I'm telling you. I don't know. I hoped it was my money but it clearly wasn't."

"So where is it?"

"On the bike."

240

"On the bike?"

"In the case on the back. You'll need a key." He nodded towards his jacket pocket. I reached inside, took the keys and handed them to Danny. He went outside to retrieve it. I waited for him to return. He was back within a minute with the envelope. The tape had been ripped open.

"We're getting there," I said. "Have you removed anything from the envelope?"

"No."

"And I should believe you because?"

"I just fucking haven't. I was looking for my money."

"So what do you know about the Scottish woman? Was she working for Serraillier?"

Kirk just laughed.

"Well?"

He shook his head.

"Nah. He didn't trust her. She's mental."

Danny opened the envelope and reached inside for the disk. But it wasn't a disk. It was a passport. He looked inside it.

"What the fuck?" he said.

"What's up?"

He held it up to show me.

"It's my passport."

I reached out and he passed it to me.

"But you gave that to March," I said. And suddenly nothing seemed to make sense again.

241

CHAPTER TWENTY-NINE

WE asked a few more questions, but it became obvious that Kirk was going to be of limited further use. We didn't know what to do with him. We couldn't call the police now it was abundantly clear that DCI March was implicated somehow, but we couldn't leave him there either. In the end, Danny suggested a compromise. Kirk wasn't looking for us. We'd let him go, but we'd take his gun. And if he came anywhere near us in the future, we'd shoot him. Simple as.

I excused myself for a moment, went outside and let the air out of his tyres. It wasn't much of a protest but was strangely therapeutic. Then when I returned, Danny cut the tape while I held the weapon pointed in Kirk's general direction. I had no idea what to do with it, and just holding the thing terrified me.

We let him go. He saw his bike and swore at me, again. I just waved the gun, and he turned, took the bike off its stand, and pushed it away. I was fairly sure we wouldn't see him again.

Once he'd gone, Danny shut the studio door and I went through to the kitchen to put the kettle on.

"I had no idea you were so violent," he said when he came to join me.

"Neither did I," I said. "But I just got so pissed off. Remember never to annoy me."

"I'll try."

I looked at the gun that was on the kitchen counter.

"What are we going to do with that?" I asked. "God knows what it's been used for."

"We'll hand it in. Actually, no we can't hand it in, they'll have too many questions. We'll leave it somewhere, down a drain or something, then phone it through anonymously."

It seemed like a decent plan. Our other plan was to return to Reigate, to check in on Megan, and spend the night there in relative calm before returning to deal with our flat in daylight.

Danny helped me fix the studio door the best I could so we could lock up for the night. I took a padlock and clasp off an old storage cupboard and he fixed them to the outside of the door. It wasn't much but it would stop the casual burglar, and I thought it would do until I could get things sorted properly. By the time we'd done all that, it was nearly 1am. We were shattered but still slightly hyper after all of the drama. I was looking forward to arriving in Reigate and just crashing.

Finally we were on the road. I took the direct route through central London, hoping the traffic wouldn't be too bad. I looked at Danny, and saw a reflection of my own fragility etched in his fatigue.

"It was interesting what he said about Lisa," I said eventually, as I turned off the Westway towards Shepherd's Bush. "I still can't work out where she fits in, though."

"I've got a theory," Danny said.

"Go on."

"Well, we're working on the basis that Clare was investigating Serraillier. And Lisa was working for him. So, how about this then? We know Serraillier was involved in art theft. But maybe he's working for someone, and he's fucked up. Actually better still, Chernin fucked up, so Serraillier killed him. But whoever Serraillier was working for found out about the fuck-up so he got shot too."

"Okay, but Lisa?"

"I'm coming onto that. Lisa said she got out when things turned a bit dodgy. Assume she's straight, but got messed up in something out of her depth."

"I know that feeling."

"Likewise. Anyway, Lisa got to meet Clare, and realised who she was, so she turned into Clare's informant. So then Lisa's giving Clare information and Clare starts digging deeper. Whoever Serraillier worked for heard about it, so killed him. They've done whatever they've done with Clare, and now they're looking for Lisa."

I thought for a moment.

"Yeah, that fits. Ah, good work, Danny."

"And that explains why Lisa's looking for Clare. She feels responsible because she's the one who got her into trouble. And she needs Clare to fix things and write the story so she can come out of hiding because at the moment they're trying to find her to kill her."

"Okay, and why did she take Kirk's money?"

"She's going to need cash, isn't she? She's presumably hiding up somewhere, in a hotel maybe. It's going to cost. We already know she's stayed in the hotel in Paddington and been moving round."

"So Lisa's the missing link?"

"Looks that way, doesn't it?"

"Okay, but two things: one, where does March fit in? And two, who smashed our flat up?"

"I've got another theory."

"I like your theories. Go on."

"So we've been investigating March. That's the whole Easter

244

Bunny thing. He's bent, into all sorts. But maybe Clare's come across his link to Serraillier, and then started investigating, and realised it's a whole new story on a whole new scale."

"And that's why Lisa's saying not to trust him."

"Exactly. He's all over it, somehow."

"And the flat?"

"Well, presumably whoever it is is looking for something. If we believe it's not Kirk, and I don't see how it could be given the timescales, then it's someone else. Maybe looking for any disks or documents or anything else that they think Clare has given to me. They've searched in Sunderland, and there was nothing there. They've been through Clare's flat in London, or at least March has. So that left us."

"But you haven't got anything."

"No, because we haven't got a clue what's going on, but they don't know that."

"Okay. But why the blood?"

"I don't know." Danny shook his head. "Can't work that out. Maybe to frighten us. Maybe just blatant vandalism. Maybe a warning. Don't know. We'll have a better look tomorrow."

"Are you sure that's wise, though? Because if they're looking for disks and haven't found them, then in theory they're going to be looking for you too. Us."

"God. It's doing my head in."

I tried to change the subject for a bit, but as we drove past Richmond Park Danny started talking about Lisa again.

"There was something she said, by the canal, that I've just remembered but I can't work out."

"Go on."

"Geneva."

"Geneva?"

"Yeah, Geneva. She said what do I know about Geneva?"

"That's odd."

"I said I didn't know anything, but she asked again, if I was

245

sure. I said the only thing I could think of was the art gallery catalogue. That had an address in Switzerland on it, but that was that. I can't remember what she said then, but she kept asking questions about all sorts."

"That seems weird. Did she give any clues what she was on about?"

"No, just that. What did I know about Geneva?"

I took a moment to think.

"Oh Danny, I'm having bad thoughts," I said, eventually.

"That sounds ominous. Are you okay?"

"Yeah. It's just - what's been happening? We've been following a trail. Everything's been a trail, from when you went to the Mowbray, to Rougemont, to Hammersmith, Paddington, Sunderland, everywhere. Now Geneva."

Danny looked perplexed.

"No, can't be. Can it?"

"Oh, Danny. No, it is. I bet you. Jesus."

"In what way."

"Well, what happened when March came round? He took your passport. And now, after a fuck of a lot of effort, we've finally got hold of the envelope from Rougemont. And it's your passport come back. Why do you think that would happen?"

"Because I'm going to need it?"

"Exactly."

We pulled up outside the house in Reigate at around half past two, having discussed Switzerland, how little we knew about the place, and how we had no idea either how we'd get there or what we'd do when we arrived. Even assuming we decided to go. But it was beginning to look likely.

I parked the car and we got out into the icy night air. Danny put his arm around me as we walked over the gravel to the flat. He was becoming increasingly affectionate, which I took to be a good sign, but I didn't know if it was because he was finally coming to his senses, or he just felt guilty about getting me involved in a complete mess.

"Fancy a cup of tea before we turn in?" he asked.

"If you're making it - I'm absolutely knackered."

Danny stopped when he got to the door. It hung slightly open. There were signs of it being forced. He edged it slightly further open and peered inside. Moonlight streamed in through the windows, offering just enough light to show another scene of devastation. Like at the house in Rochester Square, everything had been smashed and turned upside down. Like at the house in Rochester Square, our lives were being torn apart.

"I don't believe this. No!" cried Danny. I was speechless. I just wanted it all to be over. We were always one step behind.

"Where's Megan?" cried Danny. "Oh my God!"

He switched on the light and saw the full horror. This time there was no hesitation. Danny stepped inside, yelling Megan's name.

There was a deathly silence in the house. He yelled again. Still silence. I followed as he checked the bathroom and the kitchen. There was destruction everywhere. We made it to the bedroom and then saw Megan, tied up and gagged, but thankfully alive. We undid her bindings, and she shook her hands, trying to revive her circulation.

We all tried to talk at once, but eventually stopped, allowing Megan to explain what had happened as I gave her a hug.

"I was in the bedroom. I heard the door getting smashed so I hid under the bed, but they lifted the mattress and saw me."

"Jesus," said Danny. "Who was it? Did you recognise them?"

"Yes, yes! The same geezers as Saturday. I got a good look at them. I thought they were going to kill me." Megan was still shaking with fear.

"Did they hurt you?"

"Not really, apart from tying me up."

"Megan, I am so sorry. We never should have left you."

"Why did they smash up the house?"

"I don't know."

"But who are they? And what time is it?"

"We just don't know. It's about 2.30."

"God! I'm so glad that you're here. I could hardly breathe."

"They've done our flat in Camden as well, the bastards. But are you all right? Can I get you anything?"

"A drink, please, Danny. Preferably a strong one. And a fag please, if anyone's got one."

It was a no go on the cigarette but Danny went off to put the kettle on and find something for Megan to calm her nerves. I stayed with her, and she clung to me as though I was protecting her from a raging storm. Which in a sense I was. Danny returned with a tray holding two cups of tea, a bottle of brandy, and three glasses. I declined the brandy, but was grateful for the tea. Could have managed a biscuit as well, but it seemed churlish to complain in the circumstances. He poured a drink for Megan.

"What do we do now, then?" I asked. "We can't stay here. We can't go back to Camden. We can't call the police or we'll get ourselves arrested. Although we'd be safer in prison."

"Safer than here," agreed Danny. "Look, you stay here with Megan. I'll go and look around the rest of the flat and take it from there."

"You can both go," said Megan, looking at me. "I'm all right here. Actually, if you can wait for a minute, I'll come with you."

I helped her up. She was understandably shaky, but clearly relieved to be mobile again. She looked pale and tired.

We surveyed the wreckage of the flat but there weren't any obvious clues to who had done it and why. Furniture had been overturned. Anything breakable was smashed to pieces.

"They're sick," I said. "Dangerous and sick."

We went outside to check the main house, but mercifully it appeared untouched. Whoever it was seemed to know what they were looking for. It was freezing cold, so I was glad to go back inside, even in the chaos. I helped Danny turn the sofa and chairs upright so we had somewhere to sit and work out a plan, all thoughts of bed on hold.

"At least we know it wasn't Kirk," I said, trying to make sense of it all. "At least we know he was telling the truth."

"But who?" said Danny. He turned to Megan. "Are you absolutely sure it was the same two who tried to kidnap you?"

"Definitely."

"It doesn't make any sense."

"It just undoes everything we were thinking," I said. I brought Megan up to speed on all of the events of the last two days. The trip to Sunderland, the night out, the pictures, the package at Rougemont, Haldane and Kirk, our flat, the studio, Danny's passport, Geneva. "We thought we knew what was happening but we were working on the basis that whoever attacked you wasn't connected. But they've got to be."

"I'm just completely fucked off with it," said Danny. I couldn't have put it any more succinctly.

"Are we calling the police?" asked Megan.

I looked at Danny.

"What do you reckon? It's outside March's area but there's going to be questions."

"I just don't know," he said. "And God knows what Philip and Claudia are going to think when they get back." I'd been thinking the same but hadn't dared say it out loud. They'd helped us out and now had their flat trashed for the privilege.

"You know what we've forgotten?" asked Danny.

"Oh God. What?"

"The Mowbray bomb. We still don't know who did that."

"That's a valid point. Are you thinking..."

"Exactly. Kirk's on his own. He's a hitman, but bombing? Doesn't seem right. But whoever these two are... Wouldn't put it past them."

"But why?"

"I don't know. It's like they're looking for something but it just seems... personal."

"They're scaring me."

And then the phone started ringing.

CHAPTER THIRTY

DANNY searched for the handset in amongst the chaos.
"Who on earth is that?" asked Anna.
Danny didn't reply.
"Hello," he said, tentatively.

"Hello, Danny? It's Lisa." It was the familiar Scottish voice.

"Lisa!" Danny looked across to Anna, who quickly moved closer to hear the overspill of the conversation. "Where are you?"

"I can't tell you that, Danny. Sorry to call so late but I'm glad to catch you."

"Jesus, Lisa, what on earth is going on?"

"I was hoping you could tell me."

"For fuck's sake. We've got no idea. This isn't funny."

"It isn't meant to be funny. You got back to London okay then?"

"Yes, but... God. Why am I telling you? You probably already know..."

"About the flat? Yes. That was unnecessary."

"But how?"

"How what, Danny?"

"How do you know? You've got to tell me what's happening. Who even are you?"

"Ah Danny, you don't need to know that. It's better not to ask."

"Lisa! I'm sorry, but this is just taking the piss."

"I'm sorry you think that way. But I do think we're getting there."

"Getting where? You've got to start talking to me."

"I am talking to you. That's why I called. You didn't call me."

"I don't have your number."

"Touché."

Danny looked at the handset in utter frustration.

"Lisa, just tell me, who smashed our flat up? Have you got any idea what we're going through here? They've attacked Megan. Twice."

"I'm sorry to hear that. Is she okay?"

"After a fashion. Who are they?"

"They're bad people, Danny. That's all I can tell you at the moment. But I've told you, you have to be careful."

"Cheers for that."

"I'm sensing a degree of hostility, Danny."

"Is it any wonder? We're running all over the country for you, getting shot at, friends attacked, home attacked, studio smashed..."

"Studio?"

"Anna's studio. Passion Fruit."

Suddenly there was silence on the other end of the line.

"Lisa? Hello? Are you still there?"

Silence.

"I think she's gone," Danny said, turning to Anna. But then he heard a voice on the line.

"Sorry Danny, I'm back. The studio?"

252

"Yeah."

"When was that?"

"This evening."

"I wasn't aware of that. That's... unfortunate."

"Pass me the phone," said Anna, reaching out her hand. Danny did so.

"Hi, Lisa, Anna here. We haven't spoken."

"Hello Anna, nice to speak to you at last."

"That's a matter of opinion. Listen, we are getting completely fucked off here. We're tired, we're scared and we're sick of feeling like you're the only person who knows anything, so can you please actually be straight with us?"

"I'm always straight with you, Anna."

"Well, you're not. You're not telling us anything. Who are you? Why are you looking for Clare? Whose side are you actually on?"

"I'm on your side, Anna. You just have to trust me. There are things I can't say."

"God, you're annoying."

Lisa laughed.

"I'm sorry, Anna. I don't mean to annoy you. Look, none of this is ideal, but hopefully it's nearly over now. Sorry about your studio."

"Somebody should be."

"Is Danny there?"

"Yes."

"Can you put him back on the line please?"

"No, not unless you tell me who you are."

"Oh Anna, I can't do that."

"Why not?"

"Because it would be dangerous. All you need to know is that I'm your friend. I'm doing everything I can to minimise the danger, but I do need you to help me."

"To help you?"

"Yes."

"How can we help you? We don't even know who you are, never mind where you are."

"Just keep doing what you're doing, and be careful."

"So you keep saying. But we wouldn't need to be careful if none of this was happening."

"I know, and I'm sorry."

"Why are you actually ringing then? Just to show off?"

"No, to check on you. And to see if you've heard any more from Richard Kirk."

"May have done."

"Oh Anna, please don't be coy with me."

"I'm not. God. Yes we met him."

"Okay. And where is he now?"

"No idea. Looking for you, probably."

"Can you put Danny back on please?"

Anna swore and passed Danny the phone and then stuck two fingers up in its general direction.

"Hi, it's Danny."

"Danny, thank you for coming back. Anna sounds angry."

"Is it any wonder?"

"I suppose not. So you met Richard?"

"Yes, at the studio..."

"Anna's studio?"

"Yes."

"This evening?"

"Yes. Why?"

"Was he civil?"

"I'm not sure I'd go that far. But we came to an understanding."

"Okay, glad to hear it. But you don't know where he is now?"

"In bed fast asleep I imagine, which is where I'd like to be. Did you get the pictures by the way?"

"I did, yes. They're very good. Anna is an excellent photographer."

"She'll be pleased to hear that. Why did you need them?"

"I'll explain when I see you."

"So I'm going to see you then?"

"Yes, sooner rather than later I hope."

"Where?"

"I don't know that yet."

"When then?"

"I don't know that either, but soon I hope. I should let you get to bed now, though. I'm sorry again for calling so late."

"Just one thing before you go."

"Okay."

"Geneva. You asked me about it. What's that got to do with anything?"

"Did I?"

"You know you did."

"Ah yes. Well, don't worry about Geneva. Not yet."

"What's that supposed to mean?"

"Just what I said. Why? What have you heard?"

"I thought I didn't have to worry about it."

"Oh, Danny, you're good. But if we're going to find Clare we can't have any secrets."

"What? It's not me who's got secrets, Lisa. Let's start with what your real name is. Charlotte?"

"Haha, no, not Charlotte. Listen, if you're going to take that kind of an attitude, I can do this on my own, but I thought we'd be better together. My mistake. Bye Danny."

"Lisa! Stop it. We're just tired, okay? Anna's been held up at gunpoint, our flat's been smashed, her studio was broken into, and the flat where we're staying now has been done over as well. It's the middle of the night. We don't have any idea what's going on, and you're not actually telling me anything."

"But Danny, you do. I think you do yourself a disservice. I think you know just about everything."

"Really? It doesn't seem like it."

"I don't think you need me any more, Danny. I thought we were going to make a good team, but I get the sense that maybe we want different things. I think we should go our separate ways."

"Lisa!"

"I'll call you if I find Clare. But otherwise you won't be hearing from me. Take care, Danny."

And with that the line went dead.

Danny looked at the handset, and then at Anna and across to Megan.

"Well, that's the end of that," he said.

"What happened?" asked Anna.

"I don't know. She just seemed to take the hump. Something about us not keeping secrets, and when I said we weren't but she was, she basically told me to fuck off and said she wouldn't be calling again."

"Bollocks to her, then," said Anna.

"But at least she seemed to know something. Without her we're nowhere."

"Let's reassess in the morning. Megan, you ready for bed?"

"If you can help me put it back together."

"Let's all go, then. Come on, Danny. Everything may look clearer in daylight. We're tired."

They headed to the bedrooms to repair the damage ahead of hopefully a good night's sleep. Nobody thought to ask how Lisa knew their number.

CHAPTER THIRTY-ONE

Thursday, February 18th, 1993

SECRETLY I'd been hoping that the magic clean-up fairies would have been round in the night, or better still that I'd wake up having dreamed everything after a cheese sandwich or some such. But alas, everywhere was still as much of a mess as ever.

It was nice to wake up next to Danny for the fourth night out of six, not that I'm counting. (I am.) But it wasn't so good to wake up and see the carnage.

Thankfully, there wasn't any blood on the walls in Reigate, but, as small mercies go, there wasn't really much else to be grateful for. I headed into the shower while the others slept, and then made tea and toast while they took turns in the bathroom. By 10am we were all dressed and ready, like three battle-scarred veterans, but without much of a plan. We still had the gun, which I felt guilty about being grateful for. The thing still terrified me but I was happy that we'd taken it out of circulation.

We agreed that we'd try to make as much of an effort to tidy things up as we could before heading back to Camden to do the same. And so we worked for a couple of hours in relative silence, each cleaning, tidying, sweeping up mess, putting furniture back upright and trying our best to make an inventory of the things we needed to replace. We agreed that we'd explain everything to our hosts on their return and offer to replace anything that was beyond repair. I just hoped there was nothing of irreplaceable sentimental value. Danny phoned an emergency locksmith to come round to repair the door, and I wondered how many more times we'd have to do that before the day was over.

Understandably, Megan didn't want to stay on her own in Reigate any more. I offered her my room at our place and said I'd sleep on the sofa. Then Danny did the same, and we almost had an argument about it, but in the end she said she'd rather go home if it was all right with us. I was secretly relieved - not so much because the sofa debate was likely to spiral out of control, but because I knew we couldn't guarantee her safety. And if we had to leave in a hurry, then knowing she was safely at home was some consolation. Having confronted her attackers the previous night, she was convinced they weren't going to trouble her again. Her theory was that if they'd wanted to harm her, they could have done it in a deserted farmhouse better than anywhere. They hadn't exactly wrapped her in cotton wool, but their violence seemed primarily aimed at property.

We still didn't know who they were, but we knew they were connected somehow. And yet if Kirk was the muscle hired by Serraillier and March, who were they working for? And what were they trying to achieve?

By 1pm we were packed up and ready to leave. Danny wrote a note for Philip and Claudia, apologising for leaving things less than pristine. We'd done our best, though, in the circumstances. He asked them to get in touch on their return so we could go round to apologise in person. I drove Megan back to her home in Dagenham and after making sure she was happy to be home, and felt secure, we gave her big hugs and set off back to Camden.

Finally, as we cut through the streets towards north London, we had a chance to discuss our situation and attempt to contrive a plan.

"So, we're on our own," I said, thinking of the bizarre middle-of-the-night phone call with Lisa.

"Looks like it," agreed Danny. "Are you worried?"

"Me? No, not worried. Well yes, extremely worried, but no more so than I was last night. She wasn't exactly much help."

Danny didn't reply immediately.

"I don't know," he said at last. "She still seems like the missing link to me. She's still the person who connects everything. It's like she knows everything and she's watching over us."

"Your guardian angel?"

"So she said."

"Well, she's shit at it, in fairness. Do you think she'll call again when she gets over her strop?"

"I don't know. It was weird. It seemed final. It was like there was a sudden switch. That's women for you."

I gave him a look. Luckily he was grinning at me or he'd have been getting the bus.

"She wasn't keen to talk to me," I said after a moment. "She didn't like it when I said she was annoying."

"No. I keep replaying the call in my head. She spoke to you then you passed her back to me. And she said she liked the pictures and would explain why she needed them when we met, which was going to be soon."

"She's all heart."

"I know, but then I asked about Geneva, and she started going on about secrets as though it was me that was keeping things from her. And that's when she turned. I challenged her on it and she just took the hump and said we wanted different things."

"But she does keep secrets."

"And we still want the same thing, unless something's happened that we've missed."

"It's odd. So what do we do? Try to find her?"

"I don't know how we can. She could be anywhere."

"She can't be far. She seems to know everything we're doing." I made a show of looking in the rear view mirror. "Oh look, there she is, right behind us. Hello, Lisa." And I waved.

Danny, to his credit, didn't turn.

"Seriously," I continued. "It wouldn't surprise me. She's following us, watching us all the time. She can't be physically too far away."

"Unless we've served our purpose."

"Do you think?"

"I don't know what to think."

I stopped to fill up with petrol again, as the tank was running low and I wanted to be prepared for anything - mercy mission, quick getaway, whatever. I paid for it this time, with my First Direct Switch card. It only seemed fair. We were in this together.

We arrived home by 3pm and the mess was every bit as bad as I'd remembered. Having spent the whole morning clearing up, I didn't really have the energy to start again, but this was our home, and the sense of violation was if anything even stronger. We put the furniture upright and swept up the worst of the mess. My light-box was ruined, and we'd need new crockery before we could contemplate entertaining.

Danny phoned another locksmith and then offered to tackle the blood on the wall and floor, which was brave of him. Just the thought made me nauseous. He'd just started when he called me.

"When did you last cut yourself?" he asked, which I thought was a bit odd, until I realised he wasn't implying I'd taken up self-harm - aside from the recent overdose of Southern Comfort.

"Can't remember. Maybe a paper cut. Why?"

"Doesn't blood congeal?"

"Is that a posh way of saying clots?"

"Okay, clots then. Blood clots. This is still wet."

I took a closer look. He had a point. It had dried a bit in places, but still seemed to have a sticky consistency in others. I was tempted to dip my finger in it to test it but I was a bit squeamish.

"It's not real," he continued. I looked closer again.

"Kensington gore," I said, largely to myself.

"What?"

"Theatrical blood. It's what they call it."

"Do they?"

"Apparently."

"Well, unless I'm wrong, this is that."

My sense of relief was only slightly tarnished by my annoyance that whoever had done this had gone to considerable effort to scare us. It wasn't spur of the moment.

"Bastards," I said. "Meaning?"

"It's either a warning or vandalism or just trying to spook us."

"That's what really pisses me off. If you want to give us a warning, why not just write it down on a piece of paper rather than making us work it out."

"Like Jimmy Ravenscroft, you mean?"

"Well, yes. I'd forgotten about him. But yes. Ah, I'm not being serious. I just don't know how much more of this I can put up with."

Danny's expression changed. And then I realised what I'd said.

261

"Hey, don't worry, I'm not abandoning you as well. I just want it over. But I'm with you for the duration."

He smiled at me.

"I've got no right to expect anything," he said.

"Oh Danny, yes you have. We're a team. Always have been, always will be."

"Do you mean that?"

I smiled, dabbed my finger in the sticky mess and touched him on the nose.

"Sealed in blood," I said with a wink.

***

It was Association Time in the tough B Wing of London's oldest prison, at Brixton. One of the inmates was standing in a bleak corridor, using a phone card to make an outside call.

"Well?"

"We've been making progress."

"Progress?"

"Yeah, getting there."

"Getting there's no fucking use. I want it finished."

"Tonight, Jimmy."

"You're not lying to me?"

"Jimmy..."

"Don't Jimmy me. Just get it done."

"We will."

"I want to read about it. Fuels my sense of irony."

"You will."

"Last 24 hours. I don't need to elaborate."

"Understood."

"I'll call tomorrow."

He put the phone down as a brass bell sounded to signal time to return to his cell.

***

I phoned out for a takeaway and when it arrived we stopped for a much-needed break. It was pizzas again, sadly, but we didn't have much by way of plates. Don't know why I said "sadly". I like pizzas.

We were just finishing off when suddenly Danny swore. I thought a filling must have come loose, but no. This was a breakthrough.

"I've been stupid," he said.

"Thinking you've got a chance with Clare when a better alternative is under the same roof already?" I didn't say.

"How?"

"Last night. Lisa. She said we shouldn't keep secrets and I said I didn't but she did and she took the arse, right?"

"Right."

"Well no, wrong. It wasn't that. She only said that after I'd mentioned Geneva. That was when she changed."

"Are you sure?"

"Definitely. She said she'd see me soon and wished us goodnight. All very amiable. Then I said there was one quick thing I wanted to ask her about, which was Geneva. She denied ever mentioning it. Then she said I didn't need to worry about Geneva. Not yet. Emphasis on the yet. And then asked what I'd heard, and that's when she started going on about secrets."

"What did she mean by 'not yet'?"

"Well, presumably, not yet, but at some stage. And when she asked what I'd heard, it was almost like I was ahead of her and she didn't like it."

"And that's when she got moody?"

"Exactly."

I took a moment to take it in.

"How soon can we get a flight?" I asked.

"Are you serious?"

"Deadly." Without further encouragement, I handed him the phone and the Yellow Pages while I went to search for my passport.

I found my passport and put it into the back pocket of my jeans for safekeeping. The locksmith arrived eventually so I left Danny to phone round the travel agents while I explained what we needed for the door. He added a heavier duty mortice as well as replacing the Yale and reinforcing the door-frame. I had no idea what the landlord would think, but in my head it could only add value. I'm so practical.

Once he'd finished, I took him over to the studio so he could do much the same there. I realised the gun was still in the boot of my car, along with Danny's passport and our overnight bags. The thought made me uncomfortable. Didn't you need a licence for that kind of a thing? Driving around with an unlicensed gun that had been used for God knows what was freaking me out. I just wanted to get rid of it as quickly as possible, but wanted to do it with Danny so we could be there to support each other in case of disaster.

Our temporary lock had held, and there'd been no further attempts to break in as far as I could tell. The locksmith mended the door frame, added another lock, and did a more thorough job of repairing the window Megan had broken than I'd managed in haste. That evening seemed like such a long time ago. While he worked, I set about tidying up, seeing which of the lights I could salvage, and trying my best to return the studio to a workable space.

Once everything was done, I locked up, admiring my collection of new keys, grateful that at least I could rest easy, knowing that everything was secure. Unlike, as it transpired, my liberty.

CHAPTER THIRTY-TWO

DANNY managed to find an agent who could sell a pair of open return Swissair flights for collection at the airport before the journey the following morning. As he read out his NatWest Access card number, he winced at the considerable expense. What if it was a wasted journey? But at that moment it seemed like the most significant step forward so far.

He found the catalogue for La Galerie du Châtelet and packed it into a rucksack along with a selection of clothes. He didn't know how many nights to pack for. One? Two? Maybe a week? He decided to travel light. In an emergency he could always buy things out there, but they might need to pack up and go in a hurry. Then he rang the night desk at the Echo to say that the leads he was following up on a new story were taking longer than he'd thought, and he might not be in for the rest of the week. And was told, in reply, that he was officially suspended, pending a disciplinary meeting with the editor. And that the editor was furious, so it wasn't likely to go well.

It was just one more crisis, but there were no shortage of those, so he tried to put it out of his mind. There seemed so much to organise, and think about, and he was desperate for Anna to come back so they could plan the trip together. They still had hotels to think about, or maybe a B&B. He was sure they'd be able to pick up a guidebook at the airport, or find a tourist office on their arrival.

The doorbell rang, and he went to answer it, assuming Anna had gone out without her new keys. But when he opened the door he found DCI Graham March and DC Amy Cranston on the doorstep.

"Danny, long time no see," said March, waving a sheet of paper. "No need to invite us in. We have a warrant."

"A warrant?" said Danny, with an immediate feeling of dread.

"Indeed, so be a good lad and stick the kettle on while we have a little look around."

March and Cranston pushed past him into the hallway. Danny's first thought was relief that he'd managed to clean up the fake blood stains. But almost immediately came the bigger question. What the hell was going on?

"Don't mind us," said March as he made his way into the front room. "Ah, pizzas. Fine dining tonight, are we? Is the lovely Anna in?"

"Anna? No. What are you actually doing here?"

"Just routine police business. No sugar in either, as you know."

"No, seriously. What the fuck are you doing?"

"Danny, are you trying to hinder the police in the course of their enquiries? I'll no doubt find a moment to talk to you once we've had a gander. But in the meantime, shut the fuck up. And a biscuit would be handy if you've got some fresher ones."

Danny went to the kitchen, feeling like he was going to be sick. He put the kettle on and found two tea bags from an old box of Typhoo that was kept for emergencies, in case the more preferable PG Tips ran out. It was a small protest, but he was powerless to do any more. He could hear noises from elsewhere in the flat. Part of him was glad Anna was being spared the humiliation. He could imagine her fury if she was with him now.

Once the tea was made, he took it through to the living room and waited. March and Cranston emerged from Anna's bedroom.

"No biscuits," he said, placing the cups on the table.

"Going somewhere?" asked March.

"No."

"Hmm, it just looked like you'd been packing a bit of an overnight bag there, for a moment. And you know my thoughts on that."

"Can you just please tell me what you're looking for?"

March turned to DC Cranston.

"What do you think, Amy? Should we tell him?"

"Tell me what?"

"Sit down, Danny."

"I'd rather stand."

"I'm afraid that's not an option, given the circumstances. I must say, in passing, that I'm slightly disappointed by the state of the place. Have you been having a party?"

"No, just a bit of spring cleaning."

"I can't pretend it's not needed. Anyway, do you mind telling me where Anna is?"

"She's gone out. She's at work I think."

"That's very convenient, but it's a bit of a shame as she's really the one I wanted to have a word with."

"Anna? Why Anna?"

"Ah, Danny, you have so much to learn about ladies, although I do have a certain degree of sympathy as I don't expect you have too much experience of them, given your, shall we say, lifestyle."

"Can you please stop fucking about? What do you want with Anna?"

"Language, Danny, please. Now sit the fuck down."

Danny reluctantly took a chair at the table. March remained standing.

"How well do you know young Anna, would you say?"

"Inside out. Why?"

"Have you known her for long?"

"Ages, yes."

"And has she ever, in all that time, shown a proclivity for what I like to call acts of violence?"

That stopped Danny. He suddenly thought of her wild fury in the studio, dropping the spiked tripod onto Kirk's leg, and the venomous look in her eyes.

"No, why?"

"Ah, Danny, you do well to cover, but I suspect you may not be as keen to do so when I tell you why I'd like to speak to her. But firstly let's cut the bullshit, and don't pretend that you've been waiting here like a good boy, like I specifically remember telling you to. I told you I'd be watching you. I know you've been away. I know where you've been. And I know exactly what you've been up to, so don't bother trying to pretend otherwise."

"So where have I been then?"

"Back to the frozen north, visiting our Geordie cousins for starters, and don't try to deny it, because I've got the bank records to prove that your credit card was used in a restaurant there as recently as yesterday."

"Okay."

"And I know what you've been up to since you got back, although why you didn't report the break-in I have no idea. Unless of course you have something to hide. I'm extremely disappointed in you, Danny."

"Look, I'm sorry. But I'm just trying to find Clare."

"Indeed and again I appreciate your loyalty, but I think I did actually tell you not to do that." He turned to Amy. "Did I tell Danny not to do that?"

"You did."

"Thank you. I thought as much. So Danny, you may be expecting me to take you away with me and sort you out with some prestigious overnight accommodation. But luckily for you I've changed my mind."

"Okay..."

"Have you got anything more to say?"

"Apart from pointing out that Geordies come from Newcastle rather than Sunderland?"

"A trifling detail, but duly noted. Anything else?"

"I just want to know why you're here."

March walked over to where DC Cranston stood by the window. He looked out, and then returned to the centre of the room.

"Women, Danny. They can be lovely, as the delightful DC here goes to prove, but get on the wrong side of them and they can have what you might call a nasty streak. Now are you sure you've never seen Anna lapse into wanton violence?"

***

I drove back to Rochester Square but annoyingly all of the parking spaces close to our flat were taken, so I ended up leaving the car in Camden Mews, which is a tiny narrow street just round the corner. As I approached the flat, I could see Danny wasn't alone. DCI March was standing at the window next to DC Cranston, looking out. He didn't see me. I panicked. I ducked back down the side street and waited for them to leave.

***

"Thanks for the warning."

"The bad ones act on jealousy or vengeance, or just sheer evil," March continued. "Amy, can you pass me the card please?"

DC Cranston passed March an envelope, from which he withdrew a greetings card.

"Do you recognise the writing, Danny?"

Danny took the card and looked at it. There was a Valentine's message on the front. Inside was his name, and a handwritten message ending in a question mark.

"It looks like Anna's." He passed it back.

"And there, Danny, is your actual evidence. It was in her top drawer. It seems like she has a little crush on you, although I hesitate to wonder why."

Danny felt himself blush despite his best intentions.

"No, that's just a joke. She's my best friend and we say we love each other but..."

"I'll stop you there and save you from embarrassing yourself."

"I..."

"Shut up. And listen. Okay? I'm going to tell you what happened to Clare."

"Okay."

"And then maybe you will change your opinion."

"I don't..." And then Danny stopped. He had a terrible feeling his world was about to implode.

"Let me start by saying I know you didn't kill Clare," March continued. "I never really thought you did because I don't think you have it in you. I'm a bit of a scholar of these things. But you didn't have an alibi for the night she disappeared, and that seemed a touch unfortunate."

"Sorry, Anna was out at work."

"Please don't interrupt, although on this occasion I'll overlook it as you make a salient point. But yes, Anna was at work. Or so she said. But actually, as she pointed out in your very kitchen, that just meant that she didn't have an alibi either."

"You're not suggesting..."

"Danny, stop. The sooner we get through this the better. So Anna has, as we've seen, got a great big crush on her flatmate, aka, you, but you spend all your time with the lovely Clare who you've admitted to being in love with, via the medium of a blush when I asked you during our second conversation. And Anna is jealous. And the jealousy builds. And she wants you for herself, although God alone understands the working of the female mind. The problem then is Clare, although if she were to disappear and Anna could help you look for her, albeit without success, she'd prove herself worthy of your affections and you'd both live happily ever after."

Danny tried to speak, but March raised his hand to stop him.

"So Anna has no alibi for the disappearance, and she says she'll help you, but as you've seen, it's a fruitless search. In fact Anna is with you every step of the way to ensure that it stays that way. Because if you found out what really happened to Clare, then maybe you wouldn't be quite so keen to walk off into the sunset, hand in hand. Of course, she cannot do this alone, so she concocts a plan with a friend. The friend pretends to be kidnapped, and Anna runs to her rescue. Except the alleged kidnapping didn't take place. They were just spending a night away, working on the finer details of the execution, if you'll excuse the phrase."

"This is madness."

"I'll continue. So you meet the mysterious Lisa, who is indeed looking for Clare, but mainly to cover her own back because she thinks the disappearance is something to do with the nasty Frenchman she's been working for. He wasn't French by the way. He was Swiss, but from the French-speaking region, so I can forgive the misconception. And then on your second visit north, Anna arranges for her friend, young Megan, to pop round to the flat and rough it up a bit, to make it look like you've had a burglary."

"But that's ridiculous. She was robbed at gunpoint."

"And again, Danny, we only have Anna's word for that. In fact the alleged robbery never happened. She left you at the flat and drove round town, maybe for a bit of shopping, who knows, they like to do that. And then when she returned she told you a fantastical story about a man on a motorbike."

"But I met him."

"Indeed you did. But unfortunately for Anna, he's somebody in my acquaintance and, let's say, he's amenable to most things for a bit of cash. So you return from Sunderland and discover the break-in, but Anna just wants to go to the studio, which is convenient. Because of course that's where she's arranged to meet our friend, to give her story from Sunderland a degree of credibility. Except she gets carried away and attacks him with a tripod, because as we now know she is indeed prone to a little bit of violence, and he wasn't best pleased because that wasn't in their agreement. To add insult to injury, she lets his tyres down. That was the final straw, and so he came to me."

"No..."

"And in the process she takes his gun. Where's the gun now, Danny?"

"It's... It's in Anna's car."

"Ah, you see, so the pieces are starting to fall into place. I think you can see where we're going with this. Megan, meanwhile, returns to Reigate and does the smashing up thing again, and when you get there, she tells you it was the same two mysterious kidnappers from the previous attack. Except they don't exist. And so now Anna is curiously absent again, except this time she's got a gun, and she's almost certainly not afraid to use it. Are you following?"

"Yes, but..."

"So we have the means, the method, and tonight we have the motive. And if you'd done as I told you to, and not gone off on a wild goose chase, we could have wrapped all this up several days ago, and possibly we'd have found out whatever she's done with the body. But Anna's gone. I just looked for her passport, but I couldn't find it. I suspect she's realised we've worked out her plan, and now she's on the run, with a gun, which is not as poetic as it sounds. I'm not going to arrest you, Danny. Being stupid is not, in itself, a crime. But I would strongly advise you to keep a low profile until we can apprehend her. We'll see ourselves out."

And with that they were gone.

Danny couldn't believe it. And yet the way it was explained, it all made sense. He knew he had to act fast. He dashed to the bedroom and finished packing his rucksack. His mind was a daze. It was time to get out, to get away, and who knew when it would ever be safe to come back.

And then he heard a key in the front door. He moved to the hallway, just in time to see Anna enter. She had a determined expression, a look in her eyes that he did not recognise. And she was holding the gun.

CHAPTER THIRTY-THREE

I WAITED until I saw March and Cranston leave and then quickly grabbed the bags and gun from the car and rushed back to the flat. I opened the door and saw Danny, terrified, looking at me.

He ran towards me.

"Thank God you're here," he said with breathless urgency, wrapping me in his arms. "We've got to go. Now!"

"Why? What's happened?"

"It's March. He's looking for you. He could be back any minute. Where's your car?"

"Camden Mews. Why?"

"Leave it. We'll get the tube. Get a bag for Geneva, quick. Two nights minimum. Seriously, now!"

I didn't waste a second. I ran to the bedroom and grabbed enough clothes for a couple of days, and threw a few toiletries into the outside pocket. Danny followed me.

"What's happened?" I asked again.

"I'll tell you on the way. Come on. Have you got your

passport?"

I patted my pocket like the woman in the Asda ad.

"Perfect. Wear a hat. Something woolly. And a scarf, everything. Bring the gun and we'll lose it on the way. Ready?"

Within just a few moments I was.

Rochester Square isn't far from Camden Town Underground station. It's a straight walk down Camden Road. But instead of turning right to take the direct route, Danny led me left toward Stratford Villas, and then, as the road turned right, we cut through a pedestrian walkway to Agar Road. Halfway through, he stopped, and pulled me close to him, under cover of a tree.

"So Danny..."

"I'll give you the summary. March came round."

"I know. I saw him."

"Christ, did he see you?"

"No, why?"

"Thank God. Basically, he came round to arrest you."

"Me? Why?"

"For murdering Clare."

"*What?*"

"Exactly. It was just excruciating. They had a warrant. Searched the flat. And then they came out with a bollocks story about how you'd murdered Clare, faked Megan's attempted kidnap, made up the story about Kirk at Rougemont, planned the whole thing with Megan, persuaded her to smash the flat up, paid Kirk to burgle the studio, and apparently now you're on the run. And you're armed and dangerous and they're out there now trying to find you."

"Again, what?" I was finding it hard to take this all in.

"Seriously, the man's gone mental."

"Jesus."

"That's why we've got to go. Now."

"But... I'm missing something. Why did I murder Clare?"

"Oh, jealousy apparently. Nice card by the way." Danny

275

grinned, despite everything.

"What card?"

"They found a card in your chest of drawers. Valentine's card, written to me."

"Ah." I blushed, but luckily it was dark.

"Don't worry. It was lovely. But that's apparently your motive. You're so in love with me you've apparently done away with Clare so you can have me to yourself."

I didn't quite know what to say. I couldn't deny the first part, but the rest just seemed surreal.

"And how have I done this?"

"Don't worry, he's worked it all out. It's quite the conspiracy. And it sounds like Kirk's made up a load of nonsense to get back at you for letting his tyres down. To give March some credit, it was quite a convincing story."

"Shit. God, you didn't think..."

"That you did it? Anna, look at me."

I looked straight into his eyes.

"This is me. Danny. You're my best friend. Soulmate. The most amazing person I know. If it's a question between you and that bent bastard, I'd trust you with my life."

I felt like I was going to cry.

"Thank you," I said. And gave him a great big hug. "So what now?"

"I've booked the flights. We leave in the morning. But we can't hang around here because they'll come back, so we need to get going. We can either go straight to the airport or stay somewhere close, but either way we're not safe here."

I pulled the hat down further. I hate the tube normally, may have mentioned it, but could see why we couldn't take my car. I just hoped March and his pals would be gentle with it. I love that car, temperamental locks and all.

We took a mazy route to Camden Town station, avoiding main roads as much as we could. On Georgiana Street we dropped the gun through the gaps in a drain cover, having wiped it clean of our fingerprints, and then Danny found a callbox to give the police an anonymous tip-off about where to find it.

He stopped at a cashpoint by the station and withdrew £100, and then we bought one-way tickets to Heathrow terminals One, Two and Three. We couldn't talk much on the train. There were too many other people, but once past Acton Town things had thinned out a bit, and we finally had seats together.

We tried to formulate a plan. Staying the night in the airport terminal was discounted. We didn't want to draw attention to ourselves, and we didn't know what we'd be facing the following day, so we didn't want to go into it already exhausted. So we decided to just get to the terminal and then take a taxi to whichever hotel looked the closest.

I've yet to reach the stage of my career where I'm offered fabulous commissions in far-flung locations, and so the novelty of air travel has yet to wear off. There's something deeply intoxicating about an airport, especially at night. They're full of buzz, with the noise of jet engines and heavy scent of kerosene adding to the sense of impending adventure. I tried not to show my excitement when we left the tube station for fear of looking too much like a tourist.

We found the taxi rank, and asked the driver to suggest a hotel that was both nearby and likely to have rooms at short notice. He recommended the Penta Hotel on Bath Road. It looked like a concrete monstrosity from the outside, but was actually quite welcoming once we were through the door. I asked for a double room before anyone suggested a twin, and Danny paid for it in cash. Apparently March had been tracing his credit card.

Our room was on the third floor. From the window we could see the airport. I could have stayed for hours, fascinated, watching the planes taxiing, but the priority was to get to sleep.

After a quick shower to wash away the stress of the day, I got into bed next to Danny for the fifth night out of seven, not that I'm counting. (I still am.) It was starting to feel normal, and we didn't even question the arrangement.

I wasn't sure how well we'd sleep. It seemed like the night before the biggest day of our lives. And yet it could just as easily be a complete waste of time. Our plan was to visit the gallery's Geneva premises and take things from there. But if that didn't work, we had no idea.

Danny was looking through the gallery's catalogue as I tried not to snuggle up beside him, even though I did a little bit. I felt like I was in an alien world. I take photographs of outfits, for heaven's sake. I do not get chased by police, held up at gunpoint, and lured to foreign countries in an attempt to solve what was increasingly looking like a murder. And Danny had said I was the most amazing person he knew. I'd settle for that.

Eventually we both turned out our lights and turned to face in opposite directions. But I couldn't resist turning back around and putting my arm round him, even if just briefly.

"Danny," I whispered.

He murmured in response.

"Thank you for believing in me."

I kissed his shoulder and then turned back, and attempted to go to sleep.

CHAPTER THIRTY FOUR

Friday, February 19th, 1993

"Enjoy the flight," said the woman at the Swissair check-in desk, with a smile.

Suddenly it began to seem even more real. We were actually going to do this. We found the check-in desk, picked up our boarding passes, found a Bureau de Change to get some Swiss francs, and then made our way through security control. And then there was no going back.

We found a coffee bar and ordered cappuccinos, feeling all cosmopolitan and European all of a sudden.

"Do you know what really puzzles me?" Danny asked, as he scooped the milk froth with a teaspoon. "How did my passport end up in Sunderland?"

It was a valid question, but just one more mystery in a week where hardly anything made sense.

"It's like, March took it on Monday night. And by Wednesday afternoon it's in an envelope at Rougemont. How did it even

279

get there?"

"Post, do you think?"

"Yeah but why? Why would he post it to somebody, and if he did, who was it? He must have sent it first thing Tuesday, but even then there was no guarantee it'd arrive before we checked the box."

"Unless somebody took it up there."

"Kirk? He was up there and seems to be March's pal."

"Can't be, though. That doesn't make sense. Why would he hold you up at gunpoint to intercept a package that he's just dropped off?"

"That's a good point. Lisa maybe?"

"But then she'd have to be working alongside March rather than against him. And if that's the case then God knows what's going on because that would undermine everything."

"All right, so whoever we were supposed to be meeting at Bentleys."

"But that was Tuesday. If it was posted it would only have been posted on Tuesday. So it must have been taken up by somebody in person. And maybe the reason they didn't turn up was because they didn't get there in time."

"Makes sense."

"But why would March be sending my passport to Lisa? And why send somebody all the way up there with it? And more than that, it seemed like he was completely oblivious of it yesterday. He went looking for yours, but made no reference to mine. So it looks like as far as he's concerned he's still got it."

"Which would mean someone else took it."

"Exactly."

I thought for a moment.

"Cranston?"

Danny stopped to take a sip of his drink and I did the same. I wanted to lick the froth off his upper lip, but thought it might be a bit inappropriate.

"It makes you think, doesn't it?" he continued. "Actually, yes!"

"Go on."

"That night at the station, when I got the lift home from Lisa. March started the interview but disappeared and she took over. And it was like she was completely different. I said something about whether he was always like that and she whispered no comment and looked at the two-way mirror. As though she was warning me he was still out there, so I should be careful."

"And you know what's been bothering me?"

"What?"

"Well, Lisa picked you up, and called herself Lisa Miller. Which means she must have known the name of the person who was supposed to be giving you a lift home was Lisa Miller. So unless it was a lucky guess, somebody must have told her."

"Oh, Anna," he said. He didn't need to say any more. Suddenly it was clear to both of us. DC Amy Cranston was the missing link.

CHAPTER THIRTY-FIVE

D ANNY got up to check the departure screens to see if our gate had been announced. It was still an hour before take-off but flight SR835 could be called at any moment. He came back, but there was no news.

"So, Cranston's Lisa's spy," I said when he sat back down. "But what does that actually mean?"

"Well, it's always seemed like she was looking out for us. March has said a couple of times that he was all for arresting me but she'd talked him out of it."

"So is she bent as well? Just in a different way to March?"

"Or maybe not bent at all. Maybe she's the one controlling everything, making sure that March doesn't do anything ridiculous. We need to speak to her."

"We can't now. We will when we get back though. Although isn't she looking for me anyway?"

"March is. Maybe she'd step in and stop him if it came to it."

"It's a bit of a risk."

And then our flight was called. We got up and started to

make our way through the busy departure lounge towards gate A22. I stopped on the way to have a quick squirt of Paris on one wrist and Poison on the other, but managed to swerve the assistant who was expecting a sale.

"Do you think this could all be a trap?" I asked as we walked, suddenly nervous.

"It's elaborate if it is," Danny replied. "They've had plenty of opportunities to get rid of us if that's what they wanted. But I can't see how it can be."

"I know, it just seems strange."

"Everything seems strange. I'll tell you something, if nothing else it's been a learning curve, all of this."

"But you're the crack investigator. My own personal Poirot."

"Not really. I just help Clare. But this is the sharp end. It's harder than it looks."

"You've had the best teacher."

Danny smiled. But it was a rueful rather than a happy one.

***

With hand luggage only, we were soon on our way once we'd cleared Swiss passport control. We stopped at a tourist information office to pick up a map of the city and then made our way to the underground train station and bought tickets for the SBB train to Cornavin, the city's main railway station. It was a refreshingly short, six-minute journey. And then we were outside, in the open air, and if anything it was even colder than London. Light snow was falling. I was glad of my hat.

We had the address of the gallery. It was in Rue de Marché on the far side of the Rhône, but Danny suggested lunch first and I was delighted to accept. I think we were both nervous.

We stopped at a cafe close to the pedestrian bridge, Pont de la Machine. I don't mind admitting, I felt completely lost. French isn't my strong point, and it looked like a busy city to me, rather than the fairy tale image I had of cuckoo clocks, and milkmaids with blonde hair delivering Alpine milk to artisan chocolate shops. The menu was in French although the cuisine was Italian. I recognised a few words from my middle school years, but thankfully the waiter was happy to translate for us. I do feel perpetually embarrassed about my lack of language skills. The satellite TV box in our flat picks up several German channels. I think I'd like to learn German as the programmes look rather saucy and exciting, but it all just seems so hard.

After lunch we crossed the bridge and headed towards the gallery. We didn't really have a plan. I'm sure our pace got slower as we approached.

And then, we were on Rue de Marché. It was a very short street with shops on both sides. And no sign of a gallery. We stopped at the end when it turned into Rue de la Croix-d'Or. Danny asked me for the map.

"Well, that's a brilliant start," he said.

"Are you sure this is the right address?" He took the gallery catalogue from his rucksack and checked the back page. He passed it to me.

"It's the right street," I said. "We must have missed it."

We walked up and down another couple of times but still there was nothing. It was deeply frustrating. All this way for a gallery that didn't even exist. I decided to ask a local for help. I showed him the catalogue and the address and he nodded, said something in French and indicated that we should follow him. Within a few seconds he was pointing at an office building and then left us to it. It wasn't a gallery. It was a shop renting mailboxes, like a mini-Swiss version of Rougemont.

"What now?" I asked.

"Presumably they must rent a mailbox here," said Danny. "I don't know. Are we supposed to be checking the box?"

"I don't know. It seems odd. It's not busy. We could go in and ask."

"But they're going to give us access are they? We haven't got a key. We haven't even got a clue if that's what they do."

"But they must do, surely. If the gallery are using this address on the catalogue then presumably they get post occasionally. So they must have a box."

"Okay. But we still don't have a key. We've got to be missing something."

"Unless that's really just it." I didn't want to suggest that the entire trip could be a complete waste of time, but I was beginning to think it. "Come on, let's think."

I could see Danny's mind working.

"What we need to do," he said at last, "is find out who the box actually belongs to. If they're using this for mail, it's either because they want a central Geneva address, or because they don't want to get stuff sent to home. But either way it's presumably someone local who comes in and picks it up occasionally."

"So what are you suggesting? That we wait until somebody goes in and then if they pick up the gallery mail we follow them?"

"No, there's no guarantee we'd recognise them. And we don't know how often they go in anyway. It might be once a month."

"Exactly."

"Presumably they have a list of names and addresses of box holders somewhere. We just need to access that."

"They're not going to just tell us."

"Valid point. So how then?"

I thought for a moment. And then I started to smile.

"Stop me if this sounds ridiculous," I said. "I've got a plan."

***

Ten minutes later, Anna staggered into the shop clutching her left arm, reached out for the counter, missed, groaned and slid to the floor, looking as though she was about to pass out.

The shocked shop assistant ran out from behind her desk to attend to the new arrival. Her high-pitched voice betrayed concern, even if the words were unintelligible to Anna, who lay on the floor, eyes pleading as they began to close.

Almost immediately, Danny ran in, carrying both of their bags.

"Help me," whispered Anna, in a faint, breathless voice. "My arm."

"What happened?" asked Danny, as he knelt on the floor.

He looked at the shop assistant, who was kneeling on the other side.

"My arm... I think, I'm...." Anna continued, as her eyes closed fully.

Danny took control.

"Veronique, do you speak English?" he asked, looking at the assistant's name badge. She nodded and pinched her thumb and forefinger together to indicate a little. On the floor, Anna continued to clutch her arm and make groaning noises.

"I saw her fall," he said. "I think she's broken her arm." And then to Anna: "Can you hear me? Do you want me to call an ambulance?"

Anna shook her head.

"Water," she said. "Just water."

Danny turned to Veronique.

"Would it be possible to get a glass of water?"

Glad to be able to help, she nodded, and disappeared into a back office, returning a few seconds later. She handed the glass to Anna, who took it in her right hand, and tried to sit up. She took a sip.

"Thank you," she said, eyes closed, voice strained.

"Can you move your arm? Have you got any movement in your hand?" asked Danny, still kneeling beside her.

Anna just shook her head. It wasn't clear whether it was to

indicate lack of movement or just that he should stop asking questions. But then her hand moved. The fingers flexed.

"Can I get you anything?" he asked. Again, she just shook her head. Danny turned to the assistant.

"I'm a doctor," he said. "I saw her fall. I don't think it's broken, just badly sprained, but I think she's in shock. Do you understand 'shock'?"

Veronique said something in French. Danny mimed shivering. She nodded.

"I think she'll be okay. She just needs to rest for a moment. Is it okay to stay here?"

"Of course," Veronique replied, in a heavy French accent.

"Thank you."

And then Anna, still holding the glass, slumped further to the floor. The glass tipped, spilling its contents onto her leg.

"One moment," said Veronique, who rushed off again and returned a moment later with some paper towels.

"I'm so sorry," whispered Anna. "The lights... So bright."

Danny turned back to the assistant. He pointed at the spotlights in the shop ceiling, then shaded his eyes.

"I think the lights are affecting her. Do you have somewhere she can sit that's maybe darker? An office? Just so she can dry out and recover?"

"Come," said Veronique. Danny helped Anna to her feet, and supported her while she tried to walk. The assistant led them through to a separate office at the back of the shop. Danny pulled out a chair and helped Anna to sit down.

"We'll just give you a minute to rest. Okay?" he said. Anna nodded. "Can I get you anything?"

"No, no thank you. Just stay for a minute," she replied.

Danny looked to Veronique.

"She'll be fine. Just let her get her breath back and dry out and then I'll take her to the hospital to get checked out. Thank you so much for helping. I can stay with her."

Veronique's face was full of concern. She gave Anna a reassuring touch on her shoulder and then left them to return to the front of the shop.

As the door closed, Anna's eyes opened.

"Top acting," whispered Danny, with a smile of acknowledgement.

"That water was bloody freezing."

Danny set to work. There were shelves with ring binders, a filing cabinet, a desk with a computer. He started rifling through, searching for anything that looked like a list of clients. Through the door he could hear two voices. It sounded like a customer had arrived. He knew he didn't have long. Veronique could return at any moment. He tried the ring binders first, but there was nothing. Invoices, delivery notes, but nothing to indicate which box belonged to which customer, and no mention of La Galerie du Châtelet. Hurrying on, he turned to the filing cabinet, but it just looked like it was used for general storage. There was an old telephone, a mess of wires, stationery catalogues, but nothing that looked of any real use.

Panic started to set in. The plan had worked beautifully, but it was only ever going to get them across the threshold. There was still no guarantee of success. The voices stopped. The door started to open. Danny just had time to shut the drawer as Veronique came back in.

"How is she?" she asked, looking worried.

"Slightly better, I think," Danny replied, sitting on the desk, trying to look calm. Anna nodded.

"Thank you," she said again. "Just fell over... My arm..."

Veronique nodded and turned to leave. As the door swung closed, Danny resumed his search, but again there was nothing. The computer screen was on so he quickly moved to the keyboard, and swept the mouse around the screen, looking for documents, or any program that might be useful.

"Anything?" asked Anna.

"No, nothing. It's all in French. It could be but I haven't got a clue. The only thing I recognise is Solitaire. Fuck."

"What if it's all out front?"

"I know. It's a nightmare. How's your head?"

"Fine, why?"

"Get a headache, now. And keep her talking."

Danny opened the door, and called to the assistant.

"Excuse me," he said, walking back to the desk. "She said she has a headache." Danny pointed to his head and grimaced. "Do you have an aspirin?"

Veronique got the message.

"I look," she said. Danny leaned on the shop counter, while she went through to the back office. He knew he might only have seconds. He ran round to the other side of the counter and looked for anything that resembled a list. But again there was nothing. Praying nobody would enter the shop, he quickly scanned the desk, the drawers, but there was just stationery, stamps, empty waybills, packaging materials, but nothing at all that looked like a list of clients.

And then he had a breakthrough.

There was a pile of post by a franking machine. It looked like mail that was being re-addressed. Maybe some of it would be for La Galerie du Châtelet. He started to flick through it but then sensed movement from the door, so quickly stopped and sprinted back to the front of the desk, just as Veronique came back through. So close.

And then Anna called out.

"Excuse me..."

Veronique turned and walked back to the office. Danny had seconds. He ran back and started rifling through the post. And then, about two-thirds of the way though the pile, he saw it. A standard DL sized envelope with a plastic window. It looked like an invoice. The name La Galerie du Châtelet could just be seen. A sticker with a forwarding address obscured the rest.

Danny didn't have time to copy the address, so he just pocketed the envelope. He'd deliver it in person. He just had to hope it wouldn't be missed.

Veronique re-emerged a split second after he'd made it back round the desk again. He smiled at her and said thank you.

"I'll see if she's up to moving," he said. "Is there a hospital nearby?"

Veronique took a pen from a desk tidy and wrote the name of the nearest hospital, on Rue Gabrielle-Perret-Gentil. He thanked her again and then went back to the office, helped Anna up from the chair, and then picked up the bags.

"Bingo," he whispered.

They walked back through to the shop front, and Anna thanked Veronique for her help. She leaned on Danny for support. Slowly, they made progress to the door. Veronique gave directions to the hospital and offered to order a taxi. Danny looked at Anna, but she declined.

"I'll be okay, I think," she said in a shaky voice. "It was just the shock. The walk will help I think. But thank you again. You have been wonderful." And with that they left, turned towards the river, and then both started to run.

CHAPTER THIRTY-SIX

"WHERE to now, Poirot?" I asked as we stopped running. We were back at the bridge.

"Let's find a cafe, get a drink, and have a look at the map." He explained about the envelope, the sticker, and how close he'd come to being caught. I was secretly impressed. We were a unit.

A cobbled footpath from the bridge led to the Riverside Cafe on Quai Bezanson-Hugues. We ordered cappuccinos and took them to a table on the terrace outside, right by the edge of the river. It was a beautiful setting, although still freezing cold, and the damp patch on my leg wasn't helping. I doubted Clare would be so keen to take one in the line of duty.

Danny took the envelope from his pocket. The address was on a printed label stuck over the original, beneath the little plastic window. He passed it to me. I had visions of a gust of wind blowing it into the river, never to be seen again, so I held it with two hands and suggested Danny copy the address onto another piece of paper as an emergency backup.

The address was in a place called Corsier. It didn't mean much to either of us. It was still in Switzerland, which was a start, but we had no idea where, nor how to get there.

"Should we open it?" I asked.

"Best not. I think that's illegal," said Danny. I found it hard to suppress a smile.

"In the way that deception and theft aren't?"

"Fair point."

"But what if it's something good? It could be a clue." I was aware I sounded like I was taking part in a treasure hunt, which in a way I suppose I was.

"I don't know, I just feel a bit awkward. How about this: we keep it with us, and we find where it is, house, office or whatever, go to have a look and see whether we think it's leading anywhere..."

"And if not, we open it?"

"Exactly."

"Good plan."

We finished the drinks and then Danny asked the waiter for directions to the nearest library. He drew us a little map showing the location of a place called the Library in English. Specifically designed for English speakers, it sounded perfect. It was back across the river, about a ten minute walk away.

It was nearly 4.30pm when we found it, sharing a building with a church close to the edge of Lake Geneva. It was due to close at 5pm so we didn't have long. We went straight to the desk and asked the librarian for assistance. It was lovely to be able to speak English without feeling guilty for my own linguistic ignorance.

We showed her the address, and she told us Corsier was about ten miles outside Geneva. She was curious about why we wanted to visit, as apparently it was just a tiny municipality (which I think is the Swiss term for village but I'm not a hundred per cent sure), but we just explained that a friend lived out there and we were hoping to visit at some stage. I think she believed us. Either way, I was encouraged that she didn't recoil in horror at the concept, declaring it a barren wasteland full of zombies. Or murderers.

She offered to get us a reference book so we could read up about the place. I was just keen to get going, but Danny thought it would be good to do some research. He had a point. We had no idea what we were getting into. As he read, I took the opportunity to ask for some suggestions for overnight accommodation. We still hadn't found a hotel for the evening, and time was moving on. I didn't fancy sleeping rough, especially in sub-zero temperatures.

With the addresses of a couple of nearby hotels that weren't as extortionate as those on the lakeside, I joined Danny at the desk, reading up about Corsier. It really was very small, with a total area of just over a square mile and population of about two thousand, of which about a third were foreign nationals. And then the librarian came to see us, apologised that the library was about to close, but wished us a pleasant stay and safe journey. I liked her.

Daylight was fading as we emerged onto the street, and the temperature was dropping even further, but I was developing a growing fondness for Geneva. The clean lake air was a welcome contrast to the carcinogenic pollution of London.

"Should we go this evening?" I asked as we walked back toward the lake to admire the view.

"Definitely, if you're up for it," Danny replied.

"I'm in. Can we find a hotel first, though? I'm sick of carrying this around." I indicated my bag. I was also growing concerned that we'd arrive back in the city late at night only to find everywhere was already full.

Danny agreed. I consulted my list and we settled on the Warwick Geneva, which was back in the direction of the train station. I thought that could be useful if we needed to make a swift getaway.

It wasn't far to walk, but I was glad of the rest when we arrived. We took a double room and I took a moment to relax on the bed while Danny unpacked his bag. We discussed going for dinner before setting off, but then decided to just get on with it. We could look forward to that this evening, depending on what we found. In truth I didn't expect to find much. We were just going to have a look at the place, scout the vicinity, and then try to formulate a plan for a daylight visit the following morning. At least, that's what I thought.

With the clock edging past 6pm, we decided it was time to make a move. The concierge offered to book us a taxi. I wasn't sure about the whole tipping protocol but Danny seemed to know what he was doing so I left it to him. Within a few minutes a large Mercedes pulled up to the door of the hotel and we went out into the cold. Danny gave the driver the address on a piece of paper, and we settled into the back seat together for the journey. The driver was listening to the radio, turned down low to a French-language talk station, and didn't seem particularly interested in engaging with us. I was quite relieved. I don't really enjoy small talk, and I wouldn't have known how to answer any questions, even assuming I'd understood them.

Instead I concentrated on Danny, who was looking pensive. It was getting too dark to see much outside, although as we left the city everywhere seemed to be covered in snow.

"Are you okay?" I asked.

He didn't reply immediately, but instead, after a moment, reached for my hand.

"I hope so," he said eventually. I knew what he meant.

"Do you think it seems a bit weird?" I asked. "We're driving through the countryside. In Switzerland of all places. It should be a massive adventure but it just seems... I don't know. Like we're stepping off the edge."

"Yeah, I feel that," he said.

"We just don't know, do we. Oooh, what if it's a really disappointing flat above a chip shop, and we knock on the door and it's a little old lady who hasn't got a clue what we're talking about."

"We could have some chips." Danny smiled, but it didn't last long.

Underpinning everything, I think, was a sense of loss. We'd faced danger, travelled hundreds of miles, been on seemingly pointless errands, and both despaired at the apparent lack of progress while at the same time making actual leaps forward in ways we hadn't foreseen. And yet beneath it all I knew Danny must be hurting. I knew how much he thought of Clare. How much he admired her. How much he loved every moment of working alongside her, sharing his life with someone he'd revered, and learning from the very best in the business. If you took my own personal agenda out of the equation, I could see why she was such a role model for him, and why he was so in awe. And yet it was over a week now since he'd last seen her, and the initial worry about her disappearance must surely have given way, at least in part, to grieving for her loss. In all of the things we'd come across, everything we'd found, everyone we'd met, and every bullet we'd dodged - physically and metaphorically - one constant remained. Nobody and nothing gave any clue to what had happened to her nor where she could be.

I replayed the events of the week in my mind. If we could guarantee a happy ending we'd be able to look back on it all as a great journey of discovery. A grand voyage. We could look back at the miles on the motorway, the highs and lows, forgetting the fear and remembering the happy times through a prism of relief, laughing at the ridiculousness of taking pictures in a nightclub while heavily intoxicated, and trying to forget my outfit which, in retrospect, was maybe out of keeping with that expected of someone who's supposed to understand fashion.

But I didn't think there was going to be a happy ending. And so what then? Maybe just the relief of finally finding the truth, and then a rebuilding process as we both came to terms with reality of bereavement. I was worried. I hated the thought of Danny in pain. I knew he'd be devastated, and it seemed like we were getting closer to that moment. Until we found the answers we could live in denial. But once it was over we could deny no more.

And yet maybe not knowing was even worse. Maybe we'd never find the answers, and we'd live for ever in a vague netherworld of uncertainty, and never be able to find any form of comfort or redemption. Maybe the only thing worse than knowing for definite is just not knowing at all.

The car started to slow. And then the driver pulled over to the side of the road. I'd been expecting a pretty chocolate-box village but the reality was different. There just seemed to be, well, nothing. We'd parked outside what looked like a large white house, but was actually a commercial building, with a bakery on one side and a post office on the other. And that was just about it, apart from a few houses. There was definitely no sign of a chip shop. The roads had been cleared of snow but were otherwise quiet. The population of two thousand all seemed to be at home.

The driver gestured to a phone box and then we understood. This was where we should call from when we were ready to go home. I gave him the international thumbs up sign and then he pulled away again, took a couple of turns, and stopped again, even more in the middle of nowhere. He pointed to the piece of paper with the address and then indicated what looked like a small farm track to our left. This time the journey was over.

Danny gave him some francs and was handed change. We got out of the car and then stood by the road, in ever-deepening darkness, surrounded by snow-covered fields, and watched him pull away.

"Where the fuck are we?" I asked, letting my confusion get the better of my language.

"I have absolutely no idea," said Danny. We looked at each other. He shrugged. It would have been funny if it hadn't been so unsettling. Suddenly the comforting warmth of a lovely hotel room had immeasurable appeal.

"Do you think this was a good idea?" I asked, in a tone of voice that implied I already knew the answer.

"It's not looking good."

"Well, there wasn't much in the village. Presumably this is the actual address." The farm track had hedges on either side. Faint tyre tracks were visible in the snow, but a fresh covering indicated that nobody had driven here recently.

"Should we come back in daylight?" he asked. It was tempting. It was dark and more than a touch scary. And yet the dark could work to our advantage. We could follow the track without being seen, assuming we didn't die of hypothermia. And on the upside, my eyes were starting to adjust to the darkness, helped by the shallow moonlight just edging its way through the snow clouds.

"Come on," I said, and reached for his hand.

We started to walk up the track. It was slippery and uneven, so progress was slow. We supported each other over the worst bits. I tried to find a positive in the conditions. At least it wasn't a mud bath, as I expected it might be when the snow melted. The track turned sharply left, and then there was a gate on the right. I climbed onto it to see if I could get a better view of anything beyond, but there was just a white expanse of nothing. The first flakes of a new snow fall caused a fog-like restriction of the long-range view.

We continued up the track. At one point it seemed to fork, but the left side stopped abruptly at a small, derelict outbuilding that may once have been a hay store. It wasn't big enough to be classed as a barn. It only had three walls, and the roof had long fallen in. We continued right. The track straightened for a bit, but we still had no idea where we were going. The hedge gave way to trees, blocking even more of the dim light. The snow was less deep underneath the trees.

And then, as we took another right turn, we saw a building. It looked like a farmhouse, although it was just a dark silhouette against the snow of its surroundings. We stopped.

"What do you think?" asked Danny.

"Come on," I said. "Be careful."

Our pace slowed as we approached. Again we were walking on virgin snow, although in places there were indentations that suggested perhaps a couple of sets of tyre tracks. It was hard to tell.

"I feel like I'm in a Scooby-Doo cartoon, approaching a haunted house," said Danny. It was hard to disagree. And then suddenly he stopped and grabbed my arm.

"Look!" he said. "The chimney."

We were still a distance away, but close enough to see smoke rising vertically from the side of the house. Somebody was home and the fire was lit.

The still night air was broken by the sound of an aeroplane. It wasn't loud but we couldn't see where it was coming from. We stopped. The snowfall was getting heavier. The sound faded and we continued.

Our pace slowed again, but then the house was right ahead of us. There was a gate, but it was open. A double garage with solid wooden doors stood to the left, separate from the main building.

"What now?" I whispered. But Danny led on. We crept through the gate, keeping close to the hedge at the front of the property. I was confident we couldn't be seen. We could hardly see each other. The curtains were closed. The house was silent.

We edged closer, working our way to the side. I was looking for a car, but if there was one it seemed to be in the garage.

Danny was significantly braver than me.

"Wait here," he whispered. He approached the side of the house, and tried to look through the windows. I ignored the instruction and followed. The curtains were closed on this side, too, but the lights seemed to be turned off. There was nothing to see. We crept back to the cover of the hedge, under the trees.

"Should we knock?" I whispered.

"No," he replied. "We'll come back tomorrow."

It seemed like an excellent idea. It was cold. It was dark. I felt like an intruder. I shivered, although I wasn't sure if it was the temperature or fear.

We continued round to the back of the house. Garden furniture was arranged on what looked like a patio, presumably ready for warmer days. It was covered in a thick layer of snow. I was worried that we'd be leaving footprints, but the fresh snow was already beginning to cover them. Again the curtains were closed. There wasn't much to see. There was a shriek as an owl flew past us, dislodging snow from the trees. I jumped.

"Come on," whispered Danny. "Let's go."

We turned back. Still the house was silent. We edged round to the side of the house, and then back towards the front.

And then we heard another sound. Like a gun being cocked, cutting the night air. Followed by a voice and a familiar Scottish accent.

"Stop there. Do not turn around." We froze.

"Lisa?" said Danny.

"Stay exactly where you are. Do not move."

The voice was unmistakable. It was exactly the same as I'd heard on the phone in Reigate.

"Lisa?" said Danny again.

"Don't make me shoot you, Danny."

I couldn't help it. I turned round. But the shock was greater than a bullet. I'd never seen Lisa before. But it wasn't Lisa holding the gun.

CHAPTER THIRTY-SEVEN

"**W**HAT the fuck?" I said. Danny turned too. Facing us, pointing a gun directly at us, unmistakeable despite the darkness, was Clare.

"Clare!" said Danny. But it was surreal. One of those moments where nothing makes sense. How was this possible? And why was she pointing a gun at us?

Clare dropped the gun to her side. That was something. Maybe she'd mistaken us for someone else. But then she'd called Danny by name. It was more than I could compute. I lost the ability to speak. I looked at Danny. He stood motionless with shock. It was not the grand reunion we'd envisaged. But on the upside, she was very much alive.

"Hi Danny," she said, "and Anna. I've been expecting you. I think you'd better come inside."

It was definitely Clare, but she looked different somehow. Older. Harder. She pointed to the front door and told us to open it. We paused to shake the snow from our shoes, and then she directed us through a wooden-floored hallway into a surprisingly well-appointed but dimly lit living room. I was expecting a rustic farmhouse, but this was modern chic. A log fire was burning, giving a pine-scented dry heat to the room. But she was still holding the gun. Danny edged closer to me, protecting me.

"Are you okay?" asked Danny, although his voice seemed to be coming from somewhere else. "And what's with the gun? We've been so worried. But... What's going on? I just don't... Lisa? Sorry, I just..." His words faded like a leaf floating away downstream.

"Let me get you a drink and I'll explain." Clare indicated the sofa. "Remove your jackets. Make yourselves at home." She switched on a small table lamp to give a soft illumination, dimmed the main lights further, and then left the room for a moment. I turned to Danny.

"What the fuck is going on?" I asked. He just shook his head. Clare returned, carrying a tray containing a bottle of champagne in an ice bucket, and three crystal glasses. She was no longer holding the gun. I wondered what she'd done with it. She removed the wire from the top of the bottle and eased out the cork.

"A small celebration," she said. She poured out three generous measures of champagne and gave one each to Danny and me. Taking a seat in the armchair opposite, she proposed a toast.

"To us. Back together again after a very traumatic week. Cheers."

I suspected she was taking the piss.

"I'm sorry for all the drama," she continued, "but welcome to my little Swiss hideaway."

"Are you okay?" asked Danny again.

"I'm fine. It's been a difficult few days."

"You're not kidding. What happened? You disappeared. We thought you were dead. I don't know whether to give you a hug or..."

"No, no hugs. I'm so sorry Danny. It wasn't ideal, but circumstances kind of forced things. Thank you for looking for me, though."

"Of course, but... Sorry, I don't understand. Were you kidnapped?"

"No."

"Hiding from somebody?"

"Kind of."

"Why didn't you get in touch?"

"I did." And then the Scottish accent returned. "DC Lisa Miller at your service." She smiled. But it was a smile as cold as the weather outside.

"Sorry, I am completely missing something here," I said. "You were Lisa?"

"Yes."

I turned to Danny.

"And you didn't recognise her because..."

"It wasn't Danny's fault. He never really saw me. The first time in the car it was dark. I dressed up. Glasses, wig. Big coat. Basic disguise really. Then in Camden the same. He only ever saw me in near total darkness."

"But the letter? The phone call? The pictures?" Suddenly my bewilderment turned to anger. "I've been fucking held up at gunpoint because of you. I'm wanted by the police. Danny was shot at. Our flat was burgled, my friend was kidnapped..."

"I know, and I'm sorry. I know you're not going to believe me, but not all of that was my fault."

"Not all of it?"

"It's been a bit complicated."

"A bit?"

Clare took a cigarette from a packet on the table beside her, and then offered one to me. I was tempted to accept, just

303

to annoy her, but declined. She lit up and blew smoke at the ceiling.

"Okay," she said. "I'll explain everything. Stop me if you have questions. But just know that you're safe now. You can leave here and explain everything. They will believe you."

"Who's they? And are you not coming back with us?"

"The police, the press, everybody. But no, sorry Danny, I can't do that."

"But why?"

She took a deep breath.

"You remember that last day, in the office, we spoke about retiring one day? This is my retirement."

"But..."

"Stop a moment. Do you remember what I said to you on the phone in Reigate when you thought I was Lisa? 'I don't think you need me any more Danny. I thought we were going to make a good team, but I get the sense that maybe we want different things. I think we should go our separate ways.' I basically told you everything."

It didn't make any sense. I took a sip of the champagne. To her credit it was an excellent bottle.

"I thought you were talking about finding Clare. Finding you."

"I know. But Danny, you know what? It's tough. I became a writer because I wanted to tell the truth. To investigate the bad people and bring them to justice. And you did the same, I think."

He nodded.

"But I suppose I just got burned out. I was writing about all of these people making millions and millions, and do you know what they all had in common?"

"They were corrupt?"

"Well, yes, but mainly they weren't as clever as they thought they were. They got caught."

304

"Okay..."

"And I just got to thinking that maybe if they weren't quite so naive, and they spent a bit less time getting self-obsessed and flaunting things, then maybe they'd be able to get away with it."

"But we made sure they didn't."

"Because they were stupid, and we were good. Oh Danny, I loved the work, I really did - at first anyway. I really did think I was making a difference - that we were making a difference. But then I just started to get fed up with all the corporate bullshit and office politics. I got disillusioned, so I started having little daydreams."

"About beaches and dogs and shouting at the sea?"

"Haha, yes. That as well. But then, what if there was a way to make millions, without anybody getting hurt, admittedly via possibly dubious methods, but doing it in a way that bypassed the whole getting caught thing. What if you could actually do it and get away with it?"

The fire crackled and a log shifted, sparks falling through the grate.

"But you're the one investigating people like that," said Danny.

"Exactly, but it was only a fantasy. I'd lie awake at night, making up stories, trying to imagine little scenarios where I could mastermind something brilliant. I never thought it'd happen, though. And then it did."

"I don't know that I want to hear this."

"Ah, Danny, try to imagine what it was like for me working at the Echo, writing exposés all day. Imagine the insight that gave me. It was okay when things were going well, but you know what? Recently it just got worse. I upset people, and not just the ones I wrote about. I wasn't exactly popular with some of the people I was working with, never mind everyone else."

"That's because you were the best and it pissed them off."

"It's kind of you to say. And maybe it's true. But I just got worn down. And that's when I started to think, maybe I could actually cross the line, do something harmless, but earn enough that I could leave everything else behind."

She stopped to have a drink of the champagne. I did the same but realised my glass was nearly empty. How had that happened? I indicated for a refill. Clare took one last drag of the cigarette and flicked it into the fire then came to top up my glass. She did the same for Danny too, although he hadn't made such good progress.

"Danny, you're a good man," she continued. "You really are. And I've been massively impressed by everything you did when we were working together, and especially everything you've done while looking for me. You know what? There are lots of people looking for me, but none have come close. You did it, with Anna of course." She raised her glass to me. "It's been brilliant. I'm so proud of you."

"Because I was terrified something had happened to you."

"I know and I'm really sorry to put you through that, but you did a brilliant job. You followed everything. The clues were cryptic, but you saw them and followed them, and here you are."

The urge to join the conversation overwhelmed me.

"Clare," I said. "I'm a photographer. This isn't my world, and you're confusing me. Can you just explain what you did, in simple terms that even I can understand? Because I'm getting lost here. Just to clarify, are you saying you're now some sort of criminal mastermind?"

She laughed.

"Anna, you're so sweet."

It was better than cute, but only just. I could feel an argument coming on.

"For me too," said Danny. "I idolised you. I can't believe I'm hearing all this."

"Okay, from the beginning?"

"Please," I said.

Clare sighed.

"So I've told you I was pissed off. Well, imagine the day when all of the knowledge I'd gathered about the working of the criminal mind came face to face with the absolutely perfect crime. The shock was that nobody had thought of it first."

"Which was?"

"I'd heard a rumour about some art fakes so I started to investigate it. All as part of the job. But as I got close, I started to see an opening. The idea was to steal works of art and replace them with near exact copies. Then you sell the originals to private collectors, no questions asked, at half what they'd cost on the open market - assuming they ever came up for sale. I say half, but the percentage varied. Anyway, these are people for whom owning the best is an obsession. It's not a question of how they've come by it. It's just the fact that they can go to bed at night in the knowledge that an original is hanging on the wall above them, and it's the real thing. The gallery doesn't notice. People still visit, so they don't mind. They don't even know that what they've got hanging on the walls are copies. Nobody gets hurt, everybody wins."

"Sounds perfect," I said. I don't know if she got the sarcasm in my voice. "Although correct me if I'm wrong, but people have been getting hurt. And killed."

"That wasn't the plan and I will come on to that. But bear with me. The clever bit was that I had the perfect alibi. Danny, Anna, you'll see - journalism opens doors. You, Anna, used my name to get in to see the Pet Shop Boys when it was sold out."

"You know about that?"

"Of course."

"You did what?" asked Danny.

"Long story," I said. And took another drink. I think I

blushed again.

"Anyway," Clare continued, "it opens doors. It's up to the individual to decide whether or not to go through those doors, but they're there nevertheless. It was all absolutely perfect. If anyone asked, I was a journalist researching a story, but I just had to make sure it never came to that."

"Pet Shop Boys?" said Danny.

"Shhh," I said. "Clare, continue."

"Okay, so I heard about this man called Benjamin Serraillier. It was his plan, really, and he recruited Dominique Chernin."

"Both of whom are now dead," I said.

"Yeah, but I'm coming onto that. It was unfortunate."

"Particularly for them."

"Indeed. Anyway, I saw what they were doing and I managed to get involved. I knew lots of people with lots of money who fitted the profile of the perfect customer."

"Criminals?" I asked.

"Some of them, but yes, generally those on the outer reaches of society, shall we say. Obviously I couldn't meet them personally but I was able to be a... conduit. Business boomed, and we were making a lot of money."

"Good for you." I raised my glass. Again I think she missed the subtext.

"But then I discovered a bit of a problem."

"Which was?"

"DCI March."

"Ah, him," I said. "We've met him. He's currently searching for me and trying to arrest me for your murder."

"Don't worry about him. He won't be a problem when you get home, and anyway you'll be left alone when they realise you haven't killed me. "

"The night is young," I said pointedly. Danny shot me a glance.

"Anyway," he said, presumably keen to return to the subject,

"DCI March?"

"Yes. Well, we were investigating him, obviously, because we know about all of his extracurriculars. But then I discovered he'd had dealings with Benjamin, and that was a little bit close to home. So I decided that maybe it was time to put an end to things. To take the profits and run."

"Very noble of you," I said.

"Can I just stop you for a minute?" asked Danny. "On the day you disappeared you said you were on the verge of a massive story and you'd tell me everything over lunch. Did you ever intend to meet me? Was there ever an actual story?"

"I did, but things got complicated when I met Benjamin."

"And what was the story?"

"There wasn't one. Not really. Not in the conventional sense. Not for me, anyway. But you've got one now."

"Thoughtful of you," I said and then realised that I'd probably best just shut up as I wasn't sure I was helping. I finished my second glass, and again Clare refilled it. I suddenly had a brief moment of panic. What if it was drugged and she was going to send us to sleep and murder us? But it was good champagne, so the panic was overruled.

"So what happened at the Mowbray?" asked Danny.

"Well, I'd mentioned I wanted out. Benjamin wasn't keen so he wanted to meet me to try to persuade me to continue, but I couldn't. It was too dangerous. Like I said, the key to not getting caught is to be clever. It's not about being greedy, but knowing when to quit. The problem was, Dominique was getting paranoid. He seemed to be under the impression that we were trying to edge him out. He thought we were planning to continue on our own, but just get rid of him. Which we weren't - but he was starting to get nasty."

"So Serraillier killed him?"

"Yes and no. Well he did, obviously, but that wasn't his plan. I expect it was in self-defence."

"He mowed him down in a car park," I pointed out.

"Yes, he did. There I can't argue with you. I don't know the full circumstances of that one, but I think it's fairly safe to say they'd fallen out and it was going to be one or the other. I expect Benjamin just took the opportunity to get in first."

"Good foresight." And then I thought I really must try harder.

"So what did you do?" asked Danny.

"I didn't really have an option. I knew that when that was investigated it could lead into all sorts of places that I'd have preferred it not to. But I'd seen it coming so I'd been working on a contingency plan which meant I could disappear. I'd been getting death threats."

"From Jimmy Ravenscroft."

"Actually no. His ex-girlfriend Sophie, it turned out. She was a bit pissed off with me. Although she only sent the one."

"Who sent all the others?"

"I did, obviously."

"To yourself?"

"Of course. It was perfect. Make it look like someone wanted me out of the way, and then when I disappeared it wouldn't look like I'd gone into hiding."

"So this is nothing to do with Ravenscroft?"

"Not exactly, Danny. That's what I mean, though, not all of this is my fault. He had a couple of his former colleagues looking for me anyway, and they were going to hurt me. They tried to blow me up for fuck's sake! They're the ones who kidnapped your friend Megan and visited your flat. I think they maybe thought Megan was me when they saw her at your studio - sorry Anna - and that's when all that happened. But that would probably have happened anyway. That's just a risk of the job. Anyway, they won't be bothering you any more."

"How do you know that?"

"I wish I could tell you, Danny, but I'm afraid some things

are probably best left unspoken. Let's just say they've ceased to pose a living threat."

"Jesus..."

"Oh come on, they were sick. The blood in your flat. That was just wrong. And they blew up a hotel just because they thought I was staying there. They were very dangerous, but thankfully very stupid. The world won't miss them." She lit another cigarette.

"Can I ask a question?" I said, realising that I should have technically asked if I could ask two questions on the basis that asking if I could ask a question was already using up my allowance if I could only ask one. But then the champagne was making my head go a little bit fuzzy. "How do you know all of this?"

"A combination of things Anna. I've been watching you - sometimes literally - and I had your house, cars, and phone bugged. You may remember your phone was playing up for a bit. That was teething trouble. Sorry about that."

"You bugged our phones?" asked Danny.

"Yes. I know. A bit naughty really. I've got keys to your flat. I copied them ages ago. The thing is, I wanted you to look for me. I needed to make sure you were always looking because I wanted you to have an amazing story. Think of it as my leaving gift. But if you ever got stuck I wanted to be able to help you. You were good, though. I just did the bare minimum. You'll go a very long way."

"I don't know whether to be shocked or grateful."

"You've got to remember that it's me who trained you, Danny. I knew exactly what methods you were likely to use because it was me that taught you. Obviously I couldn't be there all the time, so occasionally I also had to rely on contacts within the police."

"DC Cranston?"

"Exactly. She's good. Heart of an angel. She's fixated on

March, thinks he's a bent bastard, which he is, so she was willing to help me, because she thought I was just going deep undercover to get him. Which in a way I was. But yes, you can trust Amy."

"So that's how you got my passport."

"Hmmm, no. But when you're into forgery, an authentic-looking passport is no bother."

"You gave me a fake passport?"

"Yes, but it's good though. You could never tell. Amy is as straight as they come. She's not one to steal from an evidence room."

"But who's Richard Kirk then?" I asked. "He robbed me at gunpoint and broke into my studio."

"And shot at us," said Danny

"He was working for Benjamin, kind of a bodyguard. But he's best pals with March too, which is how they're linked. So when Benjamin was killed, March had Kirk investigate. He'd do anything for money. I think he was trying to kill me. Well, not me, but Lisa. I told him, as Lisa, I had the money from Benjamin, more to keep him under control than anything, but hey, I didn't ever hand it over. And yeah, it nearly backfired. I think he was running out of patience. Sorry about the canal thing. I had a suspicion he wasn't far away, which is why I was on alert when I heard the motorbike. I think you also met Sean Haldane."

"I did," I said.

"Don't worry about him. He broke into my car and stole my phone and some notebooks but they were full of rubbish. I was expecting him."

"He wanted to speak to you."

"I know. He's a bitter man. But you know what? In fairness, if he could lay off the drink and learn some morals, he'd make a bloody good investigator. He was the only one who was on to me. But Danny, you'll make a much better job of writing the story. And you'll have the benefit of authenticity and all of the evidence in my own writing." She looked at Danny again and gave him a benevolent smile.

"So," I said, "the bed and breakfast in Paddington. What was that about?"

"I stayed there twice, once looking as I do now, once, more recently, as Lisa. I needed a driving licence with that address on it so I could hire the car. That's why I stayed there the first time. As soon as it arrived I left. It was horrible. But I went back and stayed again so you'd have a trail to follow. That's why I hadn't been to my flat for a while."

"You're all heart. And the Otter Tavern?"

"I had to take Benjamin away to tell him what I knew about Dominique. I'd stayed there once before on a story and it seemed as good a place as any."

"So how come your car ended up on the M25?"

"To make it look like I'd been kidnapped. Obvious really. But even then I had to leave you clues, like the ring down the side of the chair at the hotel, and the leaflet from the Otter Tavern at the B&B just to make sure."

"So why did you need pictures from the nightclub?"

She smiled again.

"I didn't, although Anna Burgin originals may one day be worth a lot of money and I've got a liking for art as you now know. But I needed to make sure the passport got to you and I couldn't trust the post. I'm sorry it didn't arrive in time and you had to go back to Rougemont. But I hope you had a bit of time to enjoy yourselves rather than just spending the whole of it looking for me."

"God, you're such a treasure. Which just leaves Serraillier. What happened to him?"

"Ah, yes, that was unfortunate. Again, you could call it self-defence. I'd arranged to meet him in Sunderland, but after what he did to Dominique I couldn't take any chances."

"So you killed him?"

"You make it sound so cold. It was just a little misunderstanding. I just wanted to wind up the business and move abroad. He seemed to be getting increasingly irrational."

"So you killed him?" I asked again.

"I prefer to think of it as a business move. But come on! It was getting dangerous."

"You're a fraud," said Danny, spitting out the words.

"A rich fraud."

"And a murderer. God, I idolised you. And all the time you're no fucking better than the rest of them."

"Oh, I have to disagree. The difference is that I've got away with it. And the icing on the cake is that I don't now have to split it all three ways, so it ended rather well, all things considered."

Danny shifted on the sofa and then sat with his head in his hands, speechless.

I spoke for him. "So what happens now, Clare?"

"Well, after I've gone you're more than welcome to stay the night. There are another couple of bottles of champagne in the fridge. You're more than welcome to those too. I won't be needing them. But if you'd prefer to head off, you can call a taxi from here to take you back to your hotel." She turned to Danny. "I've got a couple of presents for you, too. You've done an amazing job but I thought I'd help fill in any gaps. I've got two folders for you - one with everything you need to know about March, which is everything you've got back at the office and all of the other stuff you don't yet know about. Believe me, though, it's enough to bury him."

"But we were working on that together," he said with a desperate sadness in his voice.

"I know, but for obvious reasons I had to keep some of it back. You've got it all now, though. He's finished. Amy will buy you a very large drink."

"That's not the way this was supposed to work."

"I know, and I'm sorry. But when the two worlds began to collide it was time to quit. And then there's another folder with all the details of this. You can name me of course. Everything is in there. Photographs, customers, the works. Danny, you've got what you've always wanted. I'm going to disappear now, but you've got two amazing exclusives. You've proved yourself. You can take over my job at the Echo and then have a fantastic career for as long as you can stand it."

"And you really think that's what I always wanted?"

"Isn't it?"

Danny shook his head, more in disbelief than disagreement.

The sound of a helicopter approaching through the night sky stopped the conversation. All three of us looked up to the ceiling, which seems weird now I think about it.

"That sounds like my getaway," said Clare. "Good luck Danny. And Anna. I hope I've been some help to you in your career. I'm sorry it has to end like this, but sometimes you have to do things for yourself. It's been an absolute pleasure to work with you. Anna, look after him for me. You make a great couple."

We could see flashing lights from the helicopter through the curtains.

"Where are you going?" asked Danny.

"I'm sorry. I can't tell you that. Publish the stories, become a superstar, and think of me when you're famous. You'll realise it was for the best one day. I'll look out for you. Maybe our paths will cross again. I'm extremely proud of you."

With that she walked past us, and out into the freezing night air. We followed her to the door. She walked up to the helicopter and got in. The speed of the rotor increased and as it took off Clare waved at us out of the window.

"I loved you," Danny shouted, but Clare couldn't hear. She was on her way, out of his life, seemingly for ever.

CHAPTER THIRTY-EIGHT

W E closed the door. I turned to Danny as the
helicopter disappeared into the night, kissed his
cheek and tasted the salt of his tears.

"I just don't know what to say," he said.

"There's nothing you can say. Come on, let's find the kitchen and I'll make you a cup of tea. We can decide what we're going to do."

"I just want to get away. I want to pretend this didn't happen, wind the clock back to the beginning of last week and start all over again." He wiped his eyes but couldn't fight the emotion.

I led him down the hallway. The kitchen was on the left. It was a big, typical farmhouse kitchen, with an Aga and a central island. It was all wooden, with wooden beams running in parallel across the ceiling. Best of all, when I pressed the light switch, a set of ceiling spotlights came on. There was no sign of a fluorescent strip. Anywhere else it would have been beautiful.

I walked over to the counter where the kettle stood. Beside it were two cups, each of which contained a tea bag, and an unopened pint of milk. Clare, it seemed, had thought of everything.

"I just feel like I've woken up from a nightmare only to find that real life is worse," said Danny as he surveyed the room. "'When she was born she was as pure as snow, but like the snow she drifted.'"

"What's that?"

"The notice stuck on the wall next to Clare's desk. It makes sense now. 'Your body is a book and I can't look beyond the cover. Beauty is a flower that time will devour.' It all makes sense. The signs were there. She planned it all through. I should be impressed by the ingenuity of it all."

"She was an amazingly clever woman."

"But what does it mean? What's it all for?" He leaned against the Aga while I made the tea.

"We said it though, didn't we?" he continued. "It was like somebody was leaving a trail of clues, playing a game of hide and seek. And yet I don't know if this means we've won."

"She planned everything. It was absolutely meticulous. I mean, credit where it's due, you wouldn't want to mess with her."

"No, but it's just... We spent so long looking for her. And then we finally found her, only to lose her forever."

"I think you'd lost her a long time ago, Danny. It just took this to bring it out."

He was silent for a while, before continuing, in a voice laced with regret.

"I just can't believe it. I admired her so much. She was everything I aspired to be. And yet now..."

"You're better than her." I passed him a cup of tea. "Honestly. And tonight proves it." The tea was too hot to drink. I took the milk to the fridge. There was nothing in it apart from two cold bottles of champagne.

"So what are we going to do now?" he asked.

I thought for a moment.

"I don't know about you, but I'm definitely curious to have a look round the rest of the house. But I don't really want to stay here. It's like there's a ghost."

He nodded.

"I know what you mean."

We left the tea to cool, and set off to explore, switching on all the lights as we went. There were three bedrooms. None looked like they'd been slept in. There was a four-poster bed in the main bedroom. Lying on top of the duvet were two folders. One marked March and the other Woodbrook. There was a handwritten note on top. We read it together.

> *Danny, this is everything you need. Take it and use it to make your name. Look after it, but if anything happens on the way home, don't worry. I've made copies of everything and I'll make sure you receive them.*
>
> *Many years ago my first ever editor took a chance on me when I was young and hungry. He made me promise to one day find somebody I believed in, to nurture them, and to pass on the baton so they could rise to greatness. I now understand why he did that and I could not wish to have met anyone more deserving than you.*
>
> *I understand everything may have come as a shock, but please try not to think badly of me. Ultimately, I suppose, I found I had a weakness. You don't need me any more.*
>
> *Take care and keep nailing the bad guys.*
> *Love,*
> *Clare x.*

I put my arm around him.

"Come on," I said. "Let's go and phone for a taxi."

CHAPTER THIRTY-NINE

Saturday, February 20th, 1993

DANNY returned to his office at the Echo on Saturday morning, direct from the airport. His security pass had been revoked, but he managed to talk his way past reception. After all of the challenges of the last few days, he wasn't going to give in to that one.

The editorial floor was largely deserted, with just a skeleton weekend staff keeping on top of any breaking news. There was no sign of the editor. That meeting would come in time.

His office - now his alone - was just as he'd left it. He was struck by a terrible sadness in the realisation that Clare would never return to these four walls again. The rain had started to fall again, running in small rivers down the large office window. It felt just like the day she'd left. He knew he had to stop thinking about her in the way that he had. The truth hurt, but the world was still turning. And she was right. It was time to press on alone.

He sat at his desk and looked across to Clare's chair. Her screen. Her keyboard. Her fingers would never again touch these keys. He'd never speak to her again, share special moments of tears and laughter, nor watch her play with her ring. He still had the ring. It was something to remember her by.

He turned on his screen and opened a new file with the catchline ARTCRIME, and then wondered why the words wouldn't come. There was so much to write about, but where to begin? He leafed through the folders. The research was impeccable, well ordered, verified, and damning. But when he turned to the screen it was still empty. He looked at the flashing cursor, and then at the office, and out of the window. He wanted to write, but every word was a struggle.

Relief came in the form of a knock on the door.

"Come in!" he shouted.

A weekend security guard appeared at the door, holding a large bouquet.

"Are you Danny Churchill?"

"I am."

"These are for you."

He put the flowers on the other desk - Clare's desk - and walked out of the room, closing the door behind him.

Danny got up and picked up the envelope which had been stuck to the front of the cellophane. He opened it and took out the card.

> *I know these flowers can't relieve the pain, but I hope you'll look at them and think of me. Sometimes things happen over which we have no control and sometimes life is cruel. But remember, however sad you are, that I love you. Your friend, Anna.*

Danny put down the card and felt the tears rising again.

He picked up the phone and dialled home. The answering machine clicked on. He dialled the number for the studio. On the fourth ring it was answered.

"Passion Fruit."

"Hi, Anna?"

"Danny! How are you."

"Oh Anna. I just got the flowers. Thank you so much. They're wonderful."

"Are they nice?"

"Beautiful."

"Did you read the card?"

"Yes."

"You didn't mind?"

"Didn't mind what?"

"What I said."

Danny smiled.

"No, it was lovely. As long as it's true."

Anna paused.

"How's the story coming on?"

"Not well. What are you doing?"

"Not a lot. Just trying to organise things so I can get back to work next week. Have you phoned Amy?"

"Not yet. I'm writing the Clare story first. March is next. But I don't want him getting arrested yet. Not until it's ready."

"Good plan."

"Can I take you to dinner?"

"Tonight?"

"Yeah. Your choice. Just to thank you for everything you've done for me. The very least I can do."

"Not pizzas then?"

"No, anything you like. Somewhere special."

"I'd love that."

"Brilliant. Think of where you'd like to go and I'll see you tonight."

"Shall do."

"Oh and Anna..."

"Yes."

"I don't deserve you. But thank you."

"We'll discuss that. Write something incredible and I'll meet you at the flat."

"Perfect."

He replaced the receiver and leaned back in his chair. It felt like a new chapter was opening. It was scary, but Clare was right. He was ready. He'd been taught by the master. He turned back to the screen and started typing.

***

I had two bottles of rather excellent champagne in the fridge. Well, I wasn't going to leave them in Switzerland was I?

Danny phoned again at about 6.30 to say he'd be back within the hour. I was home within ten minutes but that gave me time to take a quick shower and to change into something nice. Obviously, conventional wisdom would suggest choosing my sexiest outfit and making my move, but do you know what? This was bigger than that. We've been through too much to aspire to the superficial. I'm not averse to making an effort, but I really do believe we have a connection that transcends make-up, hair products, lingerie and sexy shoes.

That said, it was lovely to dress up after a week in jeans, sweatshirts and DMs, so all of the above made an appearance, but I was doing it for me rather than some blatant attempt at seduction. Just so we're clear. Said with a wink.

I greeted Danny with a big hug when he arrived.

"Wow," he said. "You look amazing." He blushed. I blushed back.

"It's a special night," I replied. "It seems like we've got our lives back. And thank you."

I led him through to the kitchen where I had two glasses ready. With considerably less restraint than Clare, I popped the cork on one of the bottles and it flew through the air, bouncing off a wall cupboard. I poured us both a sizeable glass, pausing while the bubbles settled.

Where dinner was concerned, I suggested Brick Lane for something spicy, and Danny was happy to oblige. We phoned for a cab. It was a night off for both of us. A chance to let go of the past, reconnect with our surroundings, and focus on ourselves for a change.

"How are you doing?" I asked when we were in the taxi on the way to the restaurant. "Was it weird being back at the office?"

"I'm all right," said Danny. "It was just a bit sad really, knowing she'll never be back there."

"I know, it must be hard."

"It is, but it's just a question of coming to terms with it all. I don't know how to say it really."

"Would talking help?"

"Oh I don't know. It's just... It's like everything I knew about her and everything she did. It just seems false somehow."

"But she still did amazing work. It's quite a legacy."

"She did. But then, I suppose, how much do we ever really know someone?"

"How much do we ever really know ourselves?"

"Haha, indeed."

"You know me, though, Danny. I promise you I'm never going to go mad and run away on a helicopter."

"Oh, Anna." He put his arm around me. "If you do, I'm done."

"It's a shame though."

"What is?"

"Well, I'd been looking forward to the wedding. All of Fleet Street's glitterati coming out to salute two of its finest. I was

323

going to still try to be your lodger though."

He laughed.

"What are you talking about?"

"You and Clare. I'd been trying on hats."

"Me and Clare?"

"Yeah, you know. Woman that just fucked off into the sunset. You haven't forgotten her already? For heaven's sake. Men..."

"You thought I was going to get married to Clare?"

"Well, I hoped not, but I don't know. I know you wanted to." God, I hoped I didn't sound needy.

"What makes you think that?" He laughed again.

"You. You said how much you loved her."

"I did. Absolutely adored her. But I wasn't 'in love' with her. You're hilarious."

"Is there a difference?"

"Of course there is. You can love your mum or love your child, and think the world of them and be willing to do anything for them. You'd give up your life for your children. That's love. But it's not being 'in love'."

Oh.

"Oh," I said.

"What's that face for?"

"What face?"

"Your face."

"What's wrong with my face?"

"Nothing's wrong with your face. It's a lovely face. It's just got a funny expression on it."

"Are you saying I've got a funny face?"

"No!"

"I still haven't completely forgiven you for taking the piss out of my outfit."

"I wasn't taking the piss."

"Well you were."

324

"Well I wasn't."

"We shall disagree. Anyway. If anything it's my thinking face."

"Really? What are you thinking about?"

Oh Danny. If only you knew.

"Thinking about what we're going to have for tea," I said. Which I wasn't.

"No you weren't," he said.

"Ooh you're so difficult."

"I'm difficult?"

"Yes."

He squeezed me tighter.

"You're difficult," he said. "But worth the effort."

Our conversation was interrupted by the cab driver, telling us we'd arrived. Danny let go, opened the door, helped me out, and then paid the driver through the window.

"Come on," he said, linking arms. "The finest food you can find. Lead on."

CHAPTER FORTY

WE had a lovely evening. We discussed the case at first but soon changed the subject. Now it was over, I realised part of me had enjoyed the excitement of the previous few days, but I was in no rush to ever repeat it. We had great food, lots of laughs, and quite a bit of wine. I thanked Danny for treating me. He thanked me for driving him up and down the country and for helping find Clare, even though, with the way it all worked out, we both agreed it seemed a hollow victory.

We were both exhausted when we finally arrived home, so we decided on a cup of tea rather than the second bottle of champagne. He came to stand with me while I made it. I took off my heels but immediately regretted it. I'd quite enjoyed being taller.

"What a week," he said. "It's just so nice being home."

"I've lost count of the number of nights I've had to share a bed with you," I said. (I hadn't.)

"Did I snore?"

"No, you've been very good."

"That's good." He paused. "You did, though."

"I didn't."

"Yes you did! Haha."

"When?"

"In Sunderland after Bentleys."

"That was your fault for getting me pissed. I do not snore."

"Right."

I gave him a look. The kind of look that says, "I've just taken my heels off and I may be about to impale you on one."

"Well, next time you want to share a bed with me, you'll just have to make sure I'm completely sober," I said.

"Shall do."

"And that rules tonight out, then."

"Looks like it."

"Good. I'll be glad of the space."

"I suppose I could make an exception though. Just for old times' sake."

"I suppose I could try not to snore."

"I don't mind," he said. "In any case, it's quite cute." And then he made a run for it.

I woke up first, feeling slightly worse for wear, but immensely secure with Danny alongside me.

In truth I don't know that it will be a regular occurrence. I'd like it to be, but as I may have mentioned, I don't have much success with relationships, and the thought of ever splitting up with Danny and losing the best friend I could ever wish for is probably too big a risk to take. I really don't understand me sometimes. It was a lovely evening, though. I fell asleep holding his hand.

As he slept on I got dressed and walked across to the garage on Camden Road for the Sunday papers. We like to do that occasionally, having a big cooked breakfast, which is also lunch, and a nice cup of tea, going through all the sections, catching up with the world. And there was so much to catch up on. We'd been away from the news for more than a week. Obviously we knew what would be making headlines over the next few days, but that was for the rest of the world to wait for.

I had a shower, got dressed, and started to cook. Danny appeared, roused I suspect by the aroma, and made us both a cup of tea. He offered to help with the food, so I assigned him toast duty while I got on with the tricky bits. He gave me a hug, which was nice.

He noticed the red light blinking on the answering machine and pressed the button.

"Danny, this is Mike Walker. Just a quick call to say great story. There are things we need to discuss, but this is excellent work. I'll see you at the morning conference. Come in early to celebrate your first front page."

I was overwhelmed with pride in my friend, and relief that his career seemed intact. Danny just smiled. There was nothing else to say.

Once we'd had breakfast we started leafing through the papers. There was the latest on a ferry disaster. The sudden death of an MP. Warnings of higher unemployment.

And then Danny stopped.

"Jesus," he said.

He passed me the paper, pointing to a story .

Headlined "Briton killed in chopper horror", it read:

> A pilot and his female British passenger are believed to have been killed when their helicopter crashed in the Swiss Alps on Friday night.
>
> Initial reports suggest that the helicopter, which was on a private chartered flight, suffered a mechanical failure as it flew in darkness through a snowstorm. It came down in a forested area near

*the village of Rougemont, about sixty miles east of
Geneva. Eyewitness reports state that it caught fire
on impact and then exploded.*

*Rescue teams worked through the night to locate
the aircraft. Flight records show that two people
were on board, but formal identification is being
hampered by the remote location and severity of
the damage sustained in the impact. It is believed
the flight was chartered by a British woman who
had been working in Switzerland.*

*Air crash investigators are on the scene and are
expected to release more details shortly."*

Clare. I felt numb. Danny was silent. He looked at me.

"The village of Rougemont?" he said.

"Let me see."

I read it again.

It was too much of a coincidence. It was a message, just for us.

"Oh Clare," said Danny. "You clever, clever, twisted, flawed genius."

EPILOGUE

WITH its famous twin spires, Cologne Cathedral is Germany's most visited landmark. Known locally as the Dom, and dating back to 1248, it's found close to the city's main train station, or Hauptbahnhof, near the west bank of the Rhine.

At certain times of the day, the cathedral's spires cast a shadow over the entrance of the opulent, five-star Hotel Excelsior Ernst on the street below. The hotel attracts a well-heeled, discerning clientele who appreciate its luxurious ambience as much as the choice of cocktails, range of champagnes and selection of eighty whiskies in the mahogany-panelled Piano Bar.

A well-dressed English woman extinguished her cigarette, and signalled to the cocktail waiter. When he arrived she ordered an Ernst 63 champagne cocktail. Her second.

She had, she reflected, come a long way. Physically and figuratively. She was tired from the drive, and although the Mercedes 190E hire car had been soothing company, it was now time to relax and think about the future.

A well-groomed man was sitting alone on a stool by the bar. She looked at him. He noticed her gaze and smiled. She looked away. It was tempting but there was no rush. Her need for privacy and anonymity was greater than any urge for physical contact.

She toyed with the ring on the third finger of her left hand. It was new. A white gold band with diamonds framing a beautiful blue Ceylon sapphire. Bigger than the last one. She returned to her English newspaper, reading the story about a helicopter crash again, before folding the paper and putting it aside. She was an admirer of the British press, but that part of her life was over.

She thanked the waiter who placed her drink on the table in front of her and returned her gaze to the man at the bar. On second thoughts... She checked her watch. Maybe there was an hour or two.

The man saw the look. He stood up, walked over, and indicated a spare chair.

"Do you mind if I join you," he asked in German-accented English.

She nodded assent, and he pulled out the chair and sat down, facing her across the table.

"I'm Steven, Steven Ponndorf," he said.

Behind her eyes, recent events played back like a film on fast forward. She reached for her cigarettes and offered him one.

She decided on a name.

"I'm Charlotte Sadler," she replied. That should do for now.

ACKNOWLEDGEMENTS

Special thanks...

Writing can, by its nature, be a solitary pursuit, but with the support of friends you're never truly alone. Special thanks, therefore, to **Mary Cafferkey** for inspiration and care above and beyond the call of duty. I do not deserve you.

Huge thanks also to my editor, **Carrie O'Grady**, for insight, encouragement and fantastic suggestions for improving the story. The typos, however, are still mine.

And finally, to **DayBehavior** for the soundtrack for all those candle-lit nights of writing.

"Something that's broken needs love and lust to heal. And sometimes my fiction can make me feel so real."

Find them at www.daybehavior.com.

Thank you for reading Cold Press. I hope you enjoyed it! If you did, I'd really, really appreciate it if you could leave a review on Amazon, Goodreads, or indeed anywhere else you fancy. It all helps enormously. Thank you.

Please also visit my web site at www.davidbradwell.com and join the mailing list for news, updates, free things and more. Don't worry - I won't share your address with anyone, but it's a great way to keep in touch. You can, of course, also send me an email via the web site.

Danny, Anna, Clare, and DCI Graham March will be back.

More soon :-)

This page is intentionally blank. So you can draw a picture, or something.

STAND BY FOR BOOK 2!

Danny, Anna, Clare & co will be back.

Join the mailing list at:

www.davidbradwell.com

for news, updates, competitions, free things and more :-)

... and if you enjoyed Cold Press please leave reviews on Amazon, Goodreads and other web sites. Your support really does make a difference and is hugely appreciated!

Thank you.

purefiction

www.davidbradwell.com